The Little White Trip

A Night in the Pines

One of the first to take this Trip.

Thanks,
Peter Gallagher
Vbock   11-06

thelittlewhitetrip.com

A Rey-Lay Book

Copyright © 2006 Peter Joseph Gallagher

If you purchased this book without a cover, you should be aware that this book is stolen property. It was reported as "unsold and destroyed" to the publisher, and neither the author nor the publisher has received any payment for this "stripped book."

All rights reserved.

Manufactured in the United States of America

All characters and events in this book are fictitious, and any resemblance to any person, living or dead, is purely coincidental.

Cover design and photography by Juwels

Published in the United States by Rey-Lay Books

ISBN: 0-9779304-3-2

thelittlewhitetrip@hotmail.com

Rey-Lay Books
P.O. Box 542
Seal Beach, CA 90740

The Little White Trip

A Night in the Pines

Written by

Peter Joseph Gallagher

Rey-Lay Books

Peter's quote:

"When it's once right you never can do it again. You only do it once for each thing. And you're only allowed so many in your life."

Ernest Hemingway, *The Garden of Eden*.

Matt's quote:

"Dying is truly one of the only noble things that you can do these days."

Grum Crumpet, *A Life Worth Killing For*.

She's giving him that look, the way she always does. He's waiting for her to speak, and then it finally comes: "I can't believe I found you…I'm so blessed."

"I'm glad that you're happy, babe."

"Happy? No, that's just too weak an emotion. The way I feel with you is ineffable."

He shakes his head and smiles at her. "Well, if there's nothing more I do in life then that's enough."

To my beautiful baby, my child in the sky, my reason for trying, my girl, Julia. Some day we'll run away together, and they'll never find us.

And I'd be a fool to leave out my mom, the one who taught me that I *was* worth a damn and that if I chased my dreams, one day I'd catch up to them and never have to open my eyes again.

People wonder why I didn't write my own book...

Do you have any idea how hard it is to write an entire book? I do, now, but not because I did it, just because I helped — a little. In truth, I'm a decent writer — short stories, song lyrics, and even the few pages that I put in here, but the hell and labor of birthing this book in its entirety I left to the one who wanted it most. Shit, I'm just a kid who some things happened to. Without the over-excitement and relentless persuasions of a virtually unheard-of writer out of Arizona, this book wouldn't be in your hands right now.

Although traditionally the "ghost writer" remains exactly that, I have decided to give Peter Gallagher his owed recognition and name him as the genuine author. In the last few months, we've spent hundreds of hours on the phone and yakking over the Internet to get this thing right. I wanted to make sure this story turned out to be a dedication to my group, who we were, not just what became of us in a night.

I want you to know right here, before the first page, that what you're about to read is not a script, nor is it a diagramed and structured storyline. This shit actually happened to me. Don't expect the good guy to get the girl, or the murderer to come back to life for that one last attack scene. Actually, don't expect there to be a good guy at all. These couple of days would turn out to be the last ones that I would ever spend as a normal kid with my friends. A force stronger than fate would send us into one of the most fucked-up situations that you could ever imagine, and what happened...happened.

To be completely honest, at first, I had no interest in bringing this story to print. Just days after my high school graduation, I witnessed the murders of some of my closest friends for little more than the dirty pleasure of some fucking maniac. Like the reaper himself, that evil creature remained in the shadows until it was too late. Innocent people suffered, a generation died, and although I feel lucky to have been left with my life, I can't help but selfishly miss what I once had.

We went through it all, for what? So it could all be commercialized and profited from? Fuck that. But Peter explained it best when he told me, "You have no choice. The story is too big. You know that it's going to be told whether we do it or not; getting there first is the only way that *you* can control what *it* becomes." He was right, and my life has been so different after everything went down that I figured putting this book together might actually be a good idea. Why not? Let's put it on paper.

Matthew Thomas

ONE

"Okay, scholars, single file, make sure you stay in this order when we head out there. Principal Stewart will be calling you for your diplomas two at a time. We must stay organized."

Mrs. Adams had been calling us "scholars" since freshman initiation and had probably annoyed many generations before with the same irksome tones. Her croaky old smoker's voice had become a morning staple around Farrell High. Being the head of the daily announcements, Mrs. A was also guilty of a ton of incredibly lame jokes. Her intentions were pure, but at the yawning hour of eight-thirty, her timing couldn't be worse.

During freshman year, my school had been upgraded with televisions in every classroom. With the new sets came the birth of a school-based program called *News Channel One*. That great advancement allowed the student body to not only hear Mrs. A, but also to see that decrepit dictator as we were urged to, "Make the most of your time here at Scottsdale's finest, Farrell High School." She made it a point to croon that same shit to us at the close of announcements every morning. God, I hated her.

Nevertheless, I always enjoyed the end of morning announcements. First off, it marked the close of amateur hour, and secondly, in my opinion, the guy behind the camera was a genius. Each morning, at the end of Mrs. A's bit, he would draw a slow zoom in on the bottom of her pasty old face. That was where the magic happened. The monitor's twenty-five square inches were consumed with enamel shapes, yellowed peach fuzz, and low-quality face paint.

The camera would be in there real tight, just in time for her famous tag line, "Make the most of your time here..." Her mouth was intoxicating. Smears of maroon lipstick arched well above her mouth in a wasted attempt to disguise her thin lizard lips, and her thick graveyard teeth had been stained a chocolate tint over the years from caffeine and nicotine breakfasts. The best and most damaging part came within the last seconds of her slogan. That's when she would brandish this great big reptilian grin and nervously hold it. The image wasn't a freeze-frame; instead, she would hold form perfectly still for like ten or fifteen seconds. Eventually, the image would dissolve into our school logo against a black screen, and she was gone.

Quite the debate broke out in my first-hour class when I pointed out how disturbing I thought it was for her to hold that polluted smile after the announcements every morning. The majority of the class disagreed with me. They said it was a still-frame; even my teacher Mr. Holton thought so.

The Little White Trip

The class couldn't see what I did. They lacked one of my only natural gifts: attention to detail. You see, at the end of her spiel, when the camera was in there real tight, no motion could be seen, or at least easily seen. But if you looked closely at the top of the screen, you could make out two dark floating ovals, her nostrils. With an even sharper eye on the left one, from the empty darkness, a renegade nose hair would appear. Under the pressure of her wheezy emissions, the normally concealed strand was blown out for a second before retreating with each new breath.

There was a unanimous disbelief in my claim that day, so the next morning I made sure to remind the class of the dispute. I even decided to up the ante and predict the number of times that disturbing little hair would appear.

Over the noise of the nonbelievers, I proclaimed, "Not only will the hair be making an appearance, but you can expect to see it two more times before the curtain."

Our teacher frowned at the class. A single nose hair had evoked more interest than any of his history lessons to date. That must have burned.

"Okay, class, settle down. Some of you should be using this time to prepare for today's *test*."

That morning the class watched Mrs. A more intently than they ever had before. When the end of the announcements came about, so did her infamous slogan. The camera pulled in tight. Her nostrils were in position and, just as I had promised the day before, for the first time the class witnessed the unknown morning show:

"The Hair and the Hole," starring our wonderful school counselor, Mrs. Adams. The room overflowed with laughter upon its first appearance.

On the second sighting, I jumped up from my chair and pointed to the screen, calling, "two," and just as the dissolve was setting in, right on time, "three." That filthy little hair made a third and final salute. The kids went bananas, comparing disgusted looks and clapping – my friend Sam actually fell out of his chair, rolling on the thin spun carpet in the aisle.

With a hairy fist, our teacher pounded bass-filled tones from his hollow desk, shouting, "All right, everybody calm down. It's just a nose hair." With his face becoming flushed, he tried repeating himself, but broke into a fit of guilty laughter instead.

That was a big accomplishment for me. I loved entertaining, and I loved being right even more. Throughout my schooling I fought to stay at the center of attention even though many times it landed my ass in the principal's office. As the laughter began to dwindle, I spun toward the class and took a graceful bow. My thick black hair swung forward with the gesture. Shaking the strands back and away from my cheeks, I presented a smile that was always awoken by civil disobedience.

The teacher, banging on his desk again, insisted from under a stiff mustached lip, "Matt, take your seat. You've already put us back a couple minutes."

He liked to play tough, forcing me to sit in the front row for most of the semester, calling home, and even sending me to see Mr. Stewart on rare occasions. I kept an eye on him the next morning at the end of the show.

He kind of shot me a little smirk and shook his head. "I know your buddy Ian runs the camera up there, Matt. I have a good mind to let Mrs. Adams know how you guys like making a fool of her," he threatened, playing that old tough guy routine again.

I don't know why, but little things like that got me off, comically. Sometime toward the end of elementary school, my dad, after pushing me onto sports teams, clubs, and advanced learning programs, gave up the hope that I would measure up to his own gifted childhood and turned me over to my free-spirited, more liberal mom, and I was a-okay with that.

Yeah, I didn't care about much in my younger years, and I was always getting into something. When I was eleven, while shamelessly peddling through a stop sign, I collided face-first into the side of a Volkswagen bus. The experience wrecked my bike, almost killed my mom with worry, and left me with a broken nose. The crash also produced two specks of blood in the white of my right eye. People tell me that the blood spots look like a red exclamation point. I've tried to look at them in the mirror but usually end up cross-eyed or crazy, trying to focus.

That crash was just one of many, but its repercussions lasted much longer. I immediately hated the bend in my nose. I thought it affected my breathing and gave my average face an unneeded touch of vulnerable character.

Of course I didn't call it "vulnerable character" when

I was eleven. "My nose is still all screwed up and crooked," I complained to our family doctor during my follow-up appointment.

He reassured me with his professional opinion, saying, "No, your nose is straight. It's your face that's crooked."

I couldn't help but laugh. Even back then, I knew that I overanalyzed things sometimes.

I should've felt lucky that my teeth stayed in place. When all my friends were picking wheat bread from their braces, my teeth were exactly where they were supposed to be. No, my teeth never gave me any problems and neither did any of my other features, for that matter. Besides my angled nose, I would consider myself an alright-looking guy. I don't mean to butter my own bread here, but hey, if I don't, who will? I'm the narrator, right?

My self-confidence didn't come with the stork; it came with time. Girls always did a good job of applauding my starry brown eyes, strong jaw, crazy silky hair, lips, my...ahhh – see? I've heard so much, and people tagged me as cocky for believing it. They always said that I walked around like I thought I was the shit, and maybe I did, but it took a lot to get there. I'll admit, I wasn't quite as self-assured as people thought I was. I had my issues just like everyone else. Although looks seemed to work out, the molding hands made sure to level me out in other areas, keep me down. Enough about that crap though. You don't expect me to start confessing my inadequacies right here in chapter one, do you? Ha! That's laughable. Let's get back to graduation night, the night it all started.

TWO

Four years of vending machine lunches, subpar grades, attempted hooky, and it was all coming to a great finale. The setting was a chilly December night in a beaten grass field at Farrell High. A couple of years ago the district took on the so-called "year-round schedule." The change wasn't as bad as it sounds. We had more breaks throughout the year, and our longest should-be-summer vacation was relocated to the winter. That's how hot it gets in Arizona; people prefer to take their summer in the winter.

I was just minutes away from receiving my biggest and last educational certificate. How did I feel? I asked myself that question as I stood, shivering, in the back of the line, single file and awaiting instruction. I was cold…that's it; that's as deep as my feelings for graduation ran. The administration had trained and conditioned most of my fellow sheep surprisingly well. They were almost ready for the drudge of college and then onto their future jobs, buried miserably low in the ranks of one faceless corporation or another. I didn't resent any of them for following that old trampled path.

Shit, I was actually kind of grateful. A world filled with people like me would probably result in pure mobocracy.* Somebody needs to take out the world's trash and wash the dishes while I'm traveling off on a tangent.

Okay, maybe I had a problem with structure and authority. I guess I always found my way more interesting – personal bias maybe.

Mrs. Adams was squawking at the rest of our graduating class and repeating herself louder as she worked her way up the line. "Order now, scholars. Single file. Got to stay organized, Mr. Stewart…"

When I could see that she was far enough along the line, I ducked out and darted around the tall chain-link fence that separated the art building and the football field. After loitering in the shadows for a few minutes, I saw one of my friends farther up the line pull the same escape and head for the meeting spot.

My group at Farrell was small in numbers, but we genuinely enjoyed each other's company. The first one around the fence was Sam; he was your token fast food eating, high-stress American. He carried a long skinny appearance, pale dangling arms covered in thin, flaxen,

---

* Note from the author: Matt has asked me to explain that these are not his exact words. For example: he would rather have used the word chaos instead of mobocracy. I thought that the expression "pure chaos" was trite and average wording. In any event, I have been granted *some* artistic license in the following pages.

moss-like hair, excited brown eyes, dirty blond hair trimmed to an acceptable length, and a few old pock marks positioned about his cheeks, reminiscent of a violent puberty.

Lately he had been sporting a heavy class of 2003 ring. The ring's wide face was decorated with discount jewels and centered with a black stamped bird. I didn't care for the school flare, but then again, in those days I didn't like much about Farrell. I knew that he enjoyed his tacky new band, and he rarely enjoyed anything, so I kept my opinions to myself.

Sam hooked a sleeve of his navy gown on the wire fence as he barreled around the corner. His white freckled shoulder popped through the torn seam.

The sleeve dangled, barely connected by a few stubborn threads. "What the *fuck*. Did you see the *blade* hanging off that thing?" he yowled, angrily bouncing a kick off the link fence beside us. "That shit almost took my arm off."

Sam had chronic bad luck; fortunately for him, it was never anything too serious. Somehow, he managed to stay in decent spirits, which was no small task considering the countless bumps, scrapes, and downright embarrassing situations he battled daily. Before Sam learned to accept the fact that he was locked into some kind of never-ending struggle with tainted karma, he tried to blend in, and in his more bold moments, he even attempted to infiltrate the hip crowd.

During freshman year, he had worked the idea into

his head that joining the football team would be an easy way to win a spot with the popular older guys. He never quite made it to that coveted jockstrap though.

Now, I didn't know Sam back then, so this is all hearsay, but the word around the lunch table was that he had a little mishap during the state-required physical exam. I guess he was not fully informed as to how the coach checked for a hernia, and in his confusion he ended up putting on an amazing and unintentional antigravity show. When Sam's turn for the old cough and check came up, something else did as well. That's right – boner time.

Supposedly my friend Brian Riney was there, and he told me that Sam just stood there shorts down, wide eyed, and pleading, "No, guys, it's not me. I'm *nervous*. It's because I'm nervous. What the fuck, man? Coach is the one who wants to see my balls."

That one stuck with him for a while. Yeah, shit happened to him all the time, some dreadful and others minor, but he had a way of amplifying each instance without discrimination. All of that stress and forced humility can wear on a man, can aggravate him. Some people think he's obnoxious, but I can't get enough of the guy.

The lined-up seniors near the parking lot took a step forward and then shuffled in place, listening to the band warm up on the field. As the minutes passed, I wondered where my other friends were. I figured that they were in line, but I hadn't actually seen them yet.

"Sam, did you see anybody else in line?"

The Little White Trip

He pointed ahead.

Julie and Ian cornered the fence and advanced toward our darkened hideout. Ian stumbled up to us with his trademark "I got into my mom's wine cellar" strut. His drinking wasn't a daily occurrence or anything serious like that; it was mostly a morning through night routine. I'm pretty sure that the early drink was what gave him the nerve to suggest the "extreme close-up smile" idea to Mrs. Adams. She thought he was the model student. "Some thinker," she would say. "He's real creative behind the camera."

And even more ridiculous than that, she had told his mom, on several occasions, that I was a bad influence on him, and that it would be best to keep us separated. His mom didn't give a shit though. She was too wrapped up in her next real estate commission to even notice him. And to even things out, his dad had taken a never-ending business trip years ago. That Peter Pan lifestyle left Ian to his own developing vises which had quickly become: booze, television, and the limitless possibilities of his mom's platinum card.

He had his way with the ladies, too. He was just over six foot, dressed in vintage rags that cost way too much, and had a kind of movie star-looking face: overgrown lips, a very thin and straight nose, and a shag of dark brown hair, that most of the time concealed a set of sleepy bright green eyes.

Julie was fiddling with Sam's gown, mentally straining for a way to tuck his ragged sleeve back into the hole.

"Julie, did you see Dura in line when you came over?" I asked, examining the train of puttering bodies.

"No, I thought she was back by you. That line was alphabetical, wasn't it?"

"That's what I thought, too. Hopefully she shows up. I heard that anyone who misses walking the aisle is not going to be allowed to go to Project Graduation," I said, beginning to stress a little.

"She would be crazy to miss Project Grad. I heard it's like a free all-night carnival," Julie said, abandoning Sam's crisis. "Besides, she already registered and everything."

"Julie," Sam insisted, "can you keep your attention over here? I'm falling apart."

"Sam, I'm trying my best to –" She stopped, noticing something in the distance. "Oh this is *fucking great.*"

"What?" Sam asked, confused.

"I knew he'd come here looking for me."

"Julie, what are you talking about?"

I knew exactly who she was talking about even before I saw him. Just by hearing her voice – she saved that particular tone to speak of only one person, Brad Phelps. He was the undying byproduct of a tormented, and highly talked about, year-and-a-half relationship of hers. He stopped to talk to somebody in line. He must have been asking about Julie because the girl he was questioning pointed him over in our direction.

Julie looked like she was contemplating bolting off down the alley.

Ian leaned his tabletop graduation hat forward, half

concealing his face. The blue and black tassel hung front and center like the nose plate of a Greek soldier's helmet. He was ready for battle.

As Brad pushed past the line, heading toward our spot, Ian, without saying a word to any of us, started casually walking in his direction. About halfway down the alley, trying to correct his timing, Ian's strides lengthened, and his gown floated at his heels. Brad reached the grass from the pavement just as Ian did the opposite.

As Julie's stalker spotted us, Ian, with his face hidden, nodded to the guy and scooted left, disappearing behind the art building. He bailed on the situation completely. What a shit bag, right? He must have known what was going to happen. He was normally bolder than that. Oh well; I was on my own, then.

My heart rate picked up a touch as he crossed the space between us. Sure, he was alone, but I had heard, and seen on one occasion, that that kid was a real head case, anger problems galore.

"What are these," he hollered at Julie, still about ten feet away, "your new boyfriends?"

She didn't respond.

"Does it take two guys to get you off these days?"

I cracked my neck, left then right.

"Fuck you, Brad," she scowled.

He looked like a reject from some aspiring boy band, and he had one of those annoying mouths that was always open an inch or so.

"Oh yeah, Julie, you wish I'd waste my sweat on you.

Those days are over. But if I did, I'd do it all on my own," he said with a laugh, thrusting the crotch of his jeans in our direction a couple of times.

He was way too close for my liking, three feet, maybe.

"You her new man?" he asked Sam, giving him a sarcastic pat on the shoulder, too rough to be friendly.

Sam wasn't okay with it, but he was no fighter either. I almost said something, but I wanted to give him the benefit, and let him handle it his way. "Didn't you get a restraining order against this *cool* guy?" Sam asked Julie, ignoring him altogether.

"Yeah, I did," she said, staring at Brad. "Why don't you just go away? Didn't you graduate in like 1980?"

His smile faded. "Why did you tell Amy I hit you?"

"Because you *did*. And she's way too good for your little uncut pecker anyway. Aren't you banned from being at this school? Just leave before you end up calling your dad crying from jail again."

That pissed him off pretty good. He sighed to keep from screaming. That prick probably did hit her. He seemed to be struggling to contain himself right then. I hadn't taken my eyes from his since he had stepped up to us, and he hadn't connected with mine yet. Confident that Sam was no threat, he turned his head to size me up. At the same time, I looked past him, noticing something entering into the light at the end of the alley. He must have taken my eyes diverting as a sign of fear because he tried to start in with me.

"Matt, right?" He chuckled. "Is this the tough one?"

The Little White Trip

It didn't take me long to register what, or who, was coming in from the light of the sidewalk and creeping drunkenly through the grass: Ian. Maybe I had branded him as a coward too early; he was crafty, shady. And when dealing with a slug like Brad, I liked that kind of thing.

"What's the matter? Don't want to admit that you're the new squeeze?"

His question made me think. What if I *was* her new squeeze? For all he knew that *was* the case, and here he was trying to talk sex to my girl, fucking with my friends, and now, obviously under the impression that I was too weak to retaliate, talking shit to me directly.

When I didn't answer, he chuckled and tried to give me that same horseplay bullshit that he had gotten away with doing to Sam. That's exactly where he fucked up. First of all, never hit a girl, and secondly, unless we're friends, don't put your fucking hands on me either, especially when my friend's closing in quickly on your back.

I smacked his hand away before it had even found my shoulder. His balance shifted, and he fell forward a step, putting him even closer to me. His breath smelled like an ashtray. He looked angry and confused all at the same time.

I shoved him back, hard. "Get the *fuck* out of my face."

Seeing the action picking up, Ian loped up from behind like a hungry panther.

Brad pulled back a foot or two and shook his head as

if he was going to leave it alone. But then, as blatant as a voice cue, he dropped his right shoulder and started cranking a fist around. And to think, before that moment, I was going to let him walk if he had decided to.

"*Get him, Ian,*" Julie screamed, noticing the ambush.

His swing hooked around, but before it was even close enough for me to dodge, Ian got him. As he ran up from behind, he turned his last stride, with his right leg, into a Super Bowl-strength punt. His foot erupted from under his draped gown and sailed catastrophically on point between Brad's legs. The toe of Ian's shoe popped through on my side as his kick jarred with a thud against Brad's testosterone sack. I ducked back to avoid the punch, but there was no need. With his balls rocketing toward his stomach, his swing went limp, and he doubled over.

Now, I hadn't been in a ton of fights outside of grade school, but my playground experience had taught me the basics. I knew that a pullback dodge like the one that I had just done was almost always to be followed up with a swing of my own. If I had had time to compute the agony that this guy was facing, I may have let Ian's blow be the only one – but then again, maybe not. He *was* a future wife beater, and I didn't have time to change the flight path of my fist anyway.

On account of Brad's stupid mouth always being open, my knuckles connected almost exclusively with teeth. For him, that may have been a good thing; otherwise, he might have ended up with one lip and two halves. His front teeth bent loose in his gums and kinked backward. Obviously, I couldn't tell then, but I heard about the bending later. His head whipped to the side, knees went slack, and clutching his bag of mush below, he dropped to the grass at our feet.

With the enemy wall fallen from between us, I got a look at the pleased expression on Ian's face. Job well done, he'd just committed the ultimate male-on-male sin; I guess karma wore a robe and smelled of booze that night.

Holding his cap in one hand, he pointed with the other, taunting, "What now, mother fucker? You want to beat on a girl; now you're the girl, *bitch*." I had seen Ian get in fights in the past, and he always ended up screaming like some Long Beach thug – either that or Joe Pesci.

All that boasting and hollering was not a good thing for a couple of kids trying to stay hidden so close to the faculty, especially the ones that just may have ended the hopes for offspring and solid food for a twenty-two-year-old moaning pile at their feet. Some of the kids in line started pointing toward the commotion and noise. Mr. Graves, the football coach, got wise to their talk and started jogging over.

Sam, who'd stayed quiet through our viper strike, stated the obvious, "We need to get the hell out of here."

THREE

We ran off through the alley between the fence and the art building. Ian, up front, boot camped it over a low gate into the school scrap yard. The rest of us did the same. My right hand cramped and stung as I pulled myself up and over. I remembered then why I had stopped punching solid things in the seventh grade; it fucking hurt. The scrap yard was at the rear of the 201 Building; upstairs was the teacher's lounge and below was the janitorial room. The dark yard was cluttered with things like old desks, filing cabinets, and bent and broken chairs.

Our gowns, like the ruffled draping of a table cloth, hovered just above ground-level but didn't interfere with the legs. Well, Sam tripped on his and took a spill, but I just marked that up to the fact that it was him. The fall excited him even more; dashing upfront to make up the time, he climbed a couple stacks of cabinets like oversized steps. I paused for a second, watching the odd spectacle. The cabinets grew higher and higher left to right like a three-group bar graph. On the top level Sam leaned forward toward the building; everything from his waist up disappeared onto a thin cement overhang. As he pulled himself the rest of the way up, his legs slid out of sight. His move was quite Indiana Jones, if you ask me, but Sam would wear the hat and the whip if it meant saving his ass. I climbed up next. Ian helped Julie and climbed up as well.

The top side of the ledge was long and thin, like a floating sidewalk; it covered the walkway below and extended all the way back to the gate that we had jumped to get in. The motion lights near the doors below had been triggered, but up top, especially with our dark gowns, all was hidden. Besides, it would be a pretty random place to go looking for somebody up there. The footing was noisy and a bit precarious. The tar and grainy stone surface at our feet was littered with cigarette butts and soda cans that had been dropped by rebellious teachers from the main balcony above.

Ian started to move along the edge of the walk past the rest of us. I steadied myself with a hand to the red brick wall. He squeezed past Sam, heading back in the direction of the grass alley.

Sam grabbed at his sleeve. "Ian, what the fuck are you doing?"

Ian motioned with his pointer finger for Sam to be quiet.

"Ian, you're going to get us caught."

He stopped and crept back to us, whispering, "We can see what's happening with them if we go over to that end. We should find out what's going on because we may have to say *fuck it* and skip graduation altogether."

"What? No, we can't —"

"Shhh, goddamn it. We've gotta do this; if not, fucking me and Matt might be going to jail," he said, and started off through the cans and moldy leaves and butts.

I decided to trail Ian. If he was spotted, we'd all be caught anyway. Climbing back down would not be a quick ordeal. Plus, maybe I could keep him from falling nine feet onto a stack of overturned chairs. As we neared the end, Ian crouched over to pick something up; it was a metal flask, dented and patchy with rust, but the cap was still intact. He started to say something about the wino teachers, but I shushed him and prompted him onward. He shook the container. The brew splashed inside and spoke to him through the rusty tin. *I'm not bad, Ian. I'm just aged now – even more potent.* He agreed, nodding and fitting the thin flask under his gown and into his back pocket.

"Move, fucker."

We found the end of the ledge along with a perfect bird's eye view of the coach and Brad.

He was still lying in the grass, and the coach, standing above him, seemed frustrated, asking, "What the hell happened to you? And why are you back on school campus?" Coach knew him. Brad had been a pain in his ass years ago when he went to Farrell.

He tried one last time. "Did you get in a fight or what? I can't help you if you don't work with me."

Brad probably knew that the coach wasn't trying to help him. He just wanted to get him for not only being on campus but coming there to fight as well. "Fuck you," he said; his painful words were slurred and brief.

"Okay, have it your way," he huffed, and then he started speaking into a walkie-talkie. "This is coach Graves. Can I get the nurse and one of the campus officers over here on the west side of the art building? We've a got a trespasser who came here to fight, and somebody bent his damn teeth back for him."

We waited in that spot until the cops had come and gone. They never searched the scrap yard or seemed to care much about what had really happened. We dropped down onto the metal cabinets, trying hard to minimize our time on the noisy and denting levels. We took the long route through the courtyards and were amazed to see that the line still hadn't moved. God bless the indolence of public school. The four of us found the back of the line, clear of Mrs. A, but our pentacle was still incomplete. Where the hell was Dura?

As we started to cover our final trek to the ceremony, a pair of cold hands reached up from over my shoulders and covered my eyes. I saw the hands for a second before I went blind. I knew those paws, and I knew the giggle that followed them even better: Dura. She made it. I didn't acknowledge her or her hands at first; I just kept walking with the line as if nothing had changed, but then something did. The line deadlocked, and I ran into Sam, ahead of me. When the brim of my cap hit his and fell off, I threw my hands out, catching him around the waist.

"*Hey*, what the hell, Matt? What are you doing? Get your damn hands off my hips."

I laughed and peeled the brown hands from my eyes.

I pulled Dura's arms over my shoulders and squatted down, hoisting her up and onto my back. I let her arms go, and she hung on. Her chin came in just over my right shoulder.

"Oh, Dura," Sam noticed, "you decided to join us."

I felt her chin pat the top of my shoulder a couple of times as she nodded yes.

Sam grabbed both of our caps up from the ground and handed mine over. "Here. Now keep your hands off my ass, *queer*."

"Sorry. I thought I heard Mrs. A call out, 'All right, fuckers – let's conga!'"

From her perch, Dura laughed loudly in my ear. Sam rolled his eyes and fit the suction cup base of his cap into position.

Dura's knees clung above my hips, but the tension of her weight was starting to produce some menacing sounds from the seams around the neck of my gown. I let her go, and before I could turn around to see her, she smacked my cap up and off my head. She was feisty that night.

She bobbed around like a prize fighter. "Come on, Matt. Let's see what you're made of."

She took a couple of jabs at my gut, penetrating my loose gown but nothing else.

I stumbled back. "Ugh," I joked, clutching my shattered ribs. "I give up."

When she came close enough and had stopped bouncing, I reached out with both arms like a mauling bear. She stepped in quickly and got me around the flanks in a big hug. That surprised me, but I returned the gesture as naturally as I could.

"This is the big night," she said, and did that extra tight squeeze thing that people always do just before they let go of a really important hug.

She pulled back, smiling. "Are you psyched or what? We're outta here."

"What?" I was still thrown by the long hug. She wasn't normally like that. She was physical but more cheap-shot-clowning-around-with-your-brother physical. "Yeah – I guess. We're outta here, right?"

"I'd be careful boxing with Matt," Sam told Dura. "He's liable to punch your mouth off."

"Very funny, Sam," I said, giving him a look that said, *shut up*.

Dura noticed. "What? What's he talking about, Matt?"

"Nothing." Dura was passive, and I knew that she wouldn't want to hear about Brad or his teeth. "Sam's just giving me shit because I used to go to a boxing gym when I was thirteen," I fibbed.

"Oh, I see. So you've got the advantage. I guess I'll have to start training a little more then." She took one last shot at my robe and threw her right arm up – victorious.

Dura's mom was a full-blooded Sicilian, and her dad was a boisterous Dominican. I don't think that I have to say this for it to be known, but with a mixture that spicy, there was a lot of attitude flying around the Lopez house. Good people, just proud as pros. I think that such a reverent waiving of flags kind of confused Dura growing up. She told me once that her parents almost made her feel like she had to pick a heritage. It all worked out though. She was proud like her parents but more proud of who she was, not what she was, if that makes any sense.

She had a soft coffee complexion, hazel eyes, long brown hair, and the heart-shaped lips of a sexy cartoon. She was the star volleyball champ up until junior year and still bore the athletic look. She dressed in warm-ups and tank tops, things like that. Not the most fashionable girl, more like a "one of the guys" type, nevertheless, she always had my attention.

Sam picked my cap up off the ground, and using the square top like a ping-pong paddle, he served the back of my head with a good pop for the game point. "Here's your cap, *again*. Do I need your mom to sew a chinstrap on this thing or…"

He was being a little too cocky for his own good: calling me a queer, becoming abusive, and then setting in again with the belittlement. He was showing off.

I reached over, got ahold of his left sleeve and, with a little jerk, disconnected it.

"*Hey*. What the *hell* did you do that for?" he growled, snatching the fabric from my hand.

"Dude, your entire shoulder was hanging out. What did you plan on doing?"

"I don't know," he admitted, swatting the blue tube at my face. "Goddamn, Matt, what am I supposed to be here, some punk rock graduate?"

I poked at the open hole in his gown. "Jesus, Sam, are

you wearing a shirt under there?"

"What the *fuck*? Nobody told me I had to wear a shirt. This thing covers me neck to toes."

I pulled at his gown a little more, unraveling some blue thread. "*Please* tell me that you're wearing pants, Sam."

He shoved my hand away.

"Holy shit," I laughed, "you've got armpit hair all over the place. Look out – I think it's headed for your wrists."

"Get off my gown, man."

My guts were splitting. "Oh, dude, I can see your nipple."

Sam began virally blushing; the red wave started at his cheeks and spread from there. His famous zigzag vein popped from his temple like a turkey timer. I smiled and nodded in encouragement. He was about to explode, but…he didn't. Whatever it was that was holding the line up had passed, and the rest of our class was leaving us. Sam decided to leave our children's games behind and walk ahead toward adulthood and diplomaville.

"Matt, you're a jackass."

Between our long-distance phone calls and visits, Matt e-mailed, and sometimes scribbled down, notes to help me with my writing. I have included a bit of his (slightly polished) text below. (PJG)

What's up, man...

Sorry I wasn't able to talk for long last time you tried me. I can tell you're running thin. But you'll like this; I've been writing down some extra notes, including the bad stuff when it all went crazy. Anything I put down on paper still seems like shit compared to being there, but I'm writing it anyway. Hopefully, you can take what I'm saying and make it better. Make it so people can see it the way that I did.

Maybe you should come up and visit me some day soon; you know my schedule – nothing but time. I'm not the best at telling stories, at least not in the kind of detail that you seem to need, but I'm getting better all the time, and with you always grilling my five senses, I know you'll come up with something good.

You laugh when I go on and on about the little random things, but I like that stuff the most. And I know that the dirt and the blood is what people really want to hear about, but just humor me and put in some of that other stuff, too.

(He talks about school and his parents. He talks about a night with his girl. He moves away from the weekend, into the times when they should've known better.)

Before he took us there, he spoke of the fallen, the charred, and the rotten. He said that the little girl's fingernails had been peeled back with something like a can opener. The other one, a boy, was burned to a black and gritty dust. He told us that that sick fuck had taken his time with the children; he stayed around with them for days.

We were off to meet the man from the stories, armed with disbelief and logic, an arsenal that normally could've defeated such a villain. We were ill-prepared though. Their warnings weren't worth shit; they wanted us to fall. I guess our future was just written that way. If we would've known what we were up against, who we were up against, we could have gotten away, but like feeder mice held within the trapping glass walls, we were pulled out, one by one, to cower before the hungry eyes of the snake.

FOUR

Positioned at the front of the line, Mrs. Adams guided the class of 2003 along the school grounds like a line of army ants. We marched out past the gym, beside the bleachers, and stopped at a chest-high steel gate that bordered the football field. Although it had already been dark for a while, the field was lit beyond that of daylight. I don't know if I should be proud of this, but I think graduation night may have been one of the only times that I had made it out to the field since freshman gym. I avoided school events whenever I had a choice.

The aluminum bleachers popped and clanged like a drunken parade. Everybody's mom, dad, sister, and stepbrother showed up, searching for the best row to squint from and speculate as to which navy blue blob was theirs. The air was thick with dust and yellow grass clippings. From where I was standing, I could barely make out what I thought were the tops of those funny hats that they put the marching band in. The ones up front must have held some kind of seniority because their hats had been upgraded with a fluffy white feather.

A loud shriek of electrical interference filled the air, and then a voice started in over the speakers. "*Tap, Tap,*

The Little White Trip

Tap, testing...test, can somebody fix this piece of...oh, here we are. Thanks, Karen." The voice continued, only this time less aggravated and deeper in tone. "Hello, ladies and gentlemen, members of the staff. We are gathered here on this beautiful night for a joyous occasion, to celebrate the accomplishments, hard work, and spirit of the graduating class of two thousand and three."

The crowd erupted into a frenzy of clapping, whistling, and stomping high in the bleachers.

The speakers boomed over the noise. "Okay, okay, yep, we sure are proud of them, too. But, we're going to have to ask you folks to please hold your applause until the end," the voice announced, creating an instant buzz kill for all but a few rebellious spectators.

"As the school principal, I can truthfully say that this has been my favorite bunch," Mr. Stewart said, casually lying to thousands of people. "Ladies and gentlemen, the class of two thousand and three."

With that, the brass army strained their tight lips and turgid cheeks to serenade us with that familiar graduation song, *baa bom bomp baa baa baa.*

Mrs. A, waving a thumbs-up and flashing her horse teeth at us, gave the signal to start in. We were sent into row upon row of cream-colored plastic folding chairs. They set us up like a line of dominos, and we were to fall into place accordingly.

Julie was the first one to drop headfirst into the obvious logic hole in our sit-together conspiracy. Her last name was Burnett, and the B's began spilling out of a row on the complete other side of the field. I figured that out a few minutes earlier, but we were already seated, so I decided to keep quiet and act surprised. Poor Julie; they called her name along with the person that she was supposed to be seated next to, and naturally, the other girl, Amy Bennington, reached the stage before her. There was a mass confusion amongst the staff when the kids weren't matching up with the diplomas.

Julie was forced to apologetically climb over seated people, who were to stay seated for hundreds of names to come. As they started calling the C's, she finally scurried up from the wrong side of the field, short of breath and glowing crimson. Although she hadn't appeared when her name was called, somehow Julie's parents spotted her, and with a small burst of applause they cheered her along.

She was not an easy girl to miss. Julie had inherited her mom's trophy wife looks. She wore a length of cascading blonde hair, had blue eyes, and traveled with a very strange walk; it was more of a hip-heavy waddle, but not without class. Sometimes she really exaggerated the walk. She would place one hand on her hip and extend the other above her waist. Her dangling hand, bent from the wrist, just kind of flopped around as she walked. Her face usually held an inquisitive look although I'd be surprised if there was ever much going on upstairs. She conveyed more of the friendly Labrador character, not that she was dumb or anything, but – I don't know – you know the type.

The odd bump and crawl went on three more times:

Sam Canton, Dura Lopez, and finally Ian Shmelts and yours truly, Matt Thomas. After Dura jumped the row ahead of ours, Mrs. A was onto us. Ian and I were the only ones left in the voided spots. That old crow aimed a stiff finger in our direction and waved us over with her other bony hand. I shook Ian from the semiconscious trance that he'd been living in since we sat down. At one point, he was actually sleeping on some poor kid's back who was seated ahead of him.

I knew how highly Mrs. A thought of Ian, and prayed that she might take it easier on me if she had to inflict my same punishment on her prized cinematographer. Ian braced himself on my shoulder as he tripped and muddled down the aisle. A few seats from the end, his foot wedged under a chair's leg and sent him lurching forward onto my back. His drunken weight almost pitched me to the grass. As I stumbled forward with Ian on my back, I beheld the wicked expression on Mrs. A's face and decided to take a second to maintenance my investment a bit.

Serving a couple of light palm taps on his red cheek, I said, "Ian, *Ian*, listen to me."

Addled, he staggered back. "What are you doing, man? Let's get on stage already. I want to get my diploma," he said through heavy lips which seemed to be moving to another story.

Grabbing his cheeks in my hands, I squeezed his mouth out puckered and warned, "No, man, they didn't call us, *she did*," I clarified by stepping to my left, so he could see our welcome party. "Understand? She's pissed because we didn't sit in our assigned seats."

He was still clueless. "Who's pissed?"

I turned once again, this time with him. Mrs. A was clawing her way down the aisle toward us.

His eyes sobered and fixed on her; he straightened up quickly. "*Shit.*" And just like that, he was clergy clean.

Pushing me aside, he started over to her. I followed but kept my distance; I knew his performance could go either way. As I neared the end of the aisle, I could feel my father's piercing eyes fixed on my back. I don't know how he knew it was me or how I could feel that it was him, but I knew that feeling.

"Please, *God*, let this work out. Let me make it to that stage," I whispered in a kind of pseudo prayer.

I caught up to them in time to hear Ian telling Mrs. Adams something like, "...so you see it was all just a big misunderstanding."

At first, the only thing I could see was the back of his head, but when I got closer, I saw a little crack of a smile on her cold face; it faded fast upon seeing me.

With an assenting pat on the back, she said, "Okay, Ian, you know we're going to miss you in the studio." Turning to me she switched gears and continued, "As for you, Mr. Thomas, you're on very thin ice. You better watch it if you want to make it to *Project* Graduation tonight."

As she enunciated the word *project*, she spit on me. I'd hate to think it was on purpose, but I didn't dare wipe her spittle off right there in front of her. She knew she did it just as well as I did. I even saw her eyes shift and watch it hit me on the chin. Toxic.

With that, she lifted her nose, ordering, "The two of you stay right here and file out as you're called."

The rest of the ceremony went along with the kind of ease that the administration demands, but never really expects to see.

I made it.

FIVE

After the ceremony, we waded through the crowd for a while, exchanging bear hugs and handshakes with dozens of forgotten relatives and acquaintances. My hand still hurt a little, but my brain wasn't making such a big deal out of it anymore. I walked the grounds, separated from my friends, and wiping a rainbow of lipstick from my cheek. The field was littered with square caps and lime green programs. Tired of bumping into duteously forced conversations, I decided to find my friends and get to the damn party already. Besides that, I wasn't sure how things were going to turn out with our little fight and thought it better to be hanging around with the nutcracker in case Brad or any of his counterparts decided to come back for more.

I found Dura and Sam in the parking lot, sitting in Dura's silver Acura. The car wasn't running, but I could see the blue digital menu scrolling across her flip screen CD player. I stood next to the car on Sam's side for a minute, waiting for one of them to roll down the window. My presence went unnoticed. A flash ignited near the steering wheel, illuminating the two of them in a strobe before going black again. Then, from the same spot, a second or two later, the light reappeared with a spark, but that time it followed through to a steady flame. Dura's face shone in golden tones as she directed the flame in toward the glass contraption at her lips. I tapped on the window. Sam's expression was dulled through the smoke and tint, but the terror that came through told me that he expected to see a badge and a gun. The lighter went out, but the small red and orange herbal ball in the pipe glowed brightly under the healthy pull of Dura's lungs. God, that girl was a badass. She didn't even pause her toke to contemplate Sam's shock beside her.

The window started to mechanically drop, and with it came the morose tones of some Radiohead song.

"Matt – you dick," Sam hissed. "Do you enjoy scaring years off my life?"

"Absolutely."

Sam was quiet. The guy on the CD was moaning something about being bulletproof.

"Hey, Matt," Dura said from across the car. "You want to get in the clamshell or what?"

"No thanks. You guys should get the hell out of there. I could already smell that skunk with the windows up. And when this cloud hits the field, they're going to call the fucking fire department."

She laughed and rolled the window up. The CD screen turned over and went out. After showering each other in some natural, magnolia-scented perfume, Dura and Sam followed me toward the event gates.

"Hey, what happened to you and Ian with Mrs. A?"

Sam laughed. "It didn't look good."

"Oh, Sam *Canton*, yeah, that was a convenient last name to have. I was stuck at the end with T. That old whore caught on real quick after you guys went. She ended up yelling at me, said I was on thin ice, and then she spit on me," I complained, still feeling pretty sour.

"She *spit* on you?"

"Yeah, spat. She spat on my chin." I couldn't help but chuckle at the absurdity of it all.

Dura wasn't listening to our dialogue; she was hungry. "Mmmm, Project Grad's right through those gates." She licked her lips. "I heard they had root beer floats with coconut ice cream last year."

I poked at her stomach with a finger, like they do to the Doughboy. She was Olympian fit but did the little giggle anyway.

"Fucking pothead," Sam criticized, trying to pretend like he wasn't in the clouds as well.

Dura wasn't one of those exaggerated and showy stoners. She was aware and alert, on or off. "Here comes Julie and Ian." She spotted them coming through the busy lot.

With the luminous field at their heels, I could see Ian draped over Julie's shoulder like a hobbled teammate. At first, I thought they were just taking part in a little post-graduate camaraderie, but as they came closer, it became clear that Julie was the only thing between Ian and a nap in the dirt. He had already passed his peak twice that night and was working on number three. Ian was not your normal human, the type that climbs the whisky hill to the brief peak and then tumbles down. Oh no – he had hills, valleys, humps, dips, crests, and just when you thought he was done, he would start it all over again.

When Julie was close enough, she pawned him off onto me, saying, "Here, it's your turn with Dr. Jekyll."

"What do you mean, Dr. Jekyll? Was Mr. Hyde out tonight?" I asked, attempting to balance his swaying.

Pointing at his hung mug, she griped, "Yeah, he was out all right. If it wasn't bad enough that I had to run like an idiot across the field in front of my family, Mr. Personality over there caught up with me while I was taking pictures with my Aunt Bonnie. He was drinking some rotten shit out of a dirty canteen or something. He was hanging all over me in the photos, throwing peace signs, and he ended up puking on my Aunt's shoes."

I pushed his heavy body away from me, holding him by the shoulders; his breath confirmed her story. "That's disgusting."

"I know," she agreed. "She was wearing open-toed shoes, too."

Ian defended himself, saying, "It's just booze, Julie. It's not food."

Julie's character was normally bubbly, but Ian had a way of causing her moods to go flat and downright bitter at times. They had a love, hate, hate thing going on.

Ian began to sob and moan. A bubble formed at his lips; it gradually inflated and popped with his apology, "I'm, I'm sor, sorry, Julie, that I made a mess all over your grandma's shoes. She's so nice, and I –"

"That was my aunt, not my grandmother," Julie grumbled. "Not that you care, but my grandmother is dead."

"I'm sorry, Julie. I'm sorry she's dead. I didn't…" he blubbered, running short of breath as if those were his dying words.

He was fully crying by that point. I had seen him like that before, but Dura hadn't, and I don't think Sam had either. I felt embarrassed for him at first, but soon I could see that his drunken melodramatics were actually working out for him.

The red tones in Julie's face washed white with cool compassion; her words were next. She scooped Ian up in her arms and gently rocked him, lulling, "It's okay, Ian. It's okay."

He let a few more sniffles go but was soon pacified.

"So are we going to go to the party, or…" Sam asked uncomfortably.

Shrugging my shoulders, I turned back to Julie and Ian. "Are you guys planning on going to Project Grad, or what's the deal? Because it's already quarter past nine, and doors opened fifteen minutes ago."

After a few minutes, Ian seemed to be in better spirits. Such a quick mood flip wasn't uncommon for Ian, drunk or dry. I think the booze just gave him a rational excuse for the whole thing.

All of us except for bare-chested Sam tossed our gowns into the back of Ian's truck on the way to the campus gates. As twisted as a few of us were, the old ladies at the admittance table, already hours past their six-thirty bedtime, didn't give a rat's ass about pink eyes or funny odors.

SIX

The administration had gone through a lot of trouble to transform Farrell High's sparse and vapid grounds to a fenced-in, seniors-only shindig to remember. Once inside the gates, my stomach brimmed with the kind of pleasant anxiety I used to feel on Christmas morning, wondering which boxes belonged to me. But at that place they were all mine: rides, food, games, and booths flashing and whistling the amenities usually reserved for some rich kid's tenth birthday. The only event I could compare Project Graduation to was my father's yearly company picnic. Those were the only two places I had been to that truly revolved around fun and, better yet, didn't cost a dime.

I imagined that was what being newly rich must feel like. Anything you want – it's yours and happily given to you by a pleasant attendant. Although the faculty hung this great night and privilege over our heads for months, hyping it up and then threatening to pull it away, that was in the past, and once inside we were in a candy land of rides, treats, games, and raffles. True, it was a great place.

So naturally, I would never have imagined that our horrible run of events would begin right there on that very night. Our terminal card would be dealt to us in the cruel mask of luck.

One of my favorite games at that place was this ridiculous one that took place inside a clear plastic tube. With your turn came the unsealing of the "cash capsule." The capsule was like a giant upright pill with a door. When it was your turn, you were ushered inside, and the door's latch was replaced. Standing ankle deep in crumpled cash, you knew the game was about to begin. With the ignition of a ready green light, a powerful fan below would growl and propel the bills in swarm-like clusters. The object of the game was simple: to grab as much flying money as you could, and when it was all over, you got to keep it. I know it sounds like that game would quickly double the national debt, but it was harder than you'd figure. The most cash that I ever made out with was eight bucks.

The best part about the games was how simple and dorky they all were like the beanbag toss or the cork gun shooting range. The mega tricycle race always had a huge line, but it was worth it. I'm not talking about your dad's Radio Flyer trikes though. These bikes were outfitted with oversized dirt wheels and handled surprisingly well on the dusty figure eight track. Sam sported the most intense game face during the races and, of course, he always lost.

Losing was okay because even last place was rewarded with one hundred dollars. Although the bills in the tube game were real, the money given out at the other games was not; it was more of a Monopoly money knockoff with the stupid Farrell bird in the center. The notes could be spent on many other things like black jack, broomstick horse racing, or roulette. Developing a meaty bankroll wasn't a hard thing to do. And in the end, the loot was used to buy raffle tickets, and the tickets were used to enter a number of drawings. It was a veritable economy of profits and losses and winnings and reinvestments.

I put a couple of tickets in each raffle tin – shotgun logic. Ian and Sam dropped most of theirs into the plane tickets drawing. The girls spread theirs around, but I did notice that Dura had dumped a whole handful of her tickets into the drawing for the trip to Flagstaff. The eastern sky, once wine dark, faded ashy shades of blue and grey, and the morning was upon us.

I asked one of the volunteers what time it was. She told me that it was already five forty-five. "Just fifteen minutes till the raffle starts," she said in a jovial songlike measure.

With the first birds chirping and dew on the grass, the others scattered back to the gaming tables, looking for a last-minute jackpot. Dura was the only person that I saw win a game. After exchanging cash for tickets, she crossed the busy grounds toward the raffle booth. I knew exactly where she was headed.

I stopped her just before she put them in. "Dura, are you sure you want to put even more tickets into that one? You already tossed a bunch in there. Besides, everybody's going for that prize; the chances are probably next to none."

She looked at me and seemed almost hurt. "Matt, I really want to win this one. Look, did you read it? You and *four* friends get an all-expense-paid trip to Flagstaff. It's a snowboarding trip — cabin, rentals, gear, food, and we'd even get a Lincoln Navigator to drive up there. You and four friends, that's us, Matt — this would be the senior trip we never got to take together."

Undoubtedly certain, she dropped at least twenty more tickets into the pot, crossed her fingers, and flashed me a hopeful little wink.

During the raffle a few of us got lucky. Dura won a mountain bike, I scored a nineteen-inch TV, and Sam picked himself up a fifty-dollar gift certificate to Paradise Valley Mall. He wasn't much of a mall crawler, so his prize followed a short assembly line, from the announcer to him to Dura. At first, she resisted. It was *his* prize.

But he said something like, "This is the worst prize up there. I don't even remember putting tickets in that one. You go to that Amarada place in the mall, don't you? Just use it there. You can take me to lunch sometime."

Dura shrugged, accepting a good deal. Sam was happy to have the so-called luck out of his hands. Julie and Ian had floated off somewhere. Supposedly, they had hooked up before, one night at some rowdy, lawless desert party, but it was always somewhat of a taboo subject.

Julie swore that she was too drunk that night to remember anything. "I'm not saying it didn't happen, and

I'm not saying it did. I just don't remember." Or at least she stood by that amnesic testimony during the following weeks of hullabaloo.

I never could figure out what the big deal was if they had or hadn't, but I must admit, I was curious to know what those two little miscreants had found that one-upped the raffle.

Dura tapped my hand, held up her tickets, and pointed at the announcer. He was standing over the grand finale of prizes, the coveted snowboarding getaway. The overacting performer lifted the bucket with both hands and gave it a good shake. He dramatically stopped, pressing an ear to the painted tin. *Were the tickets speaking to him?*

Twisting the label around to his eyes, he started reading the lavish description to us, "Beautiful Flagstaff, Arizona, all expense paid, eight-room cabin, free boarding passes…"

I watched Dura's eyes change a shade with each detail. I didn't want to see her disappointed. What if I won it for her? I did put a couple of tickets in that drawing. She would just melt for me, hmmm, like coffee ice-cream.

Back at the booth the announcer rung out in his best carnival barker's voice, calling, "Ooo-kay, who's it going to be? Who's the lucky one tonight? Let's see."

He called out the first three numbers painfully slow, "six…three…eight." He had everybody on edge because all the tickets started with six three eight. I had noticed that earlier in the callings, but Dura, like the others, was much too excited to detect anything beyond the prize.

She squeezed my hand as he called out the next two numbers "seven…nine."

My tickets were worthless by that point, but Dura had one ticket that was right there. The announcer was silent. The echo amongst the crowd was a mixture of frustration and anger.

Just before his dramatic pause had lost its novelty, in one great orgasm of sound, he called out the last number, "And the last number is…*one*."

Almost in unison the last ten or fifteen hangers-on moaned. Dura dropped her tickets to the ground and released my clammy hand. Her bottom lip popped out and folded at me. She tried to kid about it, but I could see through her cute expressions. Her eyes collected the truth in a well below the color. Although rare, at times, Dura could be emotional, not crazy emotional or female emotional, but far too delicate for this world.

"Hold on. Nobody claimed it," I realized aloud.

She looked at me for a second, registering my words. I was right, and she was happy.

Gathering her precious chances from the ground near her feet, she said, "So we still have a chance?"

The announcer's eyes bobbled around the crowd. I know that it seems crazy, but I could've sworn, almost like it was meant to be, while he scanned the crowd, the guy stopped a beat and watched Dura sort through her tickets. He seemed puzzled. That was a first for the night, six numbers but no winner.

Raising the microphone back to his lips, he said, "Anyone got that one?" Silence. "Going once, twice –"

And there it was, the screeching sound of bad news. Some horrible girl's voice called, "I've got it."

The voice grew louder as she cut forward through the crowd, getting nearer.

"I think that's me. What'd I win?"

She hadn't even been paying attention, didn't have a clue what she had. What an undeserving piece of shit.

I couldn't bear to look back at Dura. I was sure that she'd be in tears by then. The squealing voice grew closer, and finally, the girl broke through.

"Holy shit, Dura, look. It's Julie. She won it."

In all of the commotion, I didn't even recognize her voice until I actually saw her and heard the voice together.

"Hello? I've got the numbers. What'd I win?"

The announcer grabbed the ticket, looked it over, and said, "Ohhh, we've got our winner, and there goes the snowboarding trip. You and four friends will be going up north to Flagstaff for an all –"

Julie stole the microphone from his hand, screaming, "Holy shit!" Quickly masking her guilty mouth behind her free hand, she searched the crowd for Mrs. Adams. "I'm sorry. I never win anything. Ian, Matt, Dura, Sam, you guys better get packed. We've got our senior trip. Woooh, I love you guys! This is going to be the shit," she finished, covering her mouth again. "Sorry." With bashful eyes and a grin, Julie handed the microphone back to the announcer.

Notes to Peter from Matt:

An unreal amount of blood coated the area. Things that were once clean and new and luxurious were dead, ruined, slashed – the site of a slaughter, a murder. The first time wasn't as bad as the others because I wouldn't let myself accept it as real; how could I? Shock is numbness; it's novocaine for the brain. How could I run from shock after seeing what I did, when I'm staring at a piece of my friend, a severed limb, and it's no longer theirs?

Yeah, the first time was all shock; it's unavoidable. But with the others I couldn't stay that detached. It took a while for my stubborn and hardened brain to give way and allow the dent to form, that wrinkle where the realities of such gore and terror took up residence. But once the memory was stored, there was no getting away from it.

SEVEN

When I got home that night — well, actually, I guess it was early the next morning — I had a painful cramping stomachache. I didn't make a habit of staying up all night, but the few times I had, it was a given that my stomach would cramp in disapproval. Just before I passed out, I pulled a heavy sheet over my bedroom window and afterward lost all concept of time. Monday seemed like forever away. I could hardly wait to start our trip. Before splitting from Project Graduation, we had made plans for Saturday night to meet at the Pizza Pit and go over details.

I woke up to darkness and, regrettably, a slight case of the shits. I bumped around in my messy bedroom, locating a pair of green boxer shorts, and then walked downstairs. My little brother, Joey, was in mid construction of some sort of cathouse. The house was crafted of purple yarn, duct tape, tin foil, and the box that my TV had come in. He had our three-year-old Siamese cat trapped in what appeared to be the second story. A few circular windows were sporadically cut into each side. Unfortunately for Simon the cat, he popped his head through a window just big enough to squeeze out of, but like a stubborn pair of Chinese finger cuffs, the opening wouldn't work in reverse. He must have pinned his ears back to get out but didn't know the trick to return. As if to explain to me his predicament, he pulled back against the cardboard edges. His big black ears bent forward, but his position, stuck, remained.

"Joey, where's the TV from that box?" I asked in a groggy voice.

"Mom took it into the kitchen."

I knelt down beside the fort and liberated Simon from a rough Saturday. He immediately darted out of the rectangular opening next to Joey's feet. He lunged forward reaching for the cat but missed his long dark tail by an inch.

"Damn it, did you let him out?"

"Yeah, his head was stuck in that hole."

"I know. I made it like that." He pouted, "Do you know how hard it was to catch him in Mom's closet?"

Rolling my eyes, I turned for the kitchen.

My mom was seated at the kitchen table. She had the new TV up on the counter next to the toaster. Absorbed in a motherly task and some dramatically uplifting talk show, she was well into her typical Saturday routine. To her right was a pile of fresh color-printed newspaper, left was another stack of papers riddled with rectangular and square cutouts, and in front, in several neat stacks, was the finished product: coupons, twenty-cents-off apples, buy-one-get-one-free hotdogs – the necessities.

My mom spent the majority of her time around the house. On legal forms she penciled in the title "homemaker" next to the question of occupation. She even had the trademark short "I don't want to mess with it anymore" housewife haircut. After surviving in the wake of my older sister Callie's childhood, my own, and then nine years into raising my little brother, I would say that she either deserved a raise or a good retirement plan.

She dressed in a standard mom uniform: khaki shorts cut just above the knee, thin white lace-up shoes, and a Polo collared shirt with an embroidery on the left chest. Obviously she didn't wear the same thing every day, but she may as well have.

To me, being a homemaker seemed to be a noble yet arbitrary thing to do with your life. She *was* to be credited with molding and nurturing three other people. Beyond maintaining the house and kids, part of her job description was to deal with an over-worked and under-compensated man: king of the castle, man of the house, tyrant. A stressed-out father who spent the majority of his coherent hours gathering bank notes to bring home to his soul mate and biological litter. Being a homemaker – that's not a job you can leave at the office; that's life, every second of it. With all the world has to offer, I never really knew what to think about the choices of my elders.

My mom was and will always be my favorite person in the world. She's a rare being, strong, understanding, sincere, and when I was a kid she was always in my corner – even when I didn't deserve her to be. My dad and I share a strange relationship. I respect the hell out of the guy for what he has done for us financially, but even as far back as elementary school, when I got my first taste of what real forced work felt like, I knew that it was killing him to haul his life across town to the office every morning. Back then, I don't think that I ever took the time to thank him. His presence was always so tense and ominous around the house, and I never really got to know him. By the time I was older, his character was set, or at least in my mind it was.

I used to look in wonder at the photos of my newlywed parents. They had just met their twenties, and back then my mom had long brown hair that hung over her shoulders. In those old photos she always wore a great true smile, the kind I saw only once in a while around the house. I'm not sure if it was simply the "okay, say cheese" type of deal or if her spark had really changed that much over the years. But the girl I had seen in photos didn't seem to be the same person who washed my clothes. Don't get me wrong; I don't think she's unhappy. It's just that I can't imagine that her present life was what the beaming girl with flowing brown hair had envisioned twenty years down the line.

My mom, too busy with the food ads, hadn't noticed me, and through the window I saw my dad heading across the yard to the backdoor. He had an industrial green trash can slung over one shoulder and a rake over the other. His boots scratched and stomped on the bristled doormat. As the door started to open, I slid back around the wall into the living room. I knew what would happen if he caught me with my hair pressed straight and sleep in my eyes at nearly four in the afternoon. I would be right out there with him, tying grass up in burlap sacks, and breaking shrubs small enough to fit into the house dumpster. I was not going to let him get me that weekend. I just had to make it until Monday morning without getting myself in trouble or enslaved.

As I crept back to the staircase, my little brother started reprimanding me about freeing the cat. "All right, Matt, now *you* find him. My fort's all done, and you —"

I gave him the old cutthroat warning, sliding my pointer finger under my chin. "Shhh! I'll get the cat; just stop yelling. He's upstairs, right?"

Finally, back inside my dungeon of a room, I was safe from the weekend warriors and cat abusers. My parents knew that I was at Project Graduation all night, and they seemed to have enough compassion to let me rest. I think it was more of an out of sight, out of mind kind of thing. But if I were up and out there with them, I would be quickly utilized. I sunk back into my cold bed, contemplating what I would have to pack for the trip. The cabin was supposed to be "comfortably stocked," beds were made, and everything was paid for. I didn't feel like planning, so instead I closed my eyes to the sounds of John Lennon's greatest hits.

When I woke up, the CD was stuck on track eight. The skipping chord sounded like my morning alarm on speed. I lazily attempted to throw a shoe at the player but missed and ended up knocking the sheet down from my window. I squinted, ready to be confronted with way too much light, but the room remained dark. How long had I been sleeping? I picked my cell phone up from the nightstand – four missed calls, and it was already eight o'clock. I had been asleep for four more hours.

After pushing the message button on my phone, I was serenaded with the not-so-pleasant sounds of Sam. "Matt, where the *fuck* are you? This was your idea to meet up, and you're over an hour late. Call my cell. *Now*."

Dura and Ian's voices clouded the background. They were belting out the lyrics to some old song; it sounded like "Free Bird." I assumed that Sam's older brother was working at the Pit. He always charged us double for pitchers and pocketed the difference, but the place had a quarter jukebox and a couple of pool tables, and for a team of eighteen and nineteen-year-olds, there really weren't many other places you could have a couple of beers like real people. I was actually the only nineteen-year-old. I know; it's ridiculous, but I failed second grade. I was a little shit of a kid, and I figure that the demotion must have been for faculty spite. The other place where we had a drink hookup was the bowling alley, and that was exactly where Sam told me they were headed when I got ahold of him.

After stepping into a faded pair of blue jeans and finding a plain black shirt on the floor, I headed downstairs. Joey had captured the cat, and once again, its head was stuck in the same hole. He wasn't even playing with the cathouse anymore; his attention was diverted to a funnel rocket set. I stopped and asked him why he had gone through all the trouble of cutting doors, building levels, and connecting rooms when he could have just made a small set of stocks, pushed Simon's paws and head through, and called it a day.

"Whatever, man," he said, not sure whether or not he should retaliate.

I don't think he even knew what stocks were. He was a very bored nine-year-old and, sadly, Simon took the scrapes for it. Earlier that year, my mom caught Joey perched at the tip of our roof ready to make Simon history's first skydiving feline. He insisted that the cat's chute was fully functional; he had printed the plans from the Internet. Since then, the house rules required him to keep all of his projects and experiments in the living room, so my parents could veto any dangerous or illegal endeavors.

My folks were in the kitchen. The TV was still ablaze. They were wrapped up in some shit reality show "starring" a bunch of hopefuls singing and dancing all over the place. They were mesmerized and hadn't noticed me. How that garbage ever made its way into our lives was shocking. I'm not complaining; it made things a lot easier on me, and with my parents entertained by the tune of a Cindy Lauper song on the chopping block of some transvestite's vocal chords, I slid discretely out the front door.

EIGHT

The D, the E, and the N in the orange Hayden Lanes sign had burned out and since renamed itself Hay Lanes. Of course the bowling alley was going crazy when I showed up a little after eight-thirty. Saturday night was already a big one for the alley, and on top of that, most public schools in the area had let out the day before. A crowd of about too many kids hung around out front on the red curb and sidewalk. They kept busy talking on cell phones, smoking cigarettes, and waiting for their lane reservations to be called.

Ian spotted me from the crowd. "Thomas," he yelled over the blare of the brood.

I recognized the voice, but not the name, and then I heard him again. "Thomas. Matt Thomas, over here bro."

I turned and spotted Ian standing around with three girls who were leaning up against a graffitied stucco pillar. One was actually good looking, a brunette, who seemed to be either bored or annoyed with the attention she was receiving from Ian. The other two, fake blondes, were all smiles. They pretended to listen to Ian while keeping a constant gaze set on the crowd. They were careful not to miss out on any of the competing action. The two of them looked to be no older than maybe ninth grade. That didn't stop the chunky one from sharing Ian's cigarette though. From where I was standing, I could tell that she wasn't even inhaling. She would take a mouthful of smoke and let it leak out stealthily past her upper lip and nose. Ian waved me over, wearing a grin and pointing with his eyes at the girls.

He came dressed for distress, sporting a pair of two-hundred-dollar jeans, a long-sleeve button-up western shirt, and a thick, silver, mall-bought watch that told more than just time. He looked polished then, but by the end of the night, as always, he'd be spilled on, unbuttoned, missing his cell phone, and bedraggled to such an extent that only his mirror could recognize him. He wasn't always that bad, but, God, it seemed like it.

"What's up, Matt?" Ian greeted, slapping me five.

"Ian…" was all I could think to say.

He put another cigarette in his mouth, lighting the new one with the cherry of his already burning stick.

"Have a stogie," he said, handing me the fresh one.

Ian knew damn well that I didn't smoke anymore. I started with him a few years back but quit soon after.

"No thanks, man, I'm cool," I said, raising a hand between the cigarette and my face.

He somehow slipped the cigarette between my pointer and middle fingers. The girls watched us, giggling. The brunette had turned her attention our way. She bit her lower lip and let out a little sigh; it was as sexy as...well, as sexy as a lot of other things that you probably shouldn't do. Attempting to keep her interest, I put the cigarette in my mouth and took a long drag. Ian's eyes lit up. He loved to pull me away from my somewhat predictable nature.

As soon as the smoke hit my throat, I could tell that my body was not having it. My lungs filled, and my eyes watered. I began to cough a loud raspy hack that started at my knees. Smoke poured from my mouth and filled the void between the hot brunette and myself. She promptly displayed a face of disapproval. Hunching forward, I caught myself with one hand on my knee. I pinched the baneful cigarette and continued to drain puffs of smoke and dribble.

I bent upright trying to avoid teary eye contact with the girls and flicked the small ash from the tip of my cigarette, saying, "Whew, that sure hit the spot. What are these – Lucky Strikes?"

Ian laughed past his cigarette-clenched teeth. He reached over, patting me on the back, and mocked, "Well, ladies, I would like you to meet my good friend, Mr. Denis Leary."

The short chubby girl offered me her hand. "Nice to meet you, Denis. I'm Kelly."

The hot one shook her head, and yawned. "Okay, guys, I am going inside to get a drink." She walked away.

"Damn, man, you let that one get away," Ian said, attempting to smack the back of my hair forward.

Dodging his swing and rubbing the water from my eyes, I said, "Hey, man, if you want her so bad, you go chase her. I didn't even want that damn cigarette in the first place."

The other girls, obviously feeling inadequate, excused themselves. "It was nice meeting you boys, but we have to go find our friends now."

They disappeared into the crowd and out of sight.

"I don't give a shit about that girl," Ian said, and chuckled. "I was just passing the time, man. And those bowling balls are killing my hands. I think I left part of my thumb in one of those things."

That wasn't like Ian to just let a couple of birds get away that easily; if nothing else, he normally would have blamed it on the girls, their issues, and their loss.

Congratulating himself, he said, "Can you *believe* that shit with me and Julie? Mmmm..." His eyes rolled back, picturing something that I could only imagine was Julie's ivory bare ass. "She finally gave in, man. I guess I'm *good enough* for her now, or maybe it's because we're out of that lame school."

"I thought you and Julie hooked up before...at the desert thing."

"Oh yeah, we did. You know, but it was all sketchy. She said she couldn't remember and all that bullshit. We even hooked up again after that, but it was such a big deal to her that we keep it secret."

"But it's cool now?"

"*Hell yeah*. You saw us last night. I'm hyped on that

shit. She's super cool now."

He seemed genuine. I could tell that he was excited about Julie, but I wondered if another person could really tag along with his kind of lifestyle. I mean, sometimes he had to run just to keep up with himself. I was happy for him though. Julie was a good-looking girl, not bad company either.

"Dude, Matt, did you hang out with Dura last night after Project Grad or something?"

"What? No. I was fucking dead after we got out of there. I went home and crashed. Why?"

Ian smiled, like he thought I was lying or something. "I don't know – she was just acting all funny earlier when you weren't around. She was asking some funny questions about you, too."

"Funny? What are you talking about?"

"Never mind, man. I probably said too much already. But I just don't believe that you guys haven't been chillin' more than usual lately."

Fucking Ian was always suspicious about something.

"Where the hell were you anyway?" he remembered. "Sam's pissed."

I crushed what was left of my cigarette under my Vans, and Ian began to pull out another. "Wow, we got a chain smoker on our hands," I announced to an imaginary audience. "Put that away. We need to get inside and straighten some shit out."

I turned for the crowded entrance, nodding and jostling through the teenaged sea. I heaved the lofty mirrored front door open, but Ian lunged in before me.

Walking backwards ahead of me, he said, "Listen, before we go over there, are you going to bowl or…"

"I don't know, why? What does it matter? Aren't we here to –"

Ian stopped back stepping, threw an arm over my shoulders, and pulled me off to the side. We stood next to a life-sized cardboard display of a pink panther holding a bowling bag.

"See that guy over there? The one with the green visor," he whispered in spite of the noisy cover of two hundred jabbering kids.

"Yeah, I see him. That's the guy who sprays Lysol into the shoes, right?"

From inside his concealing hand Ian produced a cigarette butt, burning well into its filter. He inhaled cotton smoke and heat, and with words of noxious exhaust, he corrected me, "No, he got promoted a few weeks ago. Apparently, the old manager, Mrs. Lexon, stopped showing up, just disappeared, and he was conveniently next in line. There are a few theories going around about that whole –"

"Theories? Let me save you the trouble. Are you trying to say that Mr. Greasy over there had the old manager killed, so he could come up on a dollar-twenty-five promotion?"

"No, no, no, it's not a financial thing with him. The extra cash is great, sure, but you should see him run this place now, man. He's crazy with power – tossed a couple kids out of here earlier for entering Poo Poo Brown and Fon Duller as their screen names."

I killed his conspiracy rant, asking, "Okay, what does this have to do with us — better yet, with me?"

"Okay, it goes like this. We spent most of our money on pitchers over at the Pizza Pit earlier and —"

"Obviously," I agreed.

"No, that's not the point. When we got here, Julie had the idea to skip the shoe rental and just go in our socks. A few rolls into the first game Sam comes charging at the line, overstepped, and slid down most of the waxed lane on his back. The ball flew straight up and missed his head by an inch. Between how much he had to drink and the slick lanes, it took three lane boys to pull him out — one in each gutter, holding his arms and sliding him back, and the third one just stood around at the line insulting him as he slid limp on his back. We almost got thrown out for that, and we had to rent shoes, so…if you're going to play, you need to pick up some shoes."

"My God, if I was gonna bowl, I would rent the shoes anyway," I said, trying to squeeze around him.

"Oh yeah, Matt, he found out," he said, sullen through and through.

"Found out about what?"

"The beer lady. He fired her the first day he got his new title. This place is real Regal Prep now, man. I say we get out of here."

Ian led me along the antiquity casino-patterned carpet, past the lockers, and up to lane number thirteen. The others were finishing a game.

Upon my arrival, Sam started reading me the riot act. "Where the *hell* were you?"

I glanced up at the scoreboard and noticed that his name was conspicuously missing from the digital lineup.

"Sam, have you been rolling?" I asked, fighting back a smile.

He glared at me, not knowing if I had heard about his slip and slide. "I don't want to talk about it," he said, rubbing his elbow.

Dura flopped down in the orange-cushioned chair next to Sam and ruffled his hair. "Sam decided to sit the game out and take it easy on us amateurs. Did you know that he was part of the Golden Thumbs bowling club down in Texas?" she asked with a telling wink.

"I told you not to mention that," Sam said, grinning. "I was only trying to be fair and let you kids have some fun."

Julie bounced over. "Strike! That gives me the win. Ahhh, life's good." She celebrated by breaking into an obnoxious dance that resembled the Bill Cosby Jell-O shuffle.

"Ian, did you see that, babe? I did *good*. I *won*."

He pulled Julie down onto his lap, nervously prompting, "Let's get the hell out of here. The visor guy's freaking me out, and we have no beer."

Julie sighed, rolling her blues.

"Where should we go...back to the Pit?" Sam asked, anxious to drown the night's events in a pitcher of brew.

The Little White Trip

"No, let's not go back there; it's too noisy. If we want to plan out the trip, let's go someplace quiet. We could go to the secret spot," Dura said, hoping for some kind of input from the others.

Sam was busy eyeballing one of the lane boys who'd "helped" him earlier, and Ian and Julie were gazing deeply, or drunkenly, into each other's eyes, so I was the only one paying enough attention to have an opinion. "Let's do it," I said, clapping my hands. "To the spot."

NINE

Being the only person who hadn't been drinking that night, I quickly became the honorary designated driver. The secret spot was in south Scottsdale and served as an attraction at a local mountain reserve called Papago Park. People hiked and biked the area all the time during the day, but since the place was at a state park, closing time came around sundown, and the sun had retired a few hours earlier.

To keep the ranger off our trail, we always parked across the street at the ballpark. He made the rounds until midnight. The first time we found that place, we made the mistake of parking at the reserve, and the car was quickly discovered. The ranger beamed a search light all over the mountain and kept us trapped up there until around four in the morning. Actually, he was probably out of there when his shift ended at midnight, but Ian and Sam had the rest of us convinced that we were being staked out from behind a bush.

After that little lesson, nights on the mountain had become a lot more relaxing. With the car parked across the street, we could watch the ranger come and go without a worry.

Arizona's name for the spot was "Hole in the Rock." The name described — well, what it was, a huge void near the lava-formed mountaintop. The prehistoric bubble consumed a twenty-foot gap in the rock. Access to that special place could only be gained from the backside. That's not true. The opening could be reached from the front side, but it was a tall climb and posed much more danger than was necessary.

Hunching to fit, and leery of bats, we pushed forward. The entry cave was tight, but the sights impending could only be seen by those on the other side. Facing to the west, downtown Phoenix became a backdrop for the black nights. The city lights glittered through the valley — yellow, white, and orange. A seemingly never-ending row of red lights traveled down McDowell Road into the capital city, and opposite, the line of hot white beams made their way east over the hill to Scottsdale. If you were alone, "Hole in the Rock" could seem a bit unearthly in its darkened nooks. The nights up there stayed eerily quiet except when disturbed by a dancing lizard or, on rare occasions, a lonely coyote.

Dura came prepared with a natural blunt wrap and a few grams of high-grade pot. I always liked watching people prepare to smoke. Whether they were breaking it up, rolling, packing a bowl, or just talking about the origin of that particular bag, there was always somewhat of a ceremony before actually lighting up. First, Dura's fingers went through the cellophane bag, carefully picking out some choice nugs for the night's blunt. After pulling out and discarding a few stems, with sticky fingers, she broke the herb up into small pieces, no larger than kernels of black pepper. She unrolled the delicate blunt wrap. Typically, Dura patronized the cinnamon-flavored leaf, but for whatever reason, she had ventured off to a strawberry one that night.

She licked the inside of the soft brown wrap, and the scent of synthetic strawberry drifted in the night air. With skillfully pinched fingers the broken up greens were sprinkled in an even amount across the length of the damp wrap. With the weed inside, she tightly rolled the leaf and pinched one end. Locating a yellow lighter in an overcrowded satchel, she turned the blunt over a small flame like a drug rotisserie. The finished product was perfect in every way. It had an even thickness end to end, and cooking the leaf over the open flame had dried and constricted it around the buds inside. The tip, crisp and cured, formed the perfect shape for a mouthpiece.

After she clicked the stubborn flint a few times, Dura's lighter produced a small torch illuminating her cupped hand and face. Her eyes squinted in the new light. Holding it just in front of the blunt's end, she inhaled. The flame leaned in her favor and ignited the open tip. The cherry sparked and glowed bright as she pulled through. Dura passed to Ian, exhaling a stream of thick grey that could be seen even through the screen of night. The blunt circled us three times before it was finally snuffed out. I normally pass on grass, but it was such a nice night that I figured a little THC could only make it a better one.

Smoking weed could send Ian in either direction, and that night, it worked him up. On an independent jaunt, he started screaming off into the distance, "You all think I'm some spoiled kid, huh? But you'll see… One day I'll *own* downtown; you'll come to *me* for a raise."

Ian forever held resentment toward the world because he was well-off. He felt detached, left out, but not enough to change his lifestyle and join the others. He wasn't going to come down and meet the world. Rather, he wanted to climb even higher and hold as much of it for ransom as he could, the price: respect.

"Come on, Ian. Don't start." Julie sighed, "Can't we spend one night here without hearing you curse the empty buildings? Besides, it's too nice to yell up here, kind of romantic. I'd like to pack a little basket one day…maybe even bring some wine and –"

Ian was disgusted by her lack of understanding. "Don't kid yourself, Julie. They're not asleep; corporate America never sleeps. They're all too miserable to sleep. But they'll need more –"

"Ian, pontificate on your own time." Dura had heard enough. "Stop acting like such a child; you're an accomplished *scholar*, for God's sake."

Earlier that year Dura had informed us that she was tired of the classic teenage slang. She picked up a seven-dollar thesaurus and began exchanging common words for those with higher letter counts and equally opposite clarity. She replaced words like talkative with loquacious. Her new vocabulary, although used correctly, usually earned her a confused nod by classmates and teachers alike. At the height of Dura's conversions, her dialogue was occasionally a little painful to decipher, but the new words fell by the wayside with her discovery of Japanese small talk. In those days, she usually reserved her complex synonyms just to fuck with people.

Sam pointed out a few hidden satellites living amongst the stars. I never knew satellites could be seen without a telescope. They looked just like stars but were constantly moving in a set direction and speed. It was a clear December night, and the stars were overwhelming in their numbers. We talked about many things that night but planning the trip was not one of them.

A night like that one would never come along again. I mean we'd hang out, but it's just different; everything changes. And even as dysfunctional as we may have seemed, we had fun; we were happy, and – what I would come to miss most – we were all together.

Notes to Peter from Matt:

I don't know why I'm spending my time, my welcome tranquility, writing to you about such disturbing things. But this is what you need, right? I told you that we'd get this done, and we will.

When you're slaving over the pile of paper in front of you, remember how we set this thing up; it's your deal. I don't need any part of it, the book or the money or whatever. Being where I'm at now, and you know this, book royalties aren't going to change my life much.

Sometimes we made it too easy for him. When you dash blindly into the jaws of a predator, you can't expect to beat nature. His sharpened blade - like fangs, his dark and hidden perch - like ambush - he waited with blood on his breath and struck with little effort. I just remember the knife, never really seeing it because every time it slid out he would punch it right back in. He just stabbed and stabbed and stabbed. It's disgusting to think what the human body can endure and still stay in one piece. I mean, how many times can you open someone up before what's inside comes out altogether?

When I look back on it, out of everybody that was taken from me out there, I almost expected it that last time.

TEN

I spent most of Sunday dodging my parents and grouping a few things together for the trip. One bag was really all it took: a couple changes of clothes, my toothbrush, soap, and my mom's credit card – just in case. I felt ready to head north.

We got a decent rain that afternoon, so I was able to relax around my dad, whose yard work would have to take a break, at least until it dried up. I underestimated him and foolishly overlooked an obvious male workplace, the garage. Good old Pops had decided that being forced inside would give him "a perfect opportunity to clean out the garage and maybe even change the oil in Mom's car."

He caught me in the kitchen assembling a turkey sandwich. I had seen him disappear into the garage before, but unfortunately, I hadn't put two and two together.

"Matt, when you're finished up with that sandwich, do you wanna come in here and help me with something?" he said, as if he was asking. I hate the way he words things sometimes, "Do you wanna…?" or "Why don't you come in and…?" Why don't I? Did that mean that he was under the impression that I wouldn't? Was he really asking if I wanted to? Because as far back as I can remember, there was never more than one response to his words: "Sure, Dad." That always drove me crazy. I knew that it was just a figure of speech, but it still bugged the shit out of me. Basically, after that I was stuck in cardboard, cobwebs, and ancient stories for at least an hour and a half. And, yes, we did get to change the oil in Mom's car.

Julie didn't get it so easy though. She was your classic obsessive-compulsive, neurotic, high school girl. She figured, instead of killing herself to pick four outfits she liked, she would just pack everything.

"I mean, shit, we're getting a Navigator anyway; those things are huge," she told me over the phone.

Just after packing the better part of her walk-in closet, she broke down and decided that she hated everything that she owned. She had no choice but to go shopping. If there was one thing that Julie excelled at, that one thing was shopping.

"You're going to make some lucky guy very poor someday," her dad liked to jab at her from time to time.

Julie could pick through a designer rack of eighty items in under twenty minutes, and that included time to try things on. Most pieces she crinkled her nose at and tossed onto the ground in the dressing room. She spent a good portion of that Sunday trailing her dad around the house and pleading for the American Express card. That was no easy task; Ed Burnett was a tough old goat. Even though he enjoyed spoiling his little girl occasionally, he hated rewarding her for throwing tantrums, especially when it was over money.

He'd always say, "Gee, Julie, for someone who likes money so much, it's strange that you don't have a job. You know, that's where money comes from. I mean that's where I get it."

She hated it when he said that, and she had already heard it three times in her pursuit of the credit card on that fine Sunday. In the end, old Eddie cracked when Julie turned on the drip system; she really was cute when she cried.

Sam had confided in me earlier that he was definitely not up to "sliding one hundred miles an hour down a mountain on some waxed piece of fiberglass." He sure made it seem dangerous in those terms, and given his nature, I agreed that he probably should stay off the mountain, but either way, we had to convince him to come along; the trip wouldn't be the same without his bitter apple. I didn't acknowledge his gripe when he originally let me know about his decision. Instead, I told him that I wanted to borrow his disk player, and that I would stop by his house at around six-thirty that night to pick it up. I always seemed to get what I wanted one way or another. Sam was going.

I called Dura, Ian, and Julie to inform them that we could potentially have a flake on our hands. I thought we should all go by Sam's house to strong-arm him if necessary. Everybody was to meet at Dogmires, a low-quality hot dog place on Cactus Road. The place was close to Sam's house and would give us a location to go over a plan of persuasion.

I showed up a few minutes after six; Julie and Ian were already there. Ian was seated at a brown, rubber-coated table and sloppily chomping a Dogmires' original Cornville chilidog. Julie was posted on the tabletop next to him, tapping her white shell toes on the bench seat. Ian's mouth was dirty with chili; Julie's gaze broke from the carnivorous sight as she spotted me. She was clearly over his company. Julie wasn't a girl who needed much. A chocolate malt and two bendy straws would have put the glow back in her eyes. Or maybe not, but I liked to believe that she was that simple.

After Dura showed up, the four of us sat around the table and exchanged ideas, all of which were pretty off kilter. Julie thought it would be a good idea to come into the house armed with a Polaroid camera.

She said, "When Sam isn't expecting it, either Ian or Matt will blindside him with a kiss."

Julie would snap the photo, and presto, if he didn't want to come along, copies of the photo would be sent to everyone in the yearbook. Julie was very proud of her idea, but I didn't think it was the one to use.

"Don't you guys think that would work?" she asked excitedly.

"No. I mean, maybe, but for one thing it's a little extreme, and I don't think that he would believe we would send out a picture that would humiliate one of us as well,"

I said, momentarily shattering Julie's mood.

"Anybody else have a plan?" I asked.

"Yeah, I've got one," Ian said, nodding and chewing.

"Okay, let's hear it."

He took another bite of his messy dog and, choosing his words, said, "We go into his house; you guys distract him upstairs, and I'll hide a smutty porn magazine downstairs, someplace obvious. Then, we'll tell him if he doesn't come along, we're going to leave it, and he'll have to deal with his crazy mom when she finds it."

"You guys are insane. Why don't we –"

"*Gay porn*," Ian threw in there, still plotting, concocting.

"No. My *God*, I was thinking of some kind of incentive. Like we'll only snowboard one of the days, or he gets first pick of the rooms or something. Does anyone else have a more Sam-friendly plan?" I asked my last hope, Dura.

Dura shrugged, saying, "I don't know. I guess we should just tell him that we really want him to go, and that if he didn't, we'd miss him. If he honestly wants to stay back, we shouldn't force –"

"Yes we should," Julie blurted out before Dura was even finished talking. "I won us a trip for five people, and I don't want to bring some random person along. Don Killjoy's coming; don't you worry about that."

Dura hesitated, weighing her words, maybe deciding whether to speak at all. "I don't know if I should be telling everybody about this, but since dealing with Sam has become tonight's issue, I think maybe I should."

That introduction had gathered more of Julie's attention than I had seen together in months. "Yeah, you should. Tell us...tell us what you know, Dura."

Dura reconsidered. She must have felt like she was selling tickets. "All right," she started cautiously, "Don't say anything about this, but Sam called me the other day and said that his mom and stepdad have been fighting a lot lately –"

"At least he has parents." Ian grumbled with chili on his breath. "My dad's gone, and my mom can't stand to look at the 'little clone' he left behind. She told me that," he said, wishing that somebody was speaking softly about *his* feelings.

Dura cut to the point. "Either way, he's worried about his mom. You know this is her *third* marriage, and he's worried about her. So just whatever we do, let's take it easy on him, okay?"

Standing away from the table, I gave up, saying, "It's past six-thirty now; we've got to get going. I'll think of something on the way – just follow my lead."

ELEVEN

On the way over to Sam's house, I got a call from him wondering where I was. During the conversation, he told me that he had changed his mind and wanted to go with us in the morning. Next week would be the second of two weeks that his stepbrother stayed with them at his mom's house.

He said, "The little rodent is already driving me crazy. He broke into the bathroom while I was showering and threw a glass of milk on me. *Milk* for fuck's sake."

Since he was going to be coming along, I told him that I didn't need the disk player after all, and that we would be over after we got the car.

Sam had almost escaped. That shit little stepbrother of his had no idea what he had just pushed through. I'm sure that with the passing of time he would kill himself just knowing that he helped put Sam in the place that he almost avoided. I always look back on minor things like that. Slowing at a yellow light, a two-second phone call, or even your own impatience could change your life – could end your life.

The Little White Trip

After talking with Sam, I pulled off the road into the parking lot of Sir Smoke's Hookah Lounge. Julie, Ian, and Dura followed me in and found parking spaces.

"What the hell are we doing here, Matt? Need a quick nic fix?" Ian asked, looking around at Julie and Dura to see if his remark had been funny.

It wasn't.

"I just got off the phone with Sam; it turns out he wants to come along after all."

The news put everybody at ease. We really had no plan, and Sam could be quite the stubborn animal when it came down to it.

"Do you guys want to go in and puff a bowl while we're here?" I asked, already heading for the door.

The host, whose first name I couldn't pronounce, met us in the crowded doorway. We followed the traditionally uniformed boy through a room scattered with tables, chairs, and chattering customers. Our guide stopped beside an empty booth on the far wall; it was really more of a stage, tight quarters. Colorful pillows and trinkets filled the low walls of our matchbox area. The four of us split up, staking our own personal sides. At the heart of the booth an emerald glass hookah stood tall and offered a single hose. We ordered a bowl of peach tobacco and…

"Do you guys wanna get some food?" I proposed.

After his septic chilidog, Ian winced at my use of the "F" word.

Julie looked at the menu and raised an eyebrow at the strange names next to the prices. "Oh…Indian food." She nodded at the waiter. "I think my parents like this stuff."

"Yeah, it's really good," I said, "as long as you're hungry."

The waiter chuckled. "Do you require a moment to decide?"

"I know what I want," Dura said.

The waiter licked the tip of his pen and started writing at the top of his pad. "Very good."

Without looking at the menu, Dura started, "I'll have the aloo paratha with mango chutney and… Are you guys going to want some of this? We usually share, like Thai food."

"Yeah, whatever's good," Julie agreed. "And let's get some chai tea, too." Pointing at the menu she asked our waiter, "Soy…Do you have –"

"Julie, come on, he speaks English," Ian snapped unexpectedly. "What are you talking about?"

"Soy *milk*, you idiot, I'm not speaking Spanish. He's Indian…right; you're an Indian?"

The waiter lowered his pen from the pad, saying very patiently, "Yes, I am *from* India, and no, we don't have soy milk, only milk from a cow and milk from a goat."

"I'll just have a sprite," Julie said. "Dura, you can order."

Dura finished, "Okay, we'll have a palak paneer, a chana masala, and…and another aloo paratha; I guess."

"And a round of ice water," Ian added. "Please."

Scratching the rest of our order into his pad, the waiter was off, shaking his head with a renewed veneration for the white man.

Sir Smoke's was one of about three hookah bars in town. They were popular with the high school crowd and tolerated by the college kids who hadn't yet invested in a fake ID. We were in luck; Sunday night played host to a belly dancing act starting at seven. The same girl performed every Sunday. Ian said it was the owner's wife, but I think he may have just pulled that fact directly from his ass. Regardless, she was pretty damn hot in her exotic kind of way. From where we were seated, I couldn't get a good look at the dancer except for the occasional hop or twist from behind a wall of hanging beads which separated the main sections.

An older guy with a thick silver mustache appeared at our booth. Using a pair of rusted tongs he placed a few partially burning coals on top of the moist foil-covered tobacco. After the coals were hot, Julie took the first puff, exhaling two perfect rings.

She was so excited that she forgot to blow out the rest of the smoke before applauding herself. "Did you see that?" she gurgled. Her words seemed to come from the shallows of her throat. Each syllable was accompanied by a short puff of fruity smoke.

Julie and Ian slid together, occupying one side of the booth. Dura and I connected on the other. Ian brushed Julie's honey-blonde hair back and away from her face. With pressed lips to her soft cheek he lent her a warm kiss and whispered something in her ear. Whatever he said made her blush. I'd like to believe that it was something sweet, maybe a borrowed line from some Meg Ryan film. I was beginning to like the two of them – together; theirs was a mix so strange that it just might be brilliant.

Dura was telling me a story about an away game that she went on in her sophomore year. I was daydreaming. My eyes settled on the hookah, half filled with murky water and the other half with dense smoke. Ian took the hose to his mouth and pulled through, filling his lungs with carbon and grey. Foggy water bubbled and splashed inside the glass tube, and the filtered smoke whirled and continued upward in the hose, hypnotic.

"And then Jen and Stacy went at it, right there in the showers. Jen got a hold of Stacy's hair, and it took five of us to break it up," Dura was saying, totally wrapped up in her story.

The hypnosis of smoke and water was great, but my attention was Dura's as soon as I heard, "went at it" and "in the showers" in the same sentence. "Hold on, this whole thing was going down in the *girls' showers*?" I asked, slapping a palm on my damp forehead.

"Yeah, weren't you listening, Matt?"

"Of course I was listening. Jen and Stacy... But they were fighting completely naked or...?"

Dura looked at me as if she didn't understand the question. "Yes, we *were* in the showers, but that's not the point. Stacy and Jen wanted to kill..."

I was zoning off once again, but this time it wasn't over the bubbling hookah. Two, naked, pissed off, hair-pulling girls, and then five more entering the mix;

bumping, slipping, restraining, and Dura was in the middle of the whole thing. I was in the process of mentally putting myself there when Ian handed me the hose. I looked at it and then passed it right over to Dura. She tried to hand it back, but I was gone. I was squinting through the steam, bare feet on the tile floor, and totally invisible.

Using the wooden mouthpiece, Dura gave me a sharp poke in the ribs, saying, "Come on, Matt. Take your turn. Don't fuck up the rotation."

I snatched the hose, returning her jab before taking a puff.

Dura was looking good that night. I thought that she always did, but it just hit me harder being that close to her. I imagined us together, as a couple. I know I said earlier that she wasn't the most fashionable girl, and she wasn't. That didn't matter to her. But still, she always looked good. Her legs fit well into a pair of olive pants; they bordered on dressy. I remember noticing them as we walked into Sir Smoke's. I held the door, and when Dura passed, I found myself shamelessly checking her out.

It almost seemed like the designer of those pants had Dura's ass in mind. I know I did. As far as materialistic obsessions go, a good plump ass was stronger than the almighty dollar in my mind. Besides all of that, she just looked so warm and soft wrapped in her black velour hoodie. Unfortunately, cuddling wasn't part of our friendly etiquette.

With lungs tight and smoky, I lowered the hose and

blew a thin stream to my left, showering Dura. I assumed that she would retaliate with a chop to the gut or something that would leave me coughing, but she chose a much more creative approach, using only her pointer finger. Reaching slowly across to me, she found my puckered lips and plugged the hole. I instinctively released the rest of the peach ghost through a two-lane detour, my nostrils.

Realizing that I had duped her, and I think becoming a little nervous over the fact that my lips didn't mind the company, Dura pulled back. She tried to pinch my nose, but I was already done. We horsed around a bit, as we often did, but that time was so much more painful. My injuries couldn't be seen, only felt. Aching and throbbing and tearing, how could my heart love so much pain? I was absolutely hooked, craving nothing more than another masochistic moment. Romantic – right?

My head felt spacey. Hookah smoke can give you a pretty good buzz. Sometimes, after my first couple of hits, I would get the overwhelming urge to take a crap. I know it sounds kind of lewd, but I've heard that nicotine works as a laxative. That, fortunately, wasn't the case that night. It was close to nine by then, the tobacco had long since cashed out, and our server had dropped the check into the booth soon after we stopped consuming. After loitering in the parking lot for a while, we decided that it would be a good idea to make it an early night. The car could be picked up anytime after eight in the morning, and we were all anxious to get going.

The Little White Trip

Dura called me later that night at around eleven-thirty. "Hey, Matt, how come you're not sleeping? Or were you? Did I wake you? Oh, I'm sorry," she said in quick sets.

"No, you didn't wake me. Is everything okay?"

"Yeah, I'm fine. How come you're not sleeping?"

"I don't know. I tried, but my inner schedule is all screwed up since Project Graduation."

"*Me, too,*" she said, as if we had just discovered that we had matching birthdays.

She asked if I wanted to come over and hang out and maybe have a cup of coffee or something.

I was actually starting to feel a little tired by then, but the way she was acting had me interested.

"Sure. I'll head over in a couple minutes."

When I showed up at her house, I walked in through the empty garage. The only car on the street was Dura's silver Acura. I was about to go in through the garage door, which opened up to the kitchen, but I stopped. I just stood there with my hand on the doorknob. I couldn't bring my self to twist it. For some reason, I felt compelled to be proper and go to the front door. So I did. Dura answered, wearing a pair of tan and navy pajama pants and an old gray volleyball tee; the red screen print had faded over the years.

"Why didn't you come in through the garage? I left it open for you," she said, pointing over her shoulder toward the kitchen.

"Did you? I didn't even notice," I said, feeling awkward.

As we moved upstairs, she informed me that her parents had left town earlier that day. They were going to be gone for a week in San Diego, which explained the late-night lack of their twin Explorers. Although I was with Dura all the time, it had been a while since the last time I'd hung out at her house, probably months.

Whenever Dura and I were together there always seemed to be a few other participants. Plus, up until the end of senior year she had had a boyfriend. He was an older guy, a family friend who her father approved of and had pretty much arranged. Personally, I never liked the guy, and I sometimes got the impression that Dura shared my feelings, to some extent. I don't think that they ever had sex, and I mention that for my sake more than the narrative's.

Dura plopped down on a swiveling chair in front of her computer, clicking a box at the bottom of the screen. I sat on the edge of her bed and peeled my shoes off.

"Have you seen this yet?" she asked, leaning out of the way so I could get a look.

The screen displayed an advertisement for some foreign car insurance company. I'm not sure if the image was real or not. The picture was of a cute brown squirrel perched on its hind legs and lugging an unreal set of nuts, and I'm not talking about acorns.

The tagline read, "Wasting money on car insurance is just nuts."

I stood up, taking a step toward the screen. "Are those real?" I asked, studying the photo.

The Little White Trip

Dura whirled around in her chair. "Why? Are you jealous?"

"I'm not. I was afraid you might be. Those are bigger than yours, aren't they?" I said, poking at her.

Slapping my hand away, she shoved me hard, propelling me backward onto the bed. "Jerk," she said, smiling.

I inched a little higher up, resting my head on her pillows. She must have had half a dozen of them. The assortment ranged from those long full body ones to a few normal square ones with ruffles, and a couple of thin circular ones here and there. Her room was extremely neat and looked as though it stopped maturing in the seventh grade. A white, key-locking, hope chest sat next to her TV and served as a stage for clusters of dolls and stuffed animals. Among the pack were bears, ducks, rabbits, and some of those old Cabbage Patch Kids. Johnny Depp beamed a sexy gaze from across the room. I think it was a poster from the movie *Blow*.

"So why would you invite me over here for coffee if neither of us can sleep? Seems a little counterproductive to me."

Dura didn't answer. She shutdown her computer and strolled across the carpet to the other side of the room. After looking over the animal pile for a minute, she walked toward me holding a yellow duck. The bird was wearing a leather jacket and sporting a silver hip chain. I assumed that it went to his wallet, but I thought that it was a little odd because he wasn't wearing any pants; the chain just disappeared into the yellow fuzz.

With cupped palms to the duck's nonexistent ears, Dura said in a low voice, "You see, I told Bad Boy Barkley that he could be the man of the house while my parents were out of town, but I'm questioning whether or not he's really up to it." She glanced down to make sure that Barkley couldn't hear her. "Hey, Barkley boy," she hollered. He didn't seem to notice, so she continued, "Okay, so anyway a few minutes before I called you, a gust of wind blew the wooden shutters against my window, and Barkley got so scared he peed his leather pants. They're still in the dryer now."

I nodded as she explained the situation.

As she set the half-buck duck back down, I clarified, "So what you're telling me is that I'm the new man of the house?"

Dura's eyes opened wide, and she covered the duck's ears again, saying, "Shhh, don't let *him* know. It would crush'um. And don't mention the pants either; they're kind of a sore subject."

She set Barkley back with his friends and was headed over to the bed when I blurted, "Hey, Barkley, how do you like the cut of *my jeans*?"

Dura looked frantically at Barkley and then back at me, trying to figure out who she could get to first. She dove onto the bed, accidentally jamming her knee into my side. Grabbing a pillow up, she theatrically began smothering me. I grappled with her for a minute, trying to uncover my face, but then died, letting my arms fall out limp and extend past both sides of her bed.

After my chest had grown still, she slowly lifted the pillow away and rested it on my stomach. "I think I did it. I really think I did it," she confessed to the animals as she leaned in closer, examining my face.

I could feel her warm breath on my forehead. My lips began to curl up a faint smile.

She noticed the movement and slowly reached for the pillow again, saying, "*Hey...wait a minute. What the —*"

My eyes burst open, and I let out a primal growl. She tried to pull back, but I got ahold of her with arms like anacondas.

She screamed excitedly, "Barkley, quick, hit him with your chain."

We spun around on the bed, knocking most of the pillows off in the process. Our roles reversed. She was the one on the bottom, and I had her wrists pinned to the bed. We held still like that for a second, in a worn-out stalemate, exchanging intimidating faces and wasted energy. I let her wrists go, but she left her hands above her head where they were. She wasn't even trying. I started to push away from my elbows trying to sit up, but she grabbed my shirt with one hand and pulled me back down close to her. I caught myself, falling back to my elbows, one on each side of her. I could feel her heart beating fast against my chest. Our eyes confessed what time could no longer hide.

With an unsteady voice, I started, "Dura, would you hate me if I —"

She stopped my words with her lips. We kissed with the innocence of childhood. We never went beyond kissing though; it would have cheapened it if we had.

We stayed that way for a while, living in each other's arms. She fell asleep by my side that night. I stayed with her long after her eyes had closed. She curled so delicately on my shoulder, and it took everything I had to slide away from her. I knew that existing inside any fantasy for too long would always bring me back to the same place. I was afraid that I would awaken alone in my bed, with the realization that it was all just a dream. I pulled away from her only to be doing something real, something my brain could understand, because the past couple of hours had been more suited for the world I had only dreamt of, and I knew that it couldn't last forever. I left her that night swathed in white sheets, with a gentle kiss on the brow, and a silent good night.

Notes to Peter from Matt:

The decision to fight the devil was made by someone other than me. My actions were prompted by more than just the simple fight or flight chemical reaction. I can't say that it made sense; he was much bigger than me. And even if I had won out over him, I wouldn't have been all right anyway. Safety had nothing to do with my actions.

Killing, with your hands, is not an easy task for any decent person. That didn't concern me though because I had left the realm of decency in the darkness of the woods. It was only natural for such a good and prudent way to be left out there, the same place where the bodies were taken.

To end the life of a helpless man, a beast knocked away from his consciousness, should never have felt that right, but it did then. When choosing my weapon for the coup de grâce, I wondered how much damage a man's skull would really have to fall under to render his brain worthless. I didn't wonder for too long, no time; with the hell and fire I had growing inside me, the damage would be plenty.

TWELVE

Monday morning was a harsh one. I was already dreading only five hours of sleep at best, but the seven o'clock phone call from Julie brought me to a heightened low.

Speaking in hysterics and building volume with each word, she said, "Matt, you have to go down there with me. My dad can't go."

Rolling over, I consulted with my alarm clock; it was early as hell. "Can't go where? Who is this?"

"Julie…it's Julie. I'm pulling into your driveway right now. Get ready."

Downstairs, I heard banging at the door. "Is that you?" I asked in disbelief.

"Yeah, your mom just let me in."

I could hear her words in the phone and muffled outside my bedroom door. She walked in. "Matt, let's go," she said into the receiver while standing at the foot of my bed.

I hit the off button and dropped the phone onto my sheets.

Julie gasped, looking at the black screen on her phone. "*Hey*, I can't believe you just hung up on me. That's rude."

"Julie, you're *standing in my room*. What the hell's going on? It's six-thirty."

"Seven," she corrected. "Matt, you have to go down there with me. I hate dealing with those people at the lots. There's always so much pressure."

"Pressure? You are aware that this is a car *rental* lot, right? The car you're getting has already been picked out."

"Still, you know how they are. I just need you to come along to do the talking. They'll try to sell me something."

"Julie, why the *hell* are you over here bothering me? Ian lives right next to you."

"*Come on.* He'd be no help; he probably hasn't even come home from last night. I know you're good with this kind of stuff. Just get your lazy ass up."

I was pretty sure that she wasn't going to leave my room unless I was with her, but I pulled the sheets above my head in one last desperate attempt for sleep anyway. Who knows, maybe she would totally forget that I was home. I had no such luck. She took hold of my comforter and yanked it back like a matador's cape.

We arrived at the lot a half an hour early. I felt like everybody in the place was staring at us. I downed cup after cup of complimentary waiting room-style coffee. The blend was classic: foam cup, lukewarm, and accented with a hint of yesterday's sour batch. By the time eight o'clock rolled around, I was wired and ready for anything.

The rental agent was a real character. He danced out of the office with a hand extended to Julie. "You must be the lucky lady here for the Navigator," he said with a plastic expression. His brown suit emitted an aroma of Brute aftershave, cigarettes, and social anxiety.

"Right this way, folks. We're gassing her up, so we expect a full tank when she returns."

Considering who the car was rented to, he would be lucky if he got a hubcap to remember it by. Julie screeched the tires out of the lot, and I nearly crashed her purple Jetta trying to keep the pace. Ian lived only a few blocks from Julie, so we swooped him up first. Julie took care of him with a treatment similar to the one that I had received earlier.

Next, I ran in and got Dura. She was lifelessly asleep and hadn't moved from the way that I had left her. Her arm still clung to a long pillow beside her. Gathering some nervous confidence from last night, I crawled under the down comforter and gave her warm cheek a kiss.

"Matt, you're still here? I thought you went home. What time is it?" she asked, tucking the covers up and under her chin.

"I did leave, after you went to sleep. Hey, everybody's waiting down in the car. We need to roll."

She flipped back to me, looking tired and baby talking, "No, I'm tie-ohd. I need more sweep."

I had never seen her act like that before. Goddamn, she was cute.

For being a girl and just getting out of bed, Dura got

herself together quickly and without a fuss. Being the gentleman that I am, I insisted on bringing her luggage down for her. Her bags were bulky if not plentiful. The biggest one accidentally doubled as a sled when I lost my balance near the top of the stairs.

Sam was sitting out on the curb when we pulled up. "Where the *hell* have you guys been?" he snapped, getting into the car. "You said eight o'clock."

For such a complex guy, Sam never put much into what he put on. Clothing was a necessity, the same as brushing his teeth. His mom cut him a generous check at the beginning of each school year, and considering the gear he walked around in, I figured that at least three fourths of those checks ended up in his back pocket. That day he was decked out in an awkwardly cut pair of discount blue jeans topped with a plain grey tee shirt with a fashionable front pocket. His hair was a mess and his spirits matched. Things would get better for Sam before they got worse but, goddamn, they got worse.

The SUV they had set us up with was something straight out of a booming rap video. The long silver bars of the Navigator's grill shone and stretched wide like the hungry mouth of a baleen whale. Being in the SUV's massive innards made me feel like Pinocchio, trapped inside the stomach of Monstro – well, minus the cartoon uvula and cricket conscience – but either way it was huge in there.

The interior was crafted for the ultra vain – mirrors, mirrors everywhere, but why? The reflective panels did make the place look bigger. I guess if that was the aim, it worked. Our space felt more like the rear of a limo than a sports utility craft. It must have taken a team of engineers from NASA to put this thing together, wood paneling, DVD, strip lighting, speakers in every door, and dozens of buttons, switches, and stash spots; their purpose couldn't have gone deeper than heightening price tags. The black leather interior smelled fresh, speakers crisp, and as my eyes took in the gaudy lights and reflections, I thought that what I was seeing must have been sold to some classless bastard as custom.

In our package the agent had included: driving directions, keys to the cabin, a loose itinerary, five reusable slope passes, gear tickets, free food coupons at some dive, and a manila envelope containing a per diem of one hundred dollars each.

I made the suggestion to stop for food before we left town. We found a breakfast place in Cave Creek. It was a vintage Arizona diner, booth-lined walls, brightly colored table tops, overly padded vinyl seats, and a grimy worn linoleum floor. After waiting in the doorway of the mostly empty diner for five minutes, we decided that it must have been one of those seat yourself type of joints. I love places like that, good food and bad facilities.

Julie didn't exactly share my sentiments, complaining, "Let's get out of here. This place is scummy, and it smells like an old cigar."

She knew as well as the rest of us did that we were on the edge of Cave Creek, and another breakfast spot wasn't

The Little White Trip

in the near future, so a glare was all it took to quiet her objections.

Julie's phone started playing some horribly current song, "Chingy," or some such nonsense. I guess that digital dance party meant that somebody was trying to get through to her. "Oh great, it's my mom." She pushed the green button and answered, "Hello? Yeah, yeah, *no*. Mom, no, you can't keep doing that. I know he is, but you just need to deal with it. Kick his ass outside then. Okay, well why are you calling me if you're going to do it anyway? Mom, *mom*, listen, I understand, but you can't keep giving the dog Valium every time he acts up. Okay, Mom, just deal with it; I'm on the road – What? What do you mean where? I'm going to Flagstaff, remember? Okay, either way, I'm trying to drive, so I need to go. Bye." She rolled her eyes. "I can't believe I'm related to her."

We sat in a corner booth next to a large window. The sill housed a layer of dust and a few fallen moths. They had probably spent their last few minutes flying headfirst into the glass before it all stopped. At times, I kind of felt like one of those moths. Seeing the whole world moving, with opportunity at your fingertips, but it was all happening on the other side of the glass. The way that my brain works, I'm always trying to do things on such a grand scale that failure knows me by name. The world of success just wouldn't have me, and no matter how hard I rammed my head against the glass, I couldn't get through, never even made a crack. I'm convinced that one day, when I find my calling, I will leave that window. I'll fly around the room, and after enough work and a little guidance, I'll find the open door and finally be in the world that I had only before seen through a pane of dirty glass.

Our waitress dragged her heels across the room, and before even reaching our table, said, "Okay, kids, what'll it be?"

My eyes wandered the table, feeling just as confused as everyone else looked. "I think we're gonna need a couple menus and some water, please," I said, explaining her already simplistic job.

As she lethargically slid away, Ian spun around in his seat, adding, "Can I get a large Coke, too?"

She returned with the Coke, menus, a pitcher of iced tap water, and a stack of textured plastic cups.

"I'll give you kids a minute," she said, chomping her teeth.

Ian, zoning out across the table, frowned at Sam's jewelry. "Sam, why the hell are you wearing that stupid Farrell ring? Do you wish you were still there or something?"

Sam wasn't in the mood for his shit. "Fuck off. My mom bought it for me and…I like it."

"I like it, too," Dura lied. "I like the gems, very *royal* looking." She took Sam's hand in hers and gave the bird crest a little peck, like the Italianos do. Dura's gesture seemed to make up for Ian's unwanted critique.

Ian uncapped two small Jack Daniel's bottles, the kind you see for five bucks inside the minifridge in a hotel room. Using his fork as a stirring stick he created a small whirlpool, swirling bubbles and cola high inside the tall glass. Then, with a bottle in each hand, Ian emptied the JD into the mix.

"Jesus, Ian, it's barely ten in the morning. What are you doing?" Sam questioned from across the table.

"What…you mean this? This is because of last night. They say the best cure for a hangover is to have another drink. Your body needs it."

"*Who* said that?"

"I don't know. Somebody did. Oh, I know who it was…" He paused mid-sentence, draining half of his cup, and then went on, "Jesus. Yeah, she said it." Ian punctuated his claim with a long whisky belch.

Julie smiled. I think she liked him a little more when he had a couple in him. Ian could come off as edgy at times when he was sober. I think that's true for most of us, but it was worse with him.

I used to date an older girl back in my junior year, and she made no secret out of the fact that she liked me better after I had smoked a little pot. Luckily for her, I was just beginning what would turn out to be a yearlong, everyday, smoking stint. Those were good times; her apartment had a sundry perfume of cigarettes, incense, and candle wax. Most nights I'd smoke a number, curl up on her bed and, like a curious pet, watch her sort through old photos or jot down some notes into a spiral notebook. Eventually, some little thing she would say or do would totally amaze me. It could be the smallest thing, like she would spin her long hair up into a bun using only a pencil or maybe the way she would describe a customer she had served earlier that day.

I was very complimentary and easily entertained when I was stoned. I never figured out exactly what it was that I would do or say, but whatever it was, she liked it. She really favored my other personality. I could coax and insinuate an entire night away and come up dry, but "Mathew Smiles," as she called him, wouldn't have to do much more than make himself present, and she would give him whatever he wanted. And he was a very creative boy. Unfortunately, Señor Smiles died with the habit, and our relationship soon followed.

Two guys came into the diner. They sat across the room from us. The older of the two fiddled with a bulky leather bag that he had lugged in and heaved onto the table where his breakfast should be.

Ian didn't like the other guy. He thought that maybe he was trying to hit on him. "What the hell is that guy staring at?" he grumbled to Julie.

"Babe, you *always* think people are staring at you."

"No. This fucker's giving me the dick eyes."

"You're crazy."

In hushed tones they continued to discuss whether or not Ian was really being watched. I did catch the guy looking over at him once, but I didn't think anything strange of it. The diner was small, and besides his friend, who hadn't stopped fucking with his bag since they came in, we were the only company in the room. And – yes, I think that he wanted Ian's nuts.

Our food arrived remarkably fast. Sam got apple-cinnamon oatmeal. Ian regretfully nursed a cup of water. Julie, after some negotiating and explaining with the waitress, got an egg white omelet and mixed fruit, and Dura and I, feeling only half hungry, split the lumberjack special.

In some misdirected attempt to get in touch with technology, the old diner had added a new age touchscreen jukebox. The flashing box even came equipped with Internet access for track selections. Sam begrudgingly loaned me a dollar which I used to beckon a couple of old rockers, including Jimmy, Neil, and…shit, whoever sang for T. Rex. At first, Julie held her nose up at the thought of listening to anything that old, but by the second song, she was howling along with Dura and me. Wasted-ass Ian sloppily picked up the chorus, probably because it was easy to remember. Sam chose to occupy his mouth with soggy oats.

Midway through "Get It On," a scruffy old man entered the diner. He had a bald dome with some sparse grey circling the edges. His black, long sleeved shirt was ripped on the elbows, and his jeans were twice as bad. He leaned against the checkout counter, studying the room for a second, and then rang the service bell. From the noise of the kitchen a bronze man popped his head through a hollow window on the wall behind the register. The old man didn't see the cook at first and clanged the silver bell a second time. From the kitchen, the man said something in Spanish. I could tell that the old man understood. The cook hustled out of the kitchen followed by our waitress. He seemed annoyed, gesturing to the man with his hands the way you would shoo a cat off the couch.

"No. You go. You go away. Told you last time," he said in his broken English.

The waitress, shielded by the cook, joined the browbeating, "You better get out of here. We don't have nothing for ya. Don't make me get back on the phone with the police."

The man took his hands down from the counter and stuffed them into his pockets. His eyes had been fixed on the ground since the two of them had come out of the kitchen.

He looked up in their direction for a second, and said, "I was just wondering if you had any mess-up orders, or maybe some fruit that you were going to throw away. I see it all the time back there at night, and I just thought you might be able to spare it now, so I wouldn't have to fight the cats for it later."

The waitress seemed sickened by his words.

She picked up the phone, threateningly. "Listen, what you like to do with your time is your problem. Now if you don't mind, you're bothering our customers."

I stood up from the booth. "He's not bothering *us*."

The man thanked me with a tired smile.

Glancing at Dura and then at our plate, I said, "You can have the rest of these hash browns and the toast if —"

The waitress did not agree. "No. He can't. He's not a customer. Let me do this."

She started dialing the phone and then faked a conversation with the police. I could tell she was faking because she started talking even before her finger had pushed the last key.

Defeated, the weathered old man turned away, shaking his head, and walked out. There was a strong wind outside. As he pulled the handle, the door blew open. Mother Nature held the door that way until he was gone. A stack of paper menus blew off the checkout counter and scattered on the floor. The waitress, slamming the phone down, cursed the old man. She disappeared below the counter, grunting as she collected the papers.

By the time she stood back up, we were out of the booth and waiting at the register. "We'd like to pay and get out of this dump," I said.

She nodded, poking at the register's keys and expanding a set of green digital numbers on the dark screen. The total finally settled at thirty-seven fifty-one. Julie stepped forward with the envelope of hundreds, pulled out a crisp bill, and handed it over.

The waitress sorted a few crumpled bills and coins from the till. "Thank you," she said, dropping the money on the counter top.

Julie took the money, and holding up a ten, said, "No. Thank *you* for being such a generous person. You just gave your tip to that man outside, how *nice* of you."

Ian leaned in over Julie's shoulder, shamelessly laughing in the woman's face.

On our way to the car, Julie found the man sorting through some half-dead cigarettes that he had fished out of an ash tray.

Pointing through the glass at the waitress, Julie said, "See that lady in there? She felt bad about being such a bitch, so she decided to give you the tip from our meal." She handed him the ten.

He examined the bill front and back. "See, I knew she couldn't be that bad. She *really* told you to give me this?" He was smiling and waving at the irritated waitress through the glass.

Sam piped up, "Actually, she didn't tell us to. We just thought that she owed it to you, but you should probably take off 'cause she's pissed at all of us now, and..."

The man's smile grew even wider with Sam's warning. He continued to wave for a second and then gingerly extended his middle finger. He wagged his dirty bird with one hand and then pressed the waitress' lost tip flat against the glass with his other.

THIRTEEN

I had been to Flagstaff a few times before but never cut through Cave Creek to hit the freeway. Julie insisted that she was following the directions from the packet, so I didn't worry about it. We did eventually hit the Seventeen North, and the next hour or so was pretty mellow. None of us had remembered to bring CDs, so we listened to the radio until the reception on our stations thinned and dissolved to a crackling static.

"What's up, Dura? Are you all right?" Sam asked, noticing her heavy expression.

I noticed it, too. I thought maybe she was just enjoying the scenery. Actually, that's bullshit. I knew that look, and I didn't want her tones to say the rest. Things had felt weird since we'd left the diner.

She smiled at Sam's concern. "No, I mean, yeah – I'm fine. Just tired. I feel a little off. You know what I mean?"

Sam nodded. "Oh yeah, I know what you mean." His right hand was busy fishing around behind the seat. He twisted and leaned back, half disappearing, then returned.

"Hey, maybe this will help," he offered, holding up a

bottle of flavored vitamin water. "It's orange. That's the kind you like, right? I mean, I like orange, too, that's why I picked it up. But – I remembered that you do, too. So here, take it." Dura gracefully accepted. Sam shot back behind the seat and returned with another one, grape.

The trees were beginning to thicken in the foreground. I rolled my window down, hoping to smell pine in our future.

"Roll that up, Matt," Julie said over the blasting wind. "I've got a call." And did she ever. Her portion of the conversation went, "What? *What? No.*" She hung up. "Fuck *that.*"

She looked like she was going to cry, or scream. "What's up, Julie?" I asked.

"The guy from the car place called and said that we were all supposed to sign some form, something about liability," she squealed in a horrible pitch. "I don't want to go all the way back. He wants us to come back."

"All right. Julie, chill, we don't have to go back," I said, pretending to be calm.

I didn't want to waste the day driving back and forth either, but at that point I was more concerned with Julie's emotional condition behind the wheel. She was becoming so flustered that I don't think she even remembered she was the one in the driver's seat.

There was a small town coming up in a few miles, so I had her turn off on Wisher Street. With the car safely parked at a gas station, I tried to make sense of our problem. Julie insisted that I talk to the rental guy, handing me her already ringing cell phone.

After passing a thorough screening from his secretary, I got on the line with the man in the brown suit. "Where are you kids at?" he asked.

"I don't know exactly, maybe about halfway. We got off on Winner."

"Wisher?" he corrected. "Yeah you're making some time if you're that far already. How fast are ya'll going?"

I wasn't going to answer that one. "What? Yeah, Wisher. Your secretary said there might be something that we can do about the papers from out here. What's up with that?"

After way too many details and instructions, I found out that they had another location, a sister company, he called it, and it was just three more exits north on the Seventeen. The second lot, much like any other functioning place, was defined by its actions. It was basically just a huge lot of cars and tanks like ours. A small showroom, neighboring several garages painted in grey and white, stood tall near the back of the lot. A professionally dressed woman stood expectantly outside the showroom doors. She nodded as we pulled up. The guy from the Scottsdale lot must have called her.

After three tries at negotiating a "compact only" parking spot, Julie decided to shift the car into park and leave it at a severe angle.

"Let's get this over with already," Julie said as she dropped down from the tall driver's seat to the ground.

The two lots were related, as far as ownership went,

but the original location needed a personal copy of the signed form before we could continue. Thank God for fax machines, or I did then.

The two-page form showed up from the other lot in just seconds. The final signature on our end didn't come quite as easily though. Sam was troubled by the official jargon scattered amongst the contract, or I guess the waiver…whatever it was. He complained, "I don't know. Look at all this small print; my mom would freak if she knew that I was just signing some contract without reading it over. 'Not liable for injury,' injury from what, I mean…"

Julie's disposition had rapidly altered from doomed to heated, saying, "Sam, just sign the goddamn thing. Don't piss in the seat or break anything, and you'll be fine. I'm sure this is all standard."

Sam reluctantly signed, straining to read a few last lines as Julie snatched the form and handed it over to be faxed.

"Can I get that paper after it runs through?" Sam asked the girl behind the counter.

"Yeah, you can, but their line's busy now, so you'll have to wait until we can get through."

"No thanks, we need to get going," Julie interjected. "Sam we have an itinerary to follow, and I swear to God, if you –"

"Okay, but if this comes back on me, I'm going to –"

Julie walked out before Sam could finish his empty threat.

The Little White Trip

If we would've known what lay ahead for us, we probably would have told the guy at the rental lot to go fuck himself because in reality, the car meant nothing. In the end, none of us would be accountable.

I took the wheel from there, charging through the winding mountain roads at eighty-five miles an hour. Sam faked a half heart attack every time we swung around a bend.

It's amazing to watch the turning landscapes as you travel north through Arizona. In just a few hours you can climb the polar scales from the barren and dusty south to the lush and snowy north. The first run of the trip, like most everywhere else in the Southwest, is dead or dying desert. Even the things that are alive in the wilted terrain look dead. But soon – it all starts to happen. Pushing up from the flats and falling deep beneath our asphalt trail, the earth begins to sink into time-smoothed valleys and swell back up in great mountainous bounds toward the sky.

The junipers gather in groves, ornamented with their bitter purple berries and scaly green limbs, and as the townships change, the meager trees fall back and stand down to the giant pine fence, and you've entered the forest. The tall russet trunks and quilled green tops hide the road around every icy turn. What starts as a few cottony patches beneath the trees advances to a frosty blanketing of snow, painting earthy browns white and rising high on the highway's shoulders in ashy plowed mounds.

By one-thirty, we were just breaking into town. Flagstaff is one of those burnt-out mining towns that never quite hit puberty. Besides the college kids at Northern Arizona University, most people were there spending some time at their summer homes or passing through on their way to the Grand Canyon. NAU is a quiet college compared to her siblings ASU and U of A. Downtown, there are a few bars to hop, but for the most part, people go up north to get away from everything and concentrate on their studies. The others are generally hippies or gypsies networking and eating mushrooms.

Shit, actually, how could I have forgotten about the hill; that was what we were supposed to be there for, right? Snow Bowl is a main hub for Arizona snowboarding and skiing. Supposedly, the mountain, Mt. Agassiz, could've had some of the world's best slopes, but the top half was never to be opened; those were sacred lands. To the Hopi and the Navajo, that mountain was more than just a series of hills and business opportunities; it was the sight of home and history. Mt. Agassiz is where their elders met eternal rest; those grounds were blessèd and tranquil, and to the Indians, they had to stay that way.

The cabin was farther north than I had expected. The description from our pamphlet read, "An estate-style cabin situated in the historic district close to Lake Mary. Acres of forest! Enjoy all the comforts of a resort, large upstairs hot tub, Internet connection, outdoor heating, theater-quality entertainment center, and much more."

To avoid constantly making the trek into town, we

decided to stock up on enough food and supplies to last us the next couple of days.

"Do you guys want to hit a restaurant for some lunch before we get groceries?" my gurgling stomach pressured me to ask.

Julie, eager to follow one of the only things on our itinerary, reminded everyone that our package had come with free-food coupons at a place called Donny's Steakhouse. The restaurant was easy to find. The dilapidated building consumed the first main corner, right next to the Gun and Liquor store. I thought that was hilarious; only in Arizona could you go into a mom-and-pop type of store and walk out with a handle of rum and a double barrel. I pointed it out to the gang, but they were all too hungry to pull their eyes away from the neon Donny's sign.

"I'm gonna get a thick steak and a potato," Ian said, sounding mighty proud of himself.

We pulled around back and crawled out of the SUV. The air was brisk and thin. I read the temperature from my earlobes and nose, yup – cold. I was excited to see a line of steam twist up from under a manhole cover and disappear with the gust of a passing car. I rarely made it anywhere that got below sixty degrees, and I was a dork for any picturesque signs of winter like that.

In Scottsdale, winter meant that you needed to wear taller socks with your shorts. Flagstaff was different; the winter was real up there. The snow was everywhere in the city, but the urban stuff wasn't the same as the cocaine-white spans on the highway. I found it hard to imagine that the sludge at our feet was ever free and powdered. The morning snow was bullied, plowed, scraped, and salted; it collected the byproduct of the town's preparatory wake. The growling trucks cleared the streets but soiled the snow with asphalt, oil, and tar. The end result, bunched up in the corners and gutters, looked a lot to me like mashed potatoes overloaded with coarse black pepper, but that may have just been because I was hungry as hell.

Ian ran up ahead, turning toward the Gun and Liquor place, saying, "I'll catch you guys in there in a sec."

The restaurant was dark, a cheap Reno casino kind of experience, and the air was salty with steak fumes. Besides the employees, the room was empty, and even though there were tables open all over the place, the waiter insisted that we sit at a specific spot. Julie wanted to sit at the bar "the way the yokels out here do," she reasoned, but the young waiter argued with her, saying that we had to sit in *his* section. He said that his boss was a real "stiff dick" about keeping to the sections. I just laughed and wondered if "stiff dick" was the northern equivalent for our southern "hard ass." Sounds like a good pair, right?

We were finally seated at a huge horseshoe booth, sized for ten. The table was spotlit by a single hanging bulb living inside a green canvas shade. Dura had been quiet for too long, and I was beginning to wonder if her silence had something to do with what happened between us. Ian stormed into the building, reaching our booth parallel with the waiter.

"Hello," the young waiter started, "welcome to Donny's. My name is Caswell, and I'll be –"

"Goddamn it," Ian blurted, dropping himself into the booth. "That old bastard at the drunken gun stole my ID."

Our table was quiet for a second, including the waiter, who had frozen mid-sentence and was standing there with his mouth hanging open.

Ian looked up at him and then us, saying, "What's this guy trying to do, catch flies, or –"

"As I was saying, my name is Caswell, and I will be your waiter today. Would you folks like some drinks or appetizers to start?"

Ian was in rare form over his ID, but he still managed to pull off his cocky rich boy shit. Reaching a hand to the waiter, he said, "Caswell, pleased to meet you. I'm Ian. Could you run and get me a Captain and Coke? Oh yeah, I'll take your biggest steak and a baked potato as well. Thanks."

The waiter shook Ian's hand, trying to figure out if he was joking or a nut.

Then, with a smile, he said, "No problem, sir, if I could just see some *ID*, I'll have that right up for you."

Ian stirred in his seat, groaning, "I'll just have a black coffee then."

The crew was pretty quiet after the food came, aside from the orchestra of slurping and chomping that is. We had all known each other too long to try and be polite; if we were really hungry, we just chowed.

The check was dropped off, and the never-ending debate began as to who owed what and how much of it was tax. Things started to get ridiculous just before I reminded the squabbling parties that we had free coupons and that nobody was paying for lunch.

Dura got up and set out toward the bathrooms. Seeing my chance to talk to her alone, I, too, slid out in her direction. I waited at the table for a few seconds though, so I wouldn't look suspicious. I felt silly considering things like that. *Why did it even matter?* The bathrooms were all the way on the other side of the restaurant. When I got there, Dura was standing outside the door, leaning her tense back against the wall.

"What's up, Dura? Are you waiting for someone to come out?" I asked, trying to sound casual.

She shook her head and let out a little sigh.

I knew something was definitely wrong. "What's going on? You're acting different."

Her eyes flickered up at mine and then dropped, and she confessed to my shoes, "I don't know, Matt. I don't know what's up. I keep thinking that I ruined things for us last night. What if this doesn't work? What if it gets weird? I mean, I met everyone through you, and if it gets weird with you –"

Reaching a gentle hand below her chin, I coaxed her gaze up and met her worried eyes. "Shhh, don't think so much. It's okay. Nothing's going to get weird. I really like you, Dura, and not even just because of last night either. I think you're an amazing person, and I would never do anything to mess that up. Okay?"

My words seemed to calm her, and she said in a much less urgent tone, "Well, what are we then? Are we boyfriend and girlfriend? Is this going to be weird for everyone else?"

Responding first with a small peck on the tip of her nose, I took her hand, and said, "Look, Dura, baby, this is our thing, and it's good. Besides, our friends will want us to be happy, once the shock wears off, of course."

She smiled almost in unison with Julie's arrival. She rounded the corner, and her eyes shifted from our clasped hands upward to our delinquent expressions.

Lifting Dura's hand close to my face, I studied her fingers, saying, "Damn, did that lady even say she was sorry?"

Dura was wearing a puzzled expression, the same as Julie's.

"Some lady just slammed her fingers in the door," I explained. Dura caught on, looking up at Julie with a painful nod.

"What lady? Is she in the bathroom?"

"No. It happened a few minutes ago before you came over. Dura just now let me see them," I said, hoping Julie would buy it. She wasn't that hard to fool.

"They look okay," I said to Dura. "I don't think you'll lose the nail."

Julie flared her nostrils as she considered my story. She quickly lost interest and went into the bathroom.

"Shit, that was a close one," I said, dropping Dura's hand. "Actually, why are we hiding it?"

"Oh, I thought about that one. I think we should keep things secret until the end of the trip. Because Julie and Ian are already, well, whatever they are, and if you and I hook up, what does that make Sam?"

"A fifth wheel," I agreed.

She nodded, and we left it at that. I gave her a quick kiss, and we ran back out there trying hard not to look like a happy couple.

On my way over to the booth, our waiter, Caswell, called me over to the bar. He must have been on break, sitting alone on a swiveling stool and nursing a smoke.

"Hey, buddy, where you guys headed to?" he asked, blowing smoke as he talked. "You want one?" he offered, holding up a box of cheap Cownon sticks.

"No thanks. We're going out to the Binklly…or Brinkley cabin, whatever it's called."

"Oh, are you guys a part of one of those college newspaper teams doing a story on the Brinkley files?" he asked, nodding his head as if it were a given.

"The what, what? We're staying there a couple nights; it's a part of a snowboarding trip we won."

Laughing and coughing up more smoke, he said, "I don't think so, man. You must be talking about a different place. The police seized that cabin a couple months ago, just after the murders."

I pulled the directions from my back pocket and unfolded them on the bar top. "Look, it says right here,

'Brinkley cabin.' The directions are there, too."

He studied them more closely, dropping ash on the paper as he held it under his nose. "Yeah, that's the place all right. I remember it from the newspaper photos. I don't know about these directions."

Taking a pen from his shirt pocket, he corrected a few turns in red ink, saying, "If you're really trying to get to the Brinkley place, I think this would be the right way. But I'm guessing there must have been some kind of mix-up with the photos though. Don't you watch the news? Jeff Brinkley killed his entire family in that house: trophy wife, three young kids, and I hear he even beheaded the dog.

"They say he might have been involved in some brainwash cult shit. If so, he's probably with them now 'cause the cops never caught him, missed him by a couple hours. They searched all around that lake for weeks; you know — it's pretty secluded by those old cabins. One of the officers in the search posse was found in the woods, stripped completely naked and gored through the neck with a kitchen knife. Two others turned up missing and people say they ended up the same way."

His dedication to fucking with me was more disturbing than the tale itself.

Handing the paper back to me, he raised a brow, saying, "But hey, if your school rented the cabin for you, I'm sure it's safe." Hacking a phlegm-filled laugh that made me flinch, he finished, "If I were you, I'd follow the directions your school gave you. There's no way they're putting people in Brinkley yet."

People in small towns had always seemed that weird to me, anything to scare the tourists. Boredom was a very powerful thing, but I was no sucker.

FOURTEEN

I assumed the waiter was just trying to get a reaction out of me. He probably wanted to get back at us for Ian's shit-head antics. But what he did was a little much. I couldn't figure out why he would go through so much trouble to change my directions and then feed me all that unnecessary detail. Then again, before I left, he did tell me to follow the original route. I chose not to bring it up. One of the "crazy three" would have run with it for sure. Although Ian came off as aloof, he loved to entertain a good conspiracy theory when he could. Julie and Sam…need I say more?

Outside Donny's, Sam had pulled the car around and was gassing the engine. "Get the hell in the car. What did you do – have another meal in there or…?" he yelled over the rumbling V8.

Jumping into shotgun, I asked, "How are *you* driving?"

"I have the keys, dummy," he said, pointing at the consumed ignition.

"But they were locked in the car. I didn't tell you the key code, did I?"

Ian kicked the back of my seat, announcing, "*Key code?* You left the fucking door wide-open. We just walked in."

"Bullshit."

Sam agreed with Ian, saying, "You did, Matt. I think somebody got in here, too. The shit was all open and gone through."

I couldn't believe that I had left the door open. I never did shit like that.

"Did they take anything?" I asked Sam.

"Nope, Julie brought the cash in with the coupons, and I guess our clothes weren't good enough for them. The visors were flapped open, and the seats were all fucked up though."

Ian came onto something, saying, "The people out here probably know about our trip. The cash is what they were after; I can bet you that. They hate people from the valley up here. Goddamn white-trashers."

The natural remedy to handling Ian's rants was to simply pretend that you didn't hear him, and judging by the silence that followed his words, "white-trashers," I would say that the others were trying to deal with him the naturopathic way.

Tired of idling in the parking lot and ready to change the subject, I said, "All right, get back onto Route Sixty-Six and —"

"Wait," Dura interrupted, "aren't we going to the grocery store?"

Sam nodded, blasting through the parking lot and crossing four lanes to a Safeway food and drug store.

The Little White Trip

After dividing our spending money, we took off, pushing carts and stocking up. We originally tried to stay together and just shop like a family, but we kept losing members to the fancy displays down one aisle or another, and soon enough, I was alone. I picked up tons of junk food, a few steaks, ribs, soda, a loaf of French bread, three pounds of cold cuts, and a circular Jell-O mold with bits of pear mixed in. I was the first back at the car, then Sam, Julie, and Dura. Even from seeing only some of their groceries, the ones popping above the paper bag mouths, it seemed to me that we had all picked up the same things, but combined, we had way too much.

After we had packed everything in, Sam pulled the car around to find Ian. Julie spotted him standing next to the pay phones and looking super shady. Sam honked the horn and clicked the headlights at him. Ian glared at the car and attempted to shoo us away. A minute later, a homeless-looking man walked up to Ian cradling two brown paper bags, one in each hand. With a real suave wave, Ian started walking toward us. They talked for a second next to the car. After his negotiations, Ian climbed back inside and began inventorying the bags; Julie was pleased with his buy. He had vodka, rum, gin, and for when the time came to tear the house apart, whiskey. There were also a couple of six-packs of some foreign beer that he had trouble pronouncing and four bottles of cheap champagne.

Holding up some fruity raspberry drinks, he shoved my shoulder and speaking in a shabby British accent, said,

"And for the ladies and lightweights, we have a soft fruity spritzer."

I thought about reclining my seat and crushing his legs, but I was sure that something would end up shattering in the process.

He looked over all the bottles on his lap, on the ground, and then back into the bags. "What the fuck. Sam — turn around. That old HOG shorted me," Ian insisted, sounding sure that everybody else was ready to pursue his shoulder tap gone wrong.

Sam ignored him, continuing toward the highway.

Ian's surly mood climbed to confusion and outrage. "*Sam…*"

I tried to calm him down, asking, "What's going on, Ian? What hog?"

"That sonofabitch gypped me. I gave him enough money for another bottle, and he just made off with an extra twenty. Now let's get his ass," he said, shaking a bottle of rum in my face.

I paused for a second, as if I was contemplating his proposal, and then said, "Okay, Ian, I *would* be down, but one thing that you've got to remember is that this guy is some kind of bum commando. Look at how smooth he worked *you* over. He lives on the streets, and I bet he's being sheltered by some of his street cronies by now." That disturbed him, and I continued, "They're probably splitting up the loot as we speak."

He nodded. I could see him envisioning the man. Ian was creative in his delusions; he probably pictured the guy kicking back on an old couch somewhere, in a ditch or maybe a storm drain like Penguin below Gotham City. When in reality, the guy was probably heading back into that very store to pick himself up a 40oz or on his way to buy a bag of weed or...maybe, working against all bum logic, he was going to get something to eat.

Ian put his bottles back into the bag. "Damn it, that really gets me, man. Where's the honesty?"

Julie consoled him by loosening the cap on one of the bottles.

I still hadn't decided which directions to follow. The waiter did tell me to take the original route, but I wasn't sure if he was serious about our path being wrong, or what. He probably felt bad about potentially sending us for a loop and that was why he ended up saying to go with the original ones.

Handing the paper to Sam, I said, "These are the directions. Don't pay attention to the stuff in red."

By the time we hit the highway, the Navigator's clock read four p.m. "We should be there around four-thirtyish," I said.

Sam eyeballed the directions. "Our cabin's near a lake?" he asked, carelessly drifting into the right lane.

A small red pickup truck beside us swerved onto the shoulder. The driver screamed at his windshield and pounded the dash. The truck's shrill horn caught Sam's attention.

"Holy shit," I whooped, clamping tight to my foam armrest. "Keep your eyes on the road."

He dropped the directions and got ahold of the wheel with both hands.

Finding the paper at Sam's feet, I said, "You know, I think maybe I should just tell you the directions."

I must have been nuts for letting him drive at all.

About a half an hour down the way, we were turning onto Springston Road, one of the last twists in a complicated set of directions. The scenery screamed north. Rows upon rows of giant pine trees parted only by the two-lane winding road, and from what I could tell, the unseen cabins never existed closer than two or three miles of each other. Most of the estates were set back from the paved road, displaying only a plowed dirt entrance and a lone mail drop.

Springston Road was a thin mountainous ride all the way to our turnoff on Mailer Lane. After bouncing and twisting along the old dirt road for about a quarter mile, we reached the cabin. As we pulled around to the front of the place, Julie spotted a car already parked in the driveway. Oddly stationed between two large pines was a white Suburban with a missing back bumper. At first, I thought that maybe it was somebody with information about the package, but that idea dissolved when I saw three young kids playing in the front yard. One of them, a boy, worked a red plastic bat, and another one waited ahead of him with a hollow white ball. Upon seeing our tall black cruiser, the third, a little girl, abandoned the boys and ran to the front door. The boys stood their post. By the time a few of us had made it out of the car, the girl had returned; she trailed behind a simple couple who looked to be in their late forties.

"Can I help you kids?" the man asked, eyeing us suspiciously.

Wondering if we'd taken a wrong turn somewhere, I asked, "Yeah, I guess. Is this the Brinkley cabin?"

The wife gasped at my question.

The man's shoulders widened, and he growled, "Does the road out there say Brinkley? No. It doesn't; we're the Mailers. How dare you come around here dropping that awful name?" Like a territorial wolf, he advanced on me. "What do you want with us anyway? Are you another one of those rubberneck reporting shits?"

Shaking my head, I turned to my friends who were all out of the car. Sam and Ian had stepped up beside me, to the left and right.

"What? Are you guys trying to intimidate me?" the man asked, nervously watching the two of them.

I tried to explain about the snowboarding trip and how the accommodations had been set up at the Brinkley cabin.

He looked over our directions for a minute and then, passing the paper to the woman, said, "I don't know who you're trying to fool with here, kid, but you're going to be in bad shape if you start with me, all three of you. We lost our son to that psychopath…" His words stopped, and the anger in his face diluted. It changed. The heat in his cheeks washed white. His mouth closed and brave chin quivered with true emotion.

FIFTEEN

Dura's voice was a welcome break from such a strange moment. "Excuse me, sir, who are you talking about? We don't know what's going on?"

The man stood mutedly, staring off into the trees. He seemed totally dead to her question. His jaw clenched, eyes glazed, and burying his face in his hands, he began to weep; he let go, shaking a few muffled words loose between heaving sobs. I had never seen a man cry before, except actors in the movies, but being there was so much more powerful.

The little girl ran up and clung to his leg. "Daddy, don't cry. You're going to make *me* cry," she whined, burying her face in his dirty pant leg.

The mother was strong. Gently, she reached over and squeezed the man's shoulders, saying, "It's okay, honey, it's going to be all right. Now let's go inside."

With his weathered eyes and beaten expression, the father turned away from us and moped back to the cabin.

The woman glanced down at the paper and acting just like a concerned mother, said, "If you kids really are going to the Brinkley place, I'd like to know *exactly* what's going on."

With a kindly wave, she beckoned us to follow as she started for the cabin.

"Let's get the hell out of here. These people are crazy," Julie said, and Sam agreed.

"We can't go anywhere until we get that paper," I said, pointing at the folded directions in the woman's hand.

My mind boiled, trying to remember every detail that I'd heard earlier from the waiter. Something was definitely foul, but I was still confused. I mean really, what was I supposed to think; were we stuck inside some cliché slasher movie? Shit like that doesn't happen in real life. In this world, a world where babies are slain at the hands of their mothers, where serial rape goes unavenged, and the law no longer scares the wicked, we would have been better off under Freddy's bladed glove or Vilmer's phallic chainsaw. If that were the case, as long as the girls didn't trip in the big chase scene and we avoided dark spooky places, we'd be fine. But as I said, "shit like that doesn't happen in real life." In this world, the villains are free and the victims are dead, or they wish they were.

Walking into the Mailers' kitchen was like being in an Old West exhibit; everything seemed perfect and meticulously in order. The cabin was exactly the way I'd expect a home in the sticks to be like. I guess that art didn't imitate life in that respect; they were exactly the same.

"Would any of you like a cup of coffee or some pie?" the woman asked, untying her apron.

"No thanks." Julie wasn't interested in pie; she wanted answers. "What was your husband talking about out there?"

"You say that you're heading over to the Brinkley place for some kind of school retreat, right?"

"Yeah, that's right," Julie said, eager to get on with it.

Then the woman told us the whole, somewhat censored, story. Her tale was almost identical to the waiter's, but that time everyone heard. "And what my husband was talking about earlier was our son Jason. He volunteered to help find that nut Brinkley a few days after the wife's remains were found in the lake. He left us that day, and we never saw him again. They found an officer from the same search in the woods, murdered. I don't even want to mention how he spent his last moments. Oh, poor Jason…my little boy." The painful recollections overcame and killed the strength that she seemed to have outside. She could no longer talk through the tears.

The five of us stood uncomfortably silent around the kitchen table listening to this poor woman whimper.

The father returned, stomping through a narrow hallway. Slapping a small picture on the table, he bawled, "Nineteen years old. Look at him. Nineteen fucking years old. And for what? To be murdered and raped in the forest?"

He stopped, noticing his wife by the sink, wiping her eyes with a dish towel and trying to gain composure. His mouth popped open, but his tongue didn't move. He fought back his next words. He wanted to continue but took a deep breath and went to his wife's aid instead.

With no compassion for the moment, Ian asked, "How do you know he was murdered if they never found him? And, this Brinkley guy – why would he still be in the forest?"

"One day my son's heading out to help track down a murderer and just takes off, doesn't contact us or anything? I don't think so. Brinkley's car was found abandoned a couple miles down a dirt road; it was less than a hundred feet from where they found an officer's body. They said he must have had a hideout or help. Alex was my oldest boy, and now he's gone, all because –"

"I thought his name was Jason," Sam commented, catching us all off guard.

"I think I know what my own *goddamn* son's name is," the man howled.

The wife threw her arms around him as if to hold him back, and explained to us, "Alex was the name he went by. It was his middle name. Jason Alex Mailer but I call him by the name I gave him, Jason."

The fierce expression on the man's face had faded and then returned with the mother's words. "Who the hell do you kids think you are questioning me? If you want to get your kicks in that evil house, be my guest." He tossed the paper in Sam's face; Sam caught it before it hit the ground.

Julie voiced what we were all thinking, "Okay...um, guys,

we should really get going." She smiled at the couple and started for the door.

Our exit from the cabin was fittingly tense and awkward, and the couple didn't say another word as we walked out.

I took the keys from Sam and cranked the SUV around in a half circle. I had to reverse in mid turn. The driveway was too tight.

"Am I clear back there?" I asked, seeing the Suburban's white shape growing in my rearview mirror.

"Yeah, it's close, but you've got room," Ian said, even though he clearly couldn't see from where he was seated.

I listened to him anyway.

The cars connected with the kind of crash that only two large machines can make, like thunder and compromised metal. "*Fuck*, Ian, what the –"

"Go man. Go."

"Goddamn it, Ian –"

"*Go…He's coming.*"

I slammed the gas, peeling up snow and gravel as we disappeared into the trees down Mailer Lane.

"Dude, Ian, what the *hell*, man? You said I was clear."

"You were, but not at fucking eighty miles an hour."

"This thing's touchy. It's not my fault. Was their car fucked up?"

"Nope. Theirs was fine. Ours didn't sound too good though."

"Was that guy really coming out?"

"No. I just wanted you to get us out of there. Dude,

it's fine. They didn't see anything, and even if they did, their car's fine."

Sam groaned, "I knew it. There goes the liability shit. I signed, and now *I'm* liable. See, Julie, now you see why –"

Julie didn't want to be lectured, especially by Sam. "Oh, shut up, *Sam*; they gave us insurance. And it's on Matt anyway."

"All right, guys," I said. "Chill, we haven't even seen the car yet. Let's just wait until we see before we start pointing fingers."

Knowing that, as Julie had said, I was probably going to be the one taking the insurance hit, Sam dropped it, and the others did the same. The father did see us hit the Suburban, but he didn't care. That doesn't happen every day. You smash up somebody's car in their own driveway, and they let it slide. No, he didn't give a shit about the damage. He had much bigger things on his mind.

I didn't say much as we traveled down Mailer Lane. For reasons I still don't understand, I decided not to tell my friends what the creepy waiter at Donny's had told me. Instead, I listened to their observations based on what had just happened alone.

Julie thought it was a crock of shit. "Can you *believe* those people?"

"Yeah, something's not right with that group," Sam granted. "I mean, we just happened to stumble upon the family who lost a son to the killer who owns the place we were looking for. *Right*. Some coincidence, don't you think? Besides, that guy didn't even know what his supposed son's name was." Sam was rarely that brave, but when he thought that he had something figured out, there was no changing his mind.

"I don't know, man, why would those people say all that stuff if it wasn't true?" Ian asked, sounding pretty shaken. "What do they have to gain?"

Sam followed up his first comment, saying, "Okay, another thing," He was great at breaking problems down. "How old did that guy say his dead son was? Like nineteen?"

"No," Ian interrupted, "he's not nineteen; he's dead."

"Brilliant, Ian," Sam laughed, "anyway, think about it like this. Those other kids at the cabin were only like six or seven or something. So that would mean that, if this other kid existed, they would have had him and then waited like ten years before crapping out *three* more. Yeah right, people don't do it that way. That other kid Alex – or Jason or whatever never existed. They're fucking with us."

He made a great point, and nobody said anything for a minute.

"Matt, what do you think?" Dura asked.

"I don't know what to think." And I really didn't.

"I agree that there was some strange shit happening over there," Dura contributed. "Something wasn't right though. It seemed too weird. But like Ian said, what would be their motivation? Do you guys think they might have been rival homeowners? Maybe they rent out their place, too, and wanted to start some bad press. I don't know."

The Little White Trip

Julie stepped in. "You guys are thinking *much* too far into this. It was weird; that's it. Our high school didn't send us to some graveyard."

"The school didn't provide *all* the prizes; some of them were donated," I said. "I'm not saying that anyone set us up at a place like that, but... Okay, well, what do you guys want to do about this?"

It seemed as though nobody knew the answer to that one.

Sam, riding shotgun, posed a question that somehow hadn't come up yet. "How the *fuck* did we end up at that place anyway? Matt, did you give me the right directions or what?"

"Yeah, I think so. Springston to the 280 pull off, and then down..."

"What? No, you said 208. I remember that shit," Sam corrected, grabbing the directions up from the dash. "What else did you fuck up here?"

Did I? I couldn't remember. Sam was always good with stuff like that, numbers and codes.

"I couldn't see with this fucking limo tint, and you kept bitching at me for turning on the dome light. You're like my grandpa with that shit," I retaliated, under attack.

"Well I guess this should be okay then," he said, clicking the overhead light on and studying the directions. "What's up with all this shit in red? Are these corrections?"

"Yeah, I guess they're corrections."

"Did we follow them?"

"No," I answered, wondering if I should fully explain.

Sam turned around in his seat telling the others, "Matt *royally* fucked our directions up. That's why we ended up at that other place."

The back of the car burst into conversation, and they were somehow put at ease by the news.

Sam had an idea that he figured could put an end to our suspicions. He thought that we should head over to the new place, and once we got there, just to shut Ian up, he would use the cabin computer to look this Brinkley character up on a search engine. "If it happened, we'll find it on the Net. This place is tiny, and I'm sure it would've made the local news."

He was right, and my guilty mind was finally starting to ease.

By the time we got back onto the main road, it was past five-thirty and growing darker by the minute. With everybody agreeable to Sam's plan, I followed the red pen about ten miles from where we had met the Mailers and pulled off at the final bend, reaching a snow-patched dirt road. To avoid visiting another wrong address, I jumped out at the entrance to check the mailbox number.

The black box had been knocked over and savagely smashed up. In the car's lights, I made out the engraved name, "Brinkley." Wrapped around the base of the wooden post I found a short length of yellow tape marked with black writing. The letters read "C A U" just before the severed end. Before climbing back into the car, I walked around back to see what was up with the bumper.

It was too dark to see everything, but running my hand along the back end, I knew it was fucked. *Great.*

The cracked fiberglass bumper was just a bug on the windshield compared to the damage that the SUV would endure over the next twenty-four hours. By that time tomorrow, our fifty-thousand-dollar luxury ride would be as doomed as we were.

As I pulled myself back into the driver's seat, Sam leaned in to see what I was carrying. "What's that?" he asked, reaching over.

I handed him the tape. Ian, Julie, and Dura bent forward in their seats to get a look.

"See...what the fuck, man? That's police tape. Some shit totally went down here," Ian said, grabbing the tape.

Sam held tightly to his end, and the two of them pulled until the black letters stretched out to grey, and the tape finally snapped.

"Don't snatch shit," Sam yelled.

"That was police tape, and you know it," Ian accused, throwing his half-piece over Sam's shoulder.

"Ian, get real. Caution tape is used for many things. Construction is one of them, but murders aren't," Sam laughed at Ian's observations.

As I continued into the darkness of Brinkley Drive, the car grew still. The road was even bumpier than Mailer Lane and about twice as long.

Just before reaching the cabin, we crossed a narrow bridge. The wooden planks creaked and buckled under the car's weight. The Brinkley place was much bigger than the Mailer's. Beginning with an ancient looking stone lined bridge, the new cabin presented class at first sight. Displaying a four-car garage, thick log columns, castle-style double doors, and an enormous balcony offset above the entryway, Brinkley wasn't your average dwelling.

Upon seeing the cabin, the car was filled with excitement. "Jesus, I can't even see where the thing ends," Julie said. "It's huge."

"Yeah, it's pretty amazing," Dura granted.

Sam didn't say anything, but I could tell that he was hyped just by looking at him.

Ian was stubborn. "Hope you guys like it because it's probably going to be your final resting place."

Julie pinched the back of his arm. "Oh, shut up, Ian. Don't be such a killjoy."

"Okay," he laughed. "I take it back. He'll probably chase you out into the forest. That'll be your final resting place."

Outside the car, Ian packed a handful of snow and tossed a solid ball over the hood at me. He got me good. The ball exploded on my shoulder and stung my cheek. Before I could fire back, the garage door jarred and began to slowly crank open.

Shit, I thought, *what now?*

SIXTEEN

Julie was holding a white garage door opener. "*Hell yeah.* This is the place. Look at it. It's a palace." She fished a ring of keys out of the packet and dashed over to the cabin door. The rest of us followed her, leaving our bags behind.

Any uncertainty about that place was left behind once we stepped into the entryway. It was too nice to be evil. The cabin was fully furnished, complete with artwork, lavish fixtures, and the new-house feel like we were the proud first owners. Positioned above an overgrown limestone fireplace hung an enormous moose head; its brown fuzzed antlers extended high above its frozen expression. I strolled around the cabin for a few minutes while the others dashed back and forth, poking in every cabinet and doorway.

The living room was dressed in a few pieces of perfectly placed, expensive-looking furniture. The bigger mocha-colored couch was situated directly in front of a shining wall of electronics. Shelved inside an oak entertainment center, a big screen TV, CD, DVD, VCR, and an old vinyl spinner waited to be played. Between the couch and the TV stood a lengthy, glass-topped coffee table. To the right of the long couch sat a matching loveseat, placed at a slight angle but still facing the TV. The artwork was mostly Southwestern landscapes, Indian art, and a few classic pottery pieces filled with dead roses or sunflowers. The air felt as clean and fresh inside as it did out in the trees.

The kitchen was simple; the granite counter tops followed an L formation around one wall and housed a sink and dishwasher on the other. A vertical side-by-side refrigerator sunk inconspicuously into the wall opposite the sink. Pots, pans, and a pair of large silver spoons hung from a stainless steel rack. The silver was suspended almost eye level above a checkerboard chopping block. The block was topped with many choices: cleaver, skewers, steak knives, and a couple of other knives and pokers that I could only assume would be used to kill an elephant or a dinosaur.

Away from the stove and utensils stood a plain oak table lined with six wooden chairs, oversized at the head and foot. A great rectangular window, which opened a view to the back deck and woods, occupied most of the fourth wall. The kitchen met a formal dining room through a domed archway. It was much too cultured and dreary to go into though. Everywhere except the kitchen floor was padded in a long tan shag carpet. The wooly strands raised high above the foundation and almost seemed to move under your feet.

The Little White Trip

As I walked back through the living room, I noticed what seemed to be a big black armchair. I hadn't recognized it as furniture at first because it was curiously faced away from everything else in the room. The chair was comfortable and crafted of black stuffed leather. Beside the chair's right armrest stood a small overhead reading light. The bulb was perched cold at the top of a thin rust-colored stand. A black beaded chain hung below the shade, and attached to the last bead was a length of white kite string.

I tugged on the string, and the light sparked and came to life. Yellow light glared on the back window. I pulled the string a second time, and the glass returned again to black. My eyes picked up on something moving in the glass reflection; it was Sam. He must have spotted the light turn on. He came nearer, and I slid away, hiding my head below the chair's high leather back. As he stepped around into my vision, I started to scream and convulse, tossing my limbs around like a maniac. He jumped back, nearly falling over with panic. His expression was so gruesome it almost scared me.

"What the *fuck*, man? Why were you hiding back there?" he groaned, still clenching his fists.

I always loved that. I had caught myself in the same defense before. I would hear a noise or think that I had seen something and immediately throw up my dukes. Even when I was afraid that it might be a ghost, the fists were up and ready. I never really figured that one out. What could a pair of fists do against a ghost?

"Where is everybody?" I chose to ask instead of clowning his reaction; there was only so far you could push him.

"Julie and Ian are checking out the master bedroom upstairs. Dura is on the back deck, and you are right here being a mother –"

"Wow, hey, yo, take it easy, Sam. I saw the opportunity, and I took it," I said through an apologetic smile. "I'm gonna pull the car into the garage, so we can get our shit. Tell everybody else to come out before the food goes bad."

"It's like forty degrees out there; I doubt anything's going bad," Sam objected, but started upstairs to get Julie and Ian anyway.

Outside, the SUV's windshield had already begun to frost. I hadn't noticed it before, but Dura must have brought a good stash a weed along, and the air floating around the seats and mirrors was perfumed with the musky tang of her unseen contraband. The frozen brakes creaked as I stopped just outside the open garage. I got out and eyed my roof clearance; it barely looked like the tank was going to fit. I cringed a little as I pulled the first couple of inches into the covering, but I made it in okay.

Dura and Sam were waiting inside.

"Matt, are you feeling okay?" Dura asked.

"Yeah, I'm fine. Why?"

"Oh, it's just that painful look you had on your face, and you were driving all slumped over," she said, imitating the look.

The Little White Trip

"No, I thought the roof was going to scrape. Haven't you ever done that? When you're driving under a tight space, you duck."

She looked at me with a smirk, and then at the car. "So you thought you were going to hit your head on the roof?"

I rolled my eyes. She was fucking with me.

"I know what you're talking about. I've done it, too," Sam said in my defense.

"Whatever, let's just get this shit unpacked," I said, pulling the back door open.

None of us acknowledged the damaged car as we unloaded everything into the kitchen and living room. Julie and Ian appeared, glowing at the top of the stairs, and announced, "We get the master bedroom. There are seven other awesome rooms to pick from, so –"

Sam and Dura didn't even care enough to listen.

"That's great, Julie. You guys have the master; now get down here and help us put this shit away," I hollered up at them.

Ian came charging down the stairs. "Oh yeah, my groceries," he said as if he had melting ice cream.

Come to think of it, the only thing he had come back to the car with was that crafty homeless guy and a grin. He must have assumed that he could just eat all of our food. I figured his bottles would be passed around, so we could call it a trade.

It was past six by then, and I had grown more than a little hungry. Settling into the first room at the top of the stairs, I wondered if my baby would bunk nearby. Sam was all the way at the end of the hall, past the game room. Dura looked over each room carefully and ended up picking one downstairs with a bathroom which opened up from the living room and her bedroom.

My room looked much like the rest of the house: tan, dark brown, silver, and black. A basic wooden bed frame held a king-sized mattress and a series of intricate carvings. With a few steps around the room I met a walk-in closet, a small bed stand with a ceramic lamp, and an arched window behind the bed.

As I was laying my clothes out on the bed, I heard Sam shouting. "Hey, guys, check this out. It's some kind of…" I found him at the end of the hall, staring at the ceiling and searching for the title of his new find. "…some kind of trapdoor," he finished, still yelling.

He turned around, and was startled at first sight of me. "Oh shit, I thought you guys were downstairs. Check this thing out."

Julie and Ian came out of their master room to see what all of the squawking was about. Ian's hair was pressed flat and standing straight up in the back.

"How's life on the bottom, Mr. Peacock?" I asked, with a wink.

I don't think he was picking up what I was putting down. "What are you guys yelling about?" he asked, looking around the hallway.

Sam pointed upward, and Ian's eyes followed. "It's a trapdoor," he said excitedly.

Julie was not happy to be out of her room. "Aren't trapdoors in the floor?" she queried in a snotty voice.

"No. Well, maybe. How do we get up there?" Sam asked sheepishly.

Ian was the tallest of us and easily reached the door. He poked at the wooden square, lifting it an inch or two, but besides some falling dust, nothing happened.

"Maybe you need a ladder," I said to Ian.

At about the same time, a red wooden ball tethered to a cord fell from the crack and swung side to side in Ian's face. His eyes followed the orb as if it were a cat toy.

"That rope isn't going to pull itself," Sam called, reaching a hand out.

Ian came to, lunging forward and beating Sam to the ball. Without a second thought, he gave it a yank. Ian was extremely competitive, and I don't think he was ready for the reaction stage of his action. The hatch resisted, stubborn, at first, but gravity and function prevailed. The horizontal door creaked and fell in our favor exposing a folded stair set and a lot more dust. The heavy contraption almost broke Ian's neck with its fall.

Backed against the wall and still clutching the, now disconnected, wooden ball, he said, "Well – there you go."

"That's just an attic. My house has the same kind of thing. It's probably dark and full of dust," Julie said, shaking her head at us.

Ian was climbing the stairs before Julie had finished with her assessment. Sam and I went up next. The attic was much like Julie had described it, dark and dusty. Sam found a hanging bulb and, giving it a tug, illuminated most of the room. Rows of plywood boards were laid out across the horizontal ceiling beams, forming a string of walkways. Ian viewed the backwoods through a circular window, which was split like a pie into four sections.

Sam joined Ian, scanning the empty sky and moonlit pines. "What a lookout."

I crossed the floor, discovering an object in the otherwise empty attic.

Julie, tired of waiting in the hallway, popped her head up through the open hatch. "See, guys, dark and dusty. What's the big deal?" she said, mocking our adventure.

"I found a box over here," I called out from the corner.

The tattered box was wedged in a tight space where the slanted roof and insulation met the floor. Ian and Sam hustled over, crouching next to me.

Sam, almost standing on my shoulder, asked, "What's in it?"

The box was heavy and covered with dust and pink fiberglass spines. Setting it down under the light, I peeled the clear packing tape off, freeing two cardboard flaps. Sam, Ian, and Julie had formed a half circle around the box and were speculating as to its contents. The majority of the box was filled with tiny clay dolls individually wrapped in outdated newspaper. I pulled a few out and uncovered porcelain figures and painted eyes and lips.

Ian and Sam, groaning with displeasure, scoured the other wall in hopes of greater finds.

Julie loved them. "These are antique Hummels. My aunt collects these. They're worth a ton, and I bet the people that own this place don't even know that they're up here," she said, flashing me a look which I understood to mean that she wanted to swipe them.

Ian and Sam weren't listening to a word she was saying. Disappointed, I started over to the hatch. She continued to pull newspaper shapes from the box, racking up her booty.

I had just disappeared below the hatch when I heard Julie's disturbed voice. "Oh-my-God, guys, *look*. It's true."

Curious, I paused my descent and pulled myself back into the attic. The three of them were looking at some sort of plaque. As I neared from behind, I could see that the object of interest was actually a framed photograph. Sallow light from the dingy overhead bulb glared on the glass inside the wooden frame. Julie read an inscription aloud, "The Brinkley Family." As I leaned over her shoulder, five figures within the panoramic-style family portrait became clear. The photo had been taken in the living room. Everything looked different though. There were different couches and lights, a much smaller TV, and, as far as I could see, no black armchair. The only thing that did match was the huge moose bust hanging above the mantel. *We'll take the house, but the moose stays*, I could almost hear the new buyer say with a chuckle, much to his wife's chagrin. Tacky bastard.

"This is too creepy, man. *That's* the family. That's the guy who murdered his family," Ian said, sending the hair on the back of my neck to attention.

They were exactly how the waiter had described them: three young kids, a beautiful wife, and the father — who didn't look much like a murderer to me. He was kind of chubby, thick blond hair, and had a round face bearing a postcard smile.

"This doesn't prove that the family was murdered; it just means that the neighbors knew the name of the people that lived here," I said. "Of course they would've known that. Shit — we all knew it. The directions say 'Brinkley cabin' at the top of the page."

"I don't know, Matt. Like, what do those people have to gain by lying to us? How could they be rival renters when they live at their house? It doesn't make sense," Julie said, disturbing me with her logic.

Ian pointed at the picture, saying, "Look at the dad. He looks evil. That guy did it, man, no question. If not, why would he disappear?"

Sam laughed. "Disappear? How do you know he —"

His words fell off, interrupted by a chilling voice rumbling from behind. "WHAT ARE YOU KIDS DOING IN MY ATTIC?"

Julie began screaming hysterically. The picture, too heavy for the moment, fell from her hands and shattered against the timber shafts below.

Sam whipped around so violently that his swinging elbow almost knocked me out in the commotion. His howling dissolved Julie's voice and tripled the chaos. "*Oh, fuck.*"

SEVENTEEN

"You piece of shit," Sam hissed, looking past me.

I felt a blast of laughter penetrate my back. An arm slung around my neck. It was Dura. We had all forgotten about her downstairs.

We took turns cursing her until she finally asked, "Jesus, why are you guys so edgy anyway?"

Julie picked the frame up from between two beams, and shaking bits of glass away, turned the picture toward Dura, saying, "This is the family. That's the guy who murdered them."

Dura shook her head. "Does it say that he murdered them right there in the inscription or…?"

"No, but it says the Brinkley family. Look, they're just like that lady said."

Dura didn't respond at first but then admitted, "I don't know what's up. This house does have a weird vibe to it though. Sam, have you checked the Internet?"

"No. I just finished bringing my stuff in."

I started fitting the Hummels back into the box.

Resting the broken picture on top, Julie said, "Let's

see what we find on the Net. If shit starts jumping off the walls, I'm outta here."

Downstairs, the five of us crowded around the computer. Finding the Internet was not easy; the failing dial-up connection dropped our search three times before we were finally signed in properly. Sam found a local Flagstaff news site and typed into the search box: Brinkley, murder, police, and on the loose. After informing us that "on" and "the" were very general terms, the search brought up a couple of blurbs.

"*Police bring Steve Brinkley in on drug charges. Sources say seventeen-year-old Brinkley will be tried as an adult.*" Our Brinkley definitely wasn't a minor, and the online photo didn't match any of the kids that we had seen in the portrait. Another one read, "*Brinkley family contributes talents in this year's art festival.*" That one *was* our group but still no mass murder. The next three were as insignificant as the first two.

"See? Don't you think there might have been some mention of an entire family's murder...especially in such a small community?" Sam reasoned, clicking the boxes to shut the programs down.

"Wait," Ian said. "I need to check my e-mail."

The crew seemed pacified by our find, or lack of a find. I felt better. I figured it very unlikely that a family would make the news for an arts and crafts fair, and then be ignored when the father went crazy and killed them all.

Dancing in from the kitchen and presenting two brimming bottles of liquor, Julie sang, "All right, I say we celebrate. We're *not* staying in the house of a murdered family."

Ian, abandoning his sign-in screen, bolted to Julie. "Whoa, whoa, *let's?* I spent the fazoos on this stuff," he said, trying to free his bottles.

Shocked, Julie fleered, "Oh, come on, *Ian*, don't be such a cheap ass. This isn't even your money. I won the damn trip."

"Ian's right," I countered. "He did take the initiative to shoulder tap." He was happy with my defense, but then I continued, "But, if I'm not mistaken, those bottles were all you got, right?"

He nodded. "Dude, I got gallons of this stuff. What do you mean, *that's all?*"

I smiled to the others, explaining, "Well, I figure at some point over the next couple of days you're going to need a little thing that we in the States like to call – *food.*"

"Shit," he sighed. "How'd I forget food?"

Enjoying his defeat, I called out, "Okay, barkeep, why don't you fix us some drinks, and we'll get dinner going."

Julie cackled and broke into her irritating victory dance. The rest of us drifted into the kitchen.

In spite of the frigid air, we decided to eat out back on the deck. A hefty redwood table beneath a steel and copper canopy filled most of the deck's left side. The wintry air had a sweet perfume of pine and vanilla. Dura ignited two kerosene torches at each side of a small stair set. The steps led down to the virgin powdered ground and miles of open forest. We felt like adults, like real and rich adults, and all the while we were just kids, playing house on one of the most perfect nights there ever was.

Back in the kitchen, I prepared the meat. Dura took settings. Sam mashed a pot of boiled red potatoes and chopped carrots, celery, and tomatoes for the salad. Ian and Julie worked diligently mixing a pitcher of Captain Morgan's and Coke; the only problem was that they seemed to be drinking more than they were spreading around. Sam was really putting his might into crushing those potatoes. Armed with a metal ladle, he mashed and churned garlic and an entire stick of butter into the blend.

"That smells great," Ian complimented Sam, passing him a full highball glass with two buoyant cubes.

Sam knocked back half the glass and turned down the burner, saying, "I'm just gonna let this sit for a minute." Dumping the balance of the drink down his throat, he exhaled, "I'll take another, Ian."

The kitchen was furnished with an indoor propane grill that connected beside the cooktop stove. A noisy overhead vent caught most of the BBQ smoke, but what escaped created an aroma of hickory sauce and bacon about the kitchen. After draining my first cocktail, I filled another. I could tell that Ian's mix was strong because after just one, my normally achy neck started to soften, and my face flushed with warmth.

Ian and Julie spent their time babysitting the second pitcher outside at the table. They had sparked the outdoor heaters and seemed very comfortable doing nothing to help. Julie, standing above Ian, held an animated conversation, carelessly watering his jeans with diluted rum in the process. Dura had been running in and out of the kitchen all night and was finishing the settings with origami-style napkins.

Our finished product really surprised me. The table was decorated with bright bowls of salad and steaming mashed potatoes. There were also two long silver platters; one with the candied ribs smothered in BBQ sauce and burnt at the tips, and another was overfilled with the steaks; their bacon wraps sizzled.

For the beverages we had an assortment of liquors and chasers: liter bottles, fruit juice, and cans. And if you weren't feeling creative with your concoctions, the two pitchers of Captain and Coke were full and ready.

With the help of the overhead heaters and the glow from the living room window our table was cast in that classy restaurant hue. The people who owned that cabin must have spent a mint rigging those heaters up. They had basically turned the ceiling of the canopy into one big honeycomb heating system. The way it was programmed, you could turn them on separately, but we had them all blasting, and it was warm and toasty under there. I was working on my third drink by the time I piled my first heaping plate. The drinks were swimming in my empty stomach, and I was having a great time.

Nobody really knew how many Sam had put back, but by then, he had loosened up plenty. "See those potatoes? Yeah, I made'um. Check'um-out guys. Bits of red skins, just enough butter, and a sprinkle of garlic," he announced, resembling an arrogant Sunday morning infomercial.

Dura chuckled, pouring herself a cocktail but filling her glass only halfway.

I eyed her pour, saying, "Is that cup half empty or half full? You're not going to drink tonight or...?"

Watching my exaggerated movements, she looked disappointed in me. I think she may have been a little thrown seeing me that drunk early on, and at that moment, I felt it as well.

"Nobody's touching the potatoes. What the fuck?" Sam noticed, shoveling a pile onto Julie's plate.

"Hey, Sam, I'm actually not a big potato eater," she said, bothered by his intrusion.

"Well, I almost threw my goddamn shoulder out mashing those things, so you are a 'big potato eater' *tonight*," he mocked, pointing his barbecue-dipped finger and swirling the shrinking cubes in his glass.

I had never witnessed Sam act that way before. He had a bit of rum cockiness coming through. Julie looked urgently to Ian for backup.

Ian diverted his eyes to the bowl, and with the ladle in hand, said, "Just have some potatoes, babe. They're good for you."

Julie was appalled by his lack of loyalty. "You *worm*."

Dura diced up a piece of steak and was busy mixing the chunks of beef with her potatoes.

She noticed my eyes on her creation and tried explaining, "What? You've never seen this done before?

The Little White Trip

It's steak a la king."

"A la king?" I questioned.

She nodded her head, saying, "Yeah, I think so. After the holidays, my mom used to mix turkey and potatoes and call it 'turkey a la king,' so I guess that would make this steak a la king."

Sam was listening from across the table, and observed, "So it's the mixing with the potatoes that brings it to the *king* status?"

"A la king," Dura corrected.

"Doesn't Allah mean God in the Middle East?" I asked.

She glanced up at her empty glass and, shaking her head, figured, "You better pour me another one."

I squeezed her leg under the table and filled both of our glasses to the spilling point. We emptied another pitcher before abandoning the littered table for the cabin.

The feast had helped sop up my first couple of drinks, but nothing could stop the following three from creeping up on me. I found the trouble with hard alcohol was that it always crept up slowly. By the time the first two came knocking, you were usually enjoying number five or six, and helplessly on your way to being shit-faced. None of that mattered at the cabin though; we were all there to have a good time.

Inside, Julie was performing some kind of Broadway number for Ian and Sam. She started near the top of the curved staircase, singing and dancing up and down the first couple of steps. Her left hand clasped her hip, and the other held an imaginary microphone to her drunken mouth. Ian and Sam, leaning against the long couch, seemed to be getting into the show, swaying their heads and snapping their fingers to her beat. For some reason, her routine really bugged me. I'm not sure why. Maybe it was Julie's horrible tones, or the mass of attention she required, but either way, I was irked.

Toward the song's climax, she leaned her ass up onto the banister and slid past the last seven or eight stairs. With arms open and fingers twiddling to the final tune, she held a high note most of the way down. That was until she spotted the large wooden ball that marked the banister's end. She cut the tune noticing her collision path, but by that time, it was too late; gravity had her. Leaning forward toward the stairs, she almost avoided the cantaloupe-sized cap. She connected with her left hip. Crashing with the ball gave her a spin as she dropped the distance between the railing and the ground. With a loud grunt, her body absorbed the fall and rolled out flat. Besides the initial gasps, the room was muted.

At first, I resisted the temptation, but the grandeur of that situation was bigger than my manners, and I couldn't help from exploding at the mouth. I could tell that she wasn't really hurt. She fell surprisingly well – hip, shoulder, and then roll. Given my time on a skateboard, I had that fall combo perfected. Besides, I was a fairly insensitive drunk, and I truly despised musicals, especially the nasal shit.

Although I hated the song, Julie's ending stunt

brought it all together. I had never seen a good-looking girl fall that hard before. She looked strange, projecting through the air in her high-fashion sweat suit. Julie always was style over function, and as far as her banister episode went, in my opinion, a good pair of jeans could've slowed her down enough to avoid that knob.

Ian and Sam hurried to her aid. Ian looked heatedly over his shoulder, ending my snigger works. His expression didn't look good, and I began to wonder if she *was* all right. He noticed my guilty face, and surprised me by breaking into a spell of silent laughter, shushing himself in time to help Julie to her feet. I was glad to see that he could enjoy the humor in her misfortune. Humor's a commodity; we need to get it where we can. He had to play the "good guy" though; if not, later he would be playing the "lonely guy." Sam appeared pretty shaken by the fall; he scared easily. Julie limped to the couch on Ian's arm, and in a whiny voice, ordered him to kiss her battered hip. Ian was noble; he was never one to turn down such a request. The two of them were soon giggling and enjoying each other behind a wall of pillows.

Sam joined Dura on the deck. She was sitting on the wooden steps below the flaming torches. Sam perched himself on the square railing above her. I don't think they were talking to each other at first. A cloud of smoke drifted above Dura's head; then, holding up a white stick, she offered him a toke. Balancing on the rail, he took the joint in his free hand and swallowed a hefty pull fueling the cherry a bright red and orange. After another hit, he leaned forward to return the joint, but Dura was over it. She rose on the steps, stretched, and wandered toward the cabin.

I had been watching them through the arcadia door for some time, and seeing her heading in my direction made me feel like an eerie voyeur. I had the idea to jump to my left and pretend to be looking out the other window, but it was too late. So instead, I pulled the door open as if I was just on my way out, saying, "After you, miss."

Her eyelids hung low, and a smile rode high through her cheeks. "Thank you, kind sir," she offered in a very proper voice.

Something about Dura felt especially warm, but I had to leave her for the cold if I wanted to complete my act. I must seem mad spending time and thought on nothing like that, but it seemed to happen all the time.

Sam was still holding the burning stick when I arrived. He had forgotten that it was in his hand.

"Do you think I could get a little hit off that thing?" I asked, pointing at his dangling hand.

He looked up at me for a second and then down at his hand. "Oh – yeah, sure. It's not even mind…I mean mine. Dura gave it to me." He handed the browning half joint over.

I took a lungful.

Staring off into space, he asked, "Matt – do you think there could ever be anything between Dura and me?"

That was the second-to-last thing that I would've

imagined Sam would ask me at that very moment. Coughing up grey and leaking from my eyes, I pushed out between breaths, "You… and —"

He took over, explaining feverishly, "Me and Dura. You know, like as a couple. She didn't say anything, but I can just feel it. There's something between us."

Yeah, I know how you feel. Dura and I just got together the other night. Her body's amazing. I damned that thought deeper into my mind.

What a horrible situation, everything between Dura and me was supposed to be kept quiet for Sam's sake, and now this. If he thought they were falling for each other, how was I supposed to tell him that, a) Dura was not down for him, and b) oh yeah, we had secretly hooked up as well. And, to add to my discomfort, all of that coughing had lifted me spiritually high. I'm talking zero fucking gravity. I didn't like it.

Supposedly, the harder you cough after a puff, the farther out of your head you go. Sam continued to rationalize his idea, but I couldn't focus. I started to obsess about my heart. I've heard that smoking anything, even cigarettes, can speed up your heart rate, and mine was hammering through my ribs. My friend Pensmith, from school, thinks that I have some type of anxiety and that smoking pot only makes it worse. And on the few nights that I'd had like that, I could believe him.

My breathing felt heavy. My skin was on fire, and my mind raced with diagnoses. To put it meekly, I had an exceptional talent for convincing my brain that my body was failing. It killed me to deal with that kind of trip. The smoke probably sped my heart up some, but the rest was all in my mind.

Cutting Sam's rant off short, I said, "You never know, man; you never know."

I wasn't even sure what we'd been talking about at that point, but reality had become a distant memory, and I knew that I needed to get out of there before I ran screaming into the forest.

I was that bad.

EIGHTEEN

With soft steps through the tall carpet, I discreetly crossed the living room and made for the stairs. None of the others inside noticed me – thank God. I was going inwardly mad, and if I had been forced into another conversation, I knew that such madness was sure to escape – orally.

A while back I had found out the only way that I could slow my loaded mind from racing was to overwhelm my senses. Usually touch would be the one to call, but sometimes my taste buds could deliver relief. Touch was the only sense that seemed to enjoy being perilously stoned. Sometimes even sound tripped me out. I would zero in on a random tone in the background of a song or even the clicking of an overhead fan, and my mind would convince itself that I was too fucked up.

Once upstairs, I pulled a towel from the hall closet and locked myself into the bathroom for a hot, calming shower. Dense clouds of steam drifted over the glass shower door and fogged the room. The moist air was easy to breathe and loosened my charred throat. Boiling beads of water pelted my back, transposing my white skin to blushing shades in their rolling paths.

The shower almost always quelled my anxieties. My brain, too busy computing all of the pleasant feelings, would have no time to agonize over erratic things like heart rate, shallow breathing, or strange sounds. As the sensory treatment progressed, I usually found myself in the same position: showerhead diverted to the wall, eyes closed, lying with my naked back against the tile floor, clenching a handful of conditioner, and entertaining a head rich with images much more vivid than my sober consciousness could ever supply.

The water eventually ran dead of heat, and my session was over. Outside, the cold tile tingled beneath my bare feet as I dried off in front of the sink. After wrapping the wet towel around my waist, I reached out with a dry hand and wiped a section of the steam-layered mirror clean. A familiar face appeared in the foggy clearing, and I could tell that things were better. My mind focused on some details and let others go.

Before I had learned how to counter those episodes, succumbing to an attack like that used to ruin me. One night it happened while I was on a road trip with my then girlfriend. I was at such an intense state of befuddlement that I refused to talk to her for most of *Willy Wonka and the Chocolate Factory*. I loved the Oompa Loompas when I was high, but that night their green hair and orange faces scared the shit out of me. Seeing me like that worried her, but she turned out to be a huge comfort. The last thing I remember about that night was lying on top of the bed sheets with my eyes closed as she covered my shaky body with damp washcloths.

I rarely told people about my issues. I knew that most of the trouble came from within, and figured they wouldn't understand. I stayed high, to some level, for the next couple of hours, but it was mellow, and until shit got crazy with the pounding at the front door, I actually enjoyed the buzz.

Downstairs, I found Dura watching the big screen intently. The program starred two meerkats. They sprung to their hind legs, and with a series of guttural yowls, alerted the feeding pack of an oncoming hyena. She loved nature shows.

"Where'd you disappear to?" she questioned, as I dropped onto the couch next to her.

"I decided to take a shower, so I wouldn't have to deal with it later," I said, shaking water from the tips of my hair and halfheartedly fighting back a cheesy grin.

"Are you stoned – yeah – you're stoned." She picked up on within a few seconds.

I hated getting called out on being stoned. I guess it was because when I was high, inside my loopy brain, I was struggling to appear normal. When someone called me out that quickly, I felt like I'd been caught, and I wondered what it was that gave it away so easily. I felt like I was drooling or something.

"Kind of," I answered guiltily. "I took a hit outside with Sam."

She gave me an all-knowing smirk, like that of a strict mother who was letting you off the hook, but just that one time. From where we were sitting, I could see Julie and Ian at the kitchen table playing some sort of game with a deck of cards and a bottle.

Dura jumped up from the couch and hurried to the bathroom. Just before stepping inside, she spun around and prompted me to follow. I was a bit confused but went along anyway. Once inside the bathroom, she reached around my waist and turned the lock.

"What are we –" I started to ask as she took my hand.

She pulled me past another door into her bedroom.

Releasing my hand she ran to the other end of the room. She locked the bedroom door and enlightened me, "My door's locked and so is the one in the bathroom. This way, if someone comes knocking at *my* door, we're not both stuck in here together."

"What?" I asked, a little bemused.

"If someone comes to my door, you can run into the bathroom. I'll come out of my room alone, and a few minutes later, you can go out through the bathroom," she explained through a vivacious grin.

"And that's not gonna be *obvious*?"

"Matt, I think you're overestimating our friends. Julie and Ian are falling all over themselves with playing cards licked and stuck to their foreheads. And Sam was drunk before dinner, and he's now drunk, high, and lying out on the deck convinced that he can count the stars."

She pushed me onto the bed and crawled on top. We

kissed. Our hands traveled, and bodies beamed salaciously for each other. We tossed on the bed, and I found myself on top.

I pulled away for a second, remembering my conversation with Sam. "Wait, we've got a problem," I said, dodging Dura's attempts to continue.

"What problem?"

"Sam told me he thinks he's falling for you."

"What? When?"

"Today, outside on the deck. He said he 'felt something' between you two."

"What'd you tell him?"

"I didn't really tell him anything. I was super high, and the whole situation kind of threw me off."

"Shit. That's not good," she said at the end of a deep breath.

"No, it's not."

Our quiet worry was broken by an impatient twisting on the bathroom door handle followed by a powerful kick.

"What the – *fuck*? Who's in there?" Ian's voice called. "Come on, I'm going to *piss* myself."

Our eyes nervously consulted, and then agreed on the same thing.

"I'm...I'll be out..." we *both* said, our voices froze, knowing that we had just fucked up.

The handle was still for a moment as confusion fell over its operator. "What? Is that you in there, Matt? Come on, man, I gotta go."

I thought for a second. Freeing my arms from Dura's grasp, I whispered to her, "Okay, this is a reverse deal. I'll go out now, and you hang in here for a minute. Got it?"

She nodded.

As I rolled off the bed, Ian's demands started again as did the kicking. I was slowly closing the door to Dura's room when I turned to get a last look at my girl. She curled a thick silken pillow against her chest and nuzzled my replacement as she watched me go. I hesitated a tick, then threw the door back open and sprung to her. I climbed onto the bed. Her arms untangled and drew me in, squeezing the pillow tightly between us. I stole a hurried kiss before disappearing back into the bathroom.

NINETEEN

I found Sam, as Dura had said earlier, lying out on the deck beneath the heaters and gazing out from under the canopy into the atmosphere. "What's up, Sam?" I asked, receiving no reply.

His eyes were open, but he hadn't blinked since I sat down beside him. I waved my open hand up and down, chopping his vision.

His eyes were watering. He finally blinked, squeezing tears from under his lids, and said, "Fuck, Matt." He paused, "you made me lose count."

"Lose count?"

He sat up and wiped his eyes. "Yeah, I was counting them," he said, "the stars."

I thought Dura was joking about that. Sam was a strange boy.

"How high did you get?"

"High as *hell*, dude. Dura told me she paid over three hundred bucks for an ounce of that stuff."

"Not the drugs, Sam; I meant how many *stars* did you count up to?"

Sam eyed his watch for a second, and then asked, "Who said anything about stars? Hey, you got a smoke on you?"

I think that the cold had frozen Sam's brain by that point; he was far beyond making any kind of sense. "Let's go inside," I said, getting up. "They're playing a card game in there."

Without hesitation, Sam popped up and followed me into the cabin.

The situation inside was confusing at first sight and got worse with time. Panicked, Ian dashed around the kitchen, concealing bottles and dirty shot glasses.

Julie was no help with whatever it was that he was trying to accomplish. "Jesus, Ian, what are you doing? Who is that?" she cried, peeking nervously into the living room.

"Who's what?" I asked.

My question answered itself in crashing actions. *Bang, Bang, Bang.* The front door thundered with a deep pounding. "Hello…is somebody in there? I need help," a man's voice called, carrying clear through the door.

Everybody froze. Apparently, that was the first time that the pounding trespasser had produced a voice.

"*Who the fuck is that?*" I asked.

Dura shook her head, whispering her obliviousness.

Ian, content with the kitchen, said, "We don't know, Matt. Maybe a cop…maybe Brinkley."

"Oh, stop that, Ian," Julie whined, undoubtedly thinking the same thing. "Just answer the door, or at least look through the peephole."

"There's no hole, Julie. *You* answer it. I don't want to deal with anybody," Ian said, making it obvious, at least to me, that he was more worried that it was the cops than anything else.

Julie said nothing, shaking her head feverishly.

"Fuck this." Sam suggested, "Let's just turn off all the lights. He won't even know that we're in here."

Ring, Ring, Ring. The bell let us all know that whoever was outside that door knew that somebody was inside. Besides, the cabin lights were easily seen from the woods.

Julie retreated toward the stairs. "Oh my God, fucking Ian, do something – *please.*"

"Goddamn it. Matt, were you guys being loud out there?" Ian accused, hoping for a scapegoat.

"No. That's not it anyway. We don't even have neighbors."

Ian bounced on his toes for a second, psyching himself up like a competitive runner. Leaning his head from side to side he physically shook the tension from his brain; it trailed down his neck, shoulders, and possessed his jittery fingertips. He was going to handle the situation. Pulling a long, serrated knife from the chopping block, he took a deep breath and started toward the door.

Dura was uneasy. "Ian are you sure you –"

"*Shhh,*" he hissed, fitting the stainless steel between his lower back and tight leather belt. His lengthy shirt fell over the handle as he crossed the living room toward the front door.

Bang, Bang, Bang. "I know you kids are in there. Could you just open up for a second? I need a phone."

When I heard that part, I was almost glad that Ian had armed himself. How the *fuck* did that guy know that we were kids?

Dura's eyes flared.

"Just turn out the lights," Sam pleaded. "Don't answer it."

Ian's hand was already on the door. He straightened up, gathered everything he had, and cranked it open. The man who we were confronted with hardly matched the anticipation, or the noise. He bordered on the short side and wore his charcoal beanie pulled down low. His chin and mouth were hidden beneath a neatly groomed rusty-blond goatee – just a normal guy.

Rubbing his icy hands together, he said, "Oh, thank *God* you answered. I was bringing my son in from town, and I blew a tire. I just need to use a phone, so I can call a tow service."

A long pause was shared in the doorway. Ian wasn't convinced. "You need your car towed because of a flat tire? Why don't you just change it?"

The man huffed at Ian's question. "I didn't realize that it had blown for a while. When I finally pulled over, the rubber was all tangled up in the axle. Even if I had a jack and iron, I'd need the Jaws of Life to cut it loose."

Ian nodded. His answer seemed believable.

"Where's your son?"

Leaning in, to make sure that Ian understood every

word, the man shot back, "I left him in the car. The locks still work and so does the heat. He's only twelve years old, and I didn't know how far I might have to walk. But I really should get back there, so are you going to let me use the phone, or are you going to ask me questions all night?"

Ian's arms were spread wide in the open doorway. He formed a barrier between the man and the inside of the cabin. His right hand gripped the edge of the open door, and the other leaned against the closed second door. He hadn't answered the man's question. He lowered his right arm, but not to clear the way. Instead, his free hand was sent behind his back and down toward his waistband. I couldn't believe what I was seeing.

What the fuck was he thinking?

His fingers danced along his loose shirt close to the knife.

"Here you go," I said, walking up from behind Ian with Julie's cell phone in hand.

Ian's drunken expression was hard to place. He may have just been fucking with us, or maybe he was going to chase the poor guy into the forest at knifepoint. The man accepted the cell phone but seemed annoyed with his lack of admittance. He dialed the phone and started to describe his situation into the illuminated mouthpiece. Ian slowly closed the door, easing the deadbolt across.

"What the fuck were you thinking?"

Ian's eyes were filled with conspiracy. "What do you mean? That's him, Matt. That's the guy."

Julie shuttered, chanting, "Oh shit, oh shit, oh —"

"Julie, calm down," I said. "Ian, you're fucked-up drunk. Nobody was murdered here. It wasn't on the news. It never happened."

"Dude, he's got blond hair, and what the fuck is he doing here —" Ian's words were paused by a tapping at the door. He proceeded in a whisper, *"What the fuck is he doing here in the middle of the night for, man?"*

The tapping started again. "Shhh, Ian, chill the fuck out, and go put that knife away."

He resisted for a second, but then, realizing that he was probably wrong and surely drunk, he walked away from the door and into the living room. Shaking my head, I watched him hide the blade behind a vase on top of the mantel. Planted stiffly on the edge of the coffee table, he posted close to his hidden weapon.

The deadbolt unhitched with an embarrassing click. I pulled the door open. The man and I stood face to face in the doorway. He looked relieved.

"Did you get everything figured out?" I asked, trying to act like a normal person.

His bizarre smile made me feel like he wasn't buying it. "Yeah, luckily after a couple calls, I found somebody that would come all the way out here."

He handed me the phone, eyeing around my shoulder into the house.

"The lady said they'd have a truck out here in about ten minutes. Must've had one around here already," he explained, not yet reaching his point. "Anyway, do you think I could come in for a drink of water before I go?"

I didn't feel totally comfortable with it. Not only had I never seen the guy before, but I was unsure about Ian. He could get us all in a lot of trouble.

"I mean – the hike up here already took so much out of me."

Fearing that I may have just made the wrong decision, I stepped back and let the stranger into our cabin. I could hear Julie mumbling something as she crept up the last of the stairs and out of sight. As if he knew where it was, the fidgety little man stepped through the living room and veered off into the kitchen. The atmosphere was turbulent, at best.

Sam waved uneasily at the guy as he passed. "Hi-ya," he said, casually positioning himself next to the vase on the mantel.

Ian glanced up at Sam, silently endorsing his move. Julie watched from above as Dura and I followed the man into the kitchen.

"The cups are above the dishwasher," Dura said.

He filled a glass from the tap, breathing heavily through his nose as he gulped the entire thing.

"So you live around here?" she asked a neutral question.

"Yep, I'm actually a lot closer to the lake than this cabin. This is the Brinkley place, right?"

The question surprised us both. He had said that he didn't know how far he would have to walk to find a phone. Then again, our private drive off Springston may have been labeled; the mailbox was.

"That's what we're told," Dura answered.

He smiled. "Hmmm, Brinkley, he's a nut isn't he?"

Neither of us said a word.

He clarified the statement, but not the way we worried he might. "Yeah, one of those religious freaks. He used to go into town and preach to people on the streets. Everybody hated that guy – oh, and his poor wife and kids."

Dura and I didn't know what to say; it wasn't as if he was asking us a question, but he looked at us as though he had.

"You never heard about him?" he asked the question, but failed to wait for an answer, continuing, "Yeah, they kind of chased him out of town. Not officially, but they made it hard enough for him here. Too much preaching, even the church didn't agree with him. Oh well, like Elvis said, "clean up *your own* backyard." I think he moved farther into the woods or something."

He had finished his second glass of water by then and seemed to remember what he was up to. "Oh shit, I gotta go. The truck should be there any minute."

He scrambled off through the kitchen but seemed to take his time as he walked through the living room. He was really soaking it up.

As he swung the towering door open, he said, "Thanks, guys. See'ya later." Then, looking up toward the stairs, he added, "You, too…*strange group.*"

The door sealed, and he was gone.

The Little White Trip

"What the hell was that?" Ian noticed, "That guy said, '*See'ya later.*'"

"It's a figure of speech," Dura said. "Besides, look, that's another reason not to worry about this place. He lives nearby and hadn't even heard anything about this so-called murderer."

"Yeah, that – or he didn't want to let on to what he knew."

I was about to lock the door but decided to do the opposite. I wanted to see him go. Sam, still waiting by the mantel, watched me open the door. I waved for him to follow. He did, but not before uncovering Ian's stashed knife. Outside, I closed the door at our backs. We watched the man jog across the driveway and over the bridge. Sam thought that I wanted him along for protection, but really, being free of my whirling high, I wanted to talk to him about Dura.

"Well, there he goes. Guess he's legit," he said, testing the knife's point on his palm.

"Of course he's legit. You didn't actually think –"

"All right Matt, let's get back in there. We're wasting our night."

Sam was still pretty fucked up and had no intention of taking part in my heart-to-heart.

He turned before I could speak. "BLAAHH," he screamed, raising the knife and charging into the cabin.

Nobody was there to witness his poorly-timed joke, though. I followed his misplaced footsteps through the carpet toward the kitchen.

"Sam, please put that knife down. You're scaring me."

He turned, examining me through squinted eyes. "You're scared'a me?"

"Not exactly. More scared *for* you. You're piss-drunk, and you're going to fall on that damn thing."

He handed me the knife, blade first, and traipsed off into the kitchen.

With the departure of our jabbering visitor, everybody quickly fell back into their places. Julie and Ian were throwing cards at each other and arguing over a technicality of their game, and Dura was excavating the stocked freezer.

Sam plopped himself on Julie's lap, ending their card toss. "How are you doing?" he asked, acting abnormally brazen.

Ian kind of tilted his head, watching from across the table.

"I...I'm doing *great*, Sam," Julie answered. "How are *you* doing?"

Sam ignored her question. "Because you fell down those stairs, and I —"

Pushing him from her lap, she snapped, "Oh *yeah*, I remember. I almost died, and you couldn't stop laughing at me."

Sam didn't remember what she was talking about at first. His eyes wandered around the room past Dura and then fixed on me. "I didn't laugh at you. I was helping; Matt's the one who laughed."

Julie redirected her glare at me. "It *was* you, wasn't it?"

she said, pointing a wicked finger. "I remember that jackal laugh of yours."

I looked over my shoulder, pretending to search for who she might have been accusing, certainly not me.

"Find anything good in there, Dura?" I asked, completely avoiding Julie and the subject.

She was still searching the freezer, sifting through fudgesticks, push-up pops, and mint bars. To my surprise, Julie let me slip away, just totally dropped the conversation. As I walked over to Dura, I was careful not to get within claws' reach of Julie. She was crafty, not one to be underestimated.

Dura was debating between the push-up pops or the fudgesticks.

"I can't decide. Matt, which one would you pick?" Her voice was desperate.

Taking the two boxes, one in each hand, I said, "It doesn't matter what *I* would pick because I'm not going to be the one eating it. You are."

She nodded earnestly as I continued. "It breaks down like this. You *could* go with the push-up pop, which is basically just sherbet ice cream in a tube, something light. Or, you could go with the fudgestick, a dark, rich treat you feel guilty about eating even before you've hit the stick. You need to look on your shoulders. On the left side there's a light orange push-up pop hovering with white-feathered wings and a halo. On the right side there's a dark brown fudgestick with its pelvis pumping in all directions, swinging a pointed tail, and flicking its long cloven tongue behind your back at the scared little push-up pop."

She looked even more lost after my advice than she did before.

I tilted the box toward her, saying, "Eat the damn fudgestick already."

I knew it was some stupid calorie thing that she was hung up on, and even without the sports routine, her body was still perfect.

Sam, wobbling near the kitchen window, mumbled, "I'm happy to be here."

Even through the noisy babble in the room, his words were lucid. The way he spoke, it was just different.

With his brief spotlight, he eased back, sitting on the windowsill, and explained, "I mean it. I'm really happy to be here with you guys. I know I'm not as much fun as you all, but I – you guys are my best friends."

"You're fun, Sam," Dura said, "a little crazy, but I think you're a lot of fun. We all do."

The rest of us caught on, a bit off cue, but we shared the feeling.

"Hey, hey, let's hear it for Sam. What a guy," Ian jokingly praised, bobbling his head and knocking back an unneeded whisky shot.

Dividing Dura's kind words by Ian's sarcasm, Sam added, "You know what I mean. It's just fun." With that, he swaggered off across the wooden floor and disappeared into the living room.

Dura really enjoyed her fudgestick. To be honest, so

did I, and I wasn't even having one. Just seeing her eat that thing was the highlight of my night — at least up until then. I was starting to sober up, so I decided to join in on Julie and Ian's card game. Dura sat on the other side of the table, in-between Ian and Julie. Sam was off doing something, which left me alone, facing the three of them from my side. Dura took full advantage of her positioning.

While Julie explained a list of complex rules, Dura slid three-fourths of the fudgestick down her throat and slowly pulled it back out. A drip of liquid fudge fell from the tip and landed on her bottom lip. Her eyes snapped up to mine, and with a pleased expression, she licked her lips clean. As Julie tossed a small stack of cards to me, Dura carefully ran her tongue along the frozen pop, stick to tip. The triple-X dessert went on for more than half of the first game until Dura was left only with a stick and a smile. She must have read into my "choices" speech, but I sure as hell wasn't complaining.

Dura, pushing up and out of her chair, declared, "I think I'm going to start a fire — I mean start the fire." Then, she pranced off into the living room.

Julie had been yelling at my lack of attention since the beginning of the game, and she was at it again. "Matt, *hello*, earth to Matt. Are you going to draw or trade?"

I looked across the table at Julie and her barely cognizant partner, Ian, and said, "I've got a game. How about we take a couple of shots, throw the cards in the air, and then scream across the table at each other. It's just as fun as your game, but this way we could actually get some drinking done. Your game sucks."

She glowered at me, mentally straining for some brilliant comeback.

Then, commandeering their bottle, I added, "And you might want to take little Romeo upstairs before he totally passes his peak, and your night goes down the drain." With a nod, I poured myself a shot, tossed it down, and clapped the empty glass on the table.

Julie looked at Ian, who was resting face-down on the table, and angrily slurred, "Come on, babe, that's the best idea Matt's had all night."

After they were gone, I retired the lights in the kitchen and found Dura kicked back on the loveseat, watching flames dance around the fireplace.

"Wow, that's a pretty good fire. Were you a Girl Scout?" I joked, sitting down beside her.

"No, but I did go to seventh and eighth grade at a Catholic school," she admitted. "I have the pleated skirt and everything."

"I guess that explains the disappearing fudgestick act then. You Catholic school girls are all the same."

She laughed and spun around to me. "So, did Bonnie and Clyde go up stairs for good?"

I nodded. "Yeah, What about Sam? Is he still stargazing?"

She ran her nails along the back of my scalp and down my neck. "Nope, he just went up to bed, too."

From over my shoulder I inspected the empty staircase. *Nobody there.* I inched a foot or two closer,

The Little White Trip

sharing Dura's cushion. She threw a leg around me, kind of sitting on my lap and knees. Our eyes collided and lips followed. My hands slid under her shirt. Her ambrosial skin rose with thousands of shivery bumps. I squeezed her hips. She clenched a handful of my hair and pulled my head back. It hurt, but I liked it. Then, she decided to be gentle, kissing my neck and breathing her libidinous warmth in my ear.

She pulled my shirt up and over my head. My hands glided above her hips and behind to her arched back. Without a struggle, I unhooked her bra, loosening the elastic tension and letting gravity and young skin fight for a balance. She ducked out of her shirt and slipped the black silk straps down from her shoulders. The firelight blanketed her body with the indiscriminate range of the sun. The shadows slid away as she turned to face the blaze in the wall. Shades of gold and bronze climbed her chest and neck.

Sliding back onto my knees, she reached down and pulled my button fly open. I started with the drawstring on her pajama pants, but she stopped me. Her hands met mine, and she guided my willing palms along her naked back pushing them down, deep below her waistband. Her ass rolled out to both sides in smooth humps of teenaged perfection.

There was nothing sentimental about it. Dura surprised me with her sexual intensity. Her eyes flickered and bore into my thoughts. She could see my wants and agreed completely. She moved down from my mouth, to my neck, chest, stomach, and then with her knees in the carpet and hands on my bare thighs... The camera panned off to the fireplace, flames glowing, wood crackling, and a great white puff of smoke escaping from a parting log. Or at least that's the way my big love scene is going to have to end on paper. I gotta keep it within the R rating, you know?

I didn't know it then, but I would later find out that Sam, in a failed attempt to reach the kitchen, witnessed as much of our act as time would permit. He sat motionless at the top of the stairs; his weakened body slumped, clutching the wooden railing to stay upright. He watched in silence until the rum got back on top of him and closed his lights right there in the soft shag carpet.

TWENTY

The next morning, Dura and I awoke on the couch being looked over by Julie and Sam. Although we did end up passing out together, we at least had the foresight to put our clothes back on.

"Jesus, Matt, you look like shit," I heard Sam's voice say as the fog in my eyes began to clear.

"Good morning to you, too," I yawned.

"How did you guys sleep last night?" Julie imposed, with a raised brow to Dura.

"*Holy shit*, squirrels, squirrels! No…badgers!" Ian hollered from the bottom of the staircase.

We looked over to see what he could possibly be yelling about. Ian was walking cautiously toward the back window and spying out onto the deck.

"They're all over the table," he said, pointing through the pane of glass.

Julie and Sam ran to Ian's side. "Wow, what are those things?" Julie asked.

Wondering if the sight justified the hype, I rolled over the back of the couch and walked to the window. They were ring-tailed raccoons, and the little vandals were having an all-out smorgasbord on last night's leftovers. One was buried headfirst in the salad bowl. The busy little animal paddled with its front paws spraying lettuce underhanded in a steady green stream. The dig would be stopped, only briefly, to chomp a rare carrot or celery bit. Another one appeared to be sick, stumbling around near the bowl of mashed potatoes. The long grey fur on its chest and front legs was slicked back and caked with white crusted potatoes. A few others fought over old rib bones and lapped up the last drops of sweet rum and Coke from a glass pitcher.

Sam reached for the sliding door. "We gotta stop those things. They're making a huge mess."

Ian blocked Sam's reach, saying, "I don't know if I'd screw with them, man. Badgers are mean as hell."

"Those aren't badgers," I said. "They're raccoons, and when they're hungry, they're mean as hell."

Ian, letting go of Sam's wrist, said, "Either way, coons or badgers, they're —"

"*Mean as hell?*" Sam predicted, slowly opening the arcadia door and easing out onto the deck.

"*Bad call,*" Ian warned, sealing the door behind him.

Everyone crowded around the side window to watch Sam's fatal mauling. The raccoons paid no attention to him as he crept over to the garden hose. He carefully turned the knob to full force. The hose had one of those pistol-grip sprayers fastened to the end.

"That's not gonna work," Ian said. "The hose is probably frozen solid."

"Ian, it's not *that* cold out there," I doubted.

"We'll see..."

Sam took a couple of steps toward the table, posting directly in front of the window. He was a strange hero, cloaked only in a pair of house slippers and pinstriped pajama pants. His pale back glared as it caught the morning light, and given the temperature out there even with the heaters that we had left burning all night, I'd imagine that his nipples were fit to cut glass.

He stood tall, holding the sprayer outstretched in both hands. "Hey, who invited you rats?"

Five grey heads cranked toward him with eyes glaring through black bands. The battle was about to begin. He took aim and blasted. The three on meat detail immediately split, scattering off the deck's edge. Mr. Potato Head was not so lucky. He ducked behind the potato bowl for a second but soon got anxious and with sluggish limbs made a break toward safety. Sam got him dead-on, near the edge of the cluttered table. The long fur on its swollen belly parted with the water's force. His paws slid on the wet table, sending him into what looked like some kind of drunkard's trapeze maneuver. He bounced off the bench seat and amazingly pulled a half rotation, landing feetfirst on the deck. He sidestepped a bit, looking disheveled, but wasted no time bolting for the stairs and dropping out of sight.

Sam was up four to zero, but the last coon was a real badass. When the others scattered and took cover, this one stood his ground next to the salad bowl. Sam had followed the last one with a powerful stream all the way to the stairs. As he pulled his aim back toward the table, the final bandit sprung off the top in his direction, lip curled, and sounding an awful growl.

Sam hesitated for a second glancing toward the door's safety. Then, for whatever reason, he decided to finish the job, serving the animal with a good shot to the face. The cold blast didn't seem to faze that warrior. Lowering his head, he walked with little difficulty toward Sam. He battled the water's force, growling louder as he neared. Inside, we ran from the window to the sliding glass door where Sam had retreated to. He held the sprayer steady in one hand and fumbled around with his other, finding the door's handle. With the rabid animal nearly at his toes, in one fluent motion, he slid the door open, dropped the hose, and jumped inside shrieking in defeat.

"Fucking – A, that's one tough bastard," he said, with eyes white as surrender.

The raccoon paused for a second when the water stopped, and after Sam was safely inside, the victorious animal raised its head, searching around the deck. He spotted us through the glass door. Walking up real casually he stood there dripping wet and glared at us with a look that said, *Come back out onto my deck. I dare you.*

"Fucking vegetarian, he's unstoppable," Sam grumbled, wiping his wet slippers on the carpet.

The Little White Trip

After the thrill of the fight, the kitchen came alive with hot pots and pans, egg shells, orange juice, and champagne. Breakfast became a time of persuasions.

"Just come to the mountain. You don't even have to snowboard. There's lots of things to do there," Dura said to Sam as he worked on his second helping of scrambled eggs.

He stuffed his mouth and nodded as Dura tried to convince him from across the table. Julie was the first to start in with Sam about going to the mountain. He fought with her through Mimosas and his first plateful. Dura took over once Julie tired of him. I could tell that he really did want to cave-in and go once Dura started, but he was in one of those weird stubborn situations. He had been saying no for so long that it would seem weak of him to just say okay all of a sudden. Besides, he was jackass stubborn when it came down to it.

"I really appreciate that you guys want me along, but I've been saying it from the beginning: I don't want to slide down the mountain."

"You never said anything about staying off the mountain," Dura contested.

I spoke up from the other end of the table, "Well, I don't know if I would say *never*. He told me that –"

"See, I did. I told Matt. Either way, I don't want to go. After today, half of you will be hurt or too sore to go back out, so this won't be such a big deal tomorrow. I'll have company."

Ian didn't give a shit either way. Having already spent

most of his cash on booze, he was happy to sell Sam's pass. I didn't like forcing people to do things they didn't want to, especially if they were supposed to be having fun.

"Fine, stay back if you want, but we're leaving you the car, so you can get around," Dura said, finally letting up on him.

The girls insisted that we take a cab into town, so Sam could have the car for the day, but I think that it was more because they liked being chauffeured around.

"I'm not going to leave the house, but if you really want to waste money on a cab, be my guest," he said, clearing his plate into the sink.

I was trying to tune out the breakfast debate. Julie's cell phone was sitting on the table in front of me, and I had fallen deep into a game of Snake.

"Is that my phone?" Julie asked.

"Yeah."

"Oh, call for a cab then. I want to get out of here."

My snake ate itself, and the game-over screen flashed. The service in the kitchen was horrible, barely one faint bar. I walked around, trying to find a strong spot, but it was dead all over. Then I remembered that our stranded visitor from the other night had made his calls from the front step. I walked outside, but there was still nothing. The driveway and back deck were even worse.

The phone wouldn't work anywhere. I wasn't going to be able to make the call from Julie's phone, but that's not what bothered me. Calling for the cab fell distant in my line of thoughts. I was more interested in knowing how it was possible for the guy from last night to make not just one but "a couple" of calls from the same dead spots. He hadn't, and I knew it.

Hoping to prove myself wrong, I clicked into the call history. If a call had been made, the evidence would have been stored in the history, and I could check it even without service. There was nothing from the night before. The last outgoing call had been logged when I had called the car rental lot on the way up.

My skin tingled with suspicion. Why wouldn't he have said anything about the useless phone? Why would he lie and say that he got through to somebody? What the fuck was he doing at the cabin? Better yet, inside the cabin? These were all great questions, and once again, I kept them to myself. I had a bad habit of doing things like that. I could have saved so much by not saying so little.

I ended up calling from the house line, and within forty-five minutes, our cab was out front honking its presence. I rode front row in the cab, and Ian somehow got stuck sitting bitch, in between the girls. I guess it's not as bad with girls on each side. Still, there's no place to put your arms.

Our cabby, an American Indian guy in his early thirties, tried to make conversation for the first few miles but gave up shortly after, turning the radio up a notch. Julie's voice raised two octaves with his radio. She was so excited about the day that she could hardly remember to breathe, gasping between sentences. I'm not going to lie; I was kind of happy that Sam stayed behind. Julie and Ian were joined at the hip, as usual, and without having to worry about including Sam, Dura was all mine.

She was a much better snowboarder than she let on to be. Supposedly, she had only been on the hill a few times before, but my proud machismo chose to doubt that.

After a few hours of riding, Dura and I settled in at a restaurant near the lobby bar called the Snowberg's Inn. The place had an eerie game room vibe: thick hairy carpet, glazed log walls, a chandelier made up of hundreds of antlers and lights, and the expectantly present, stuffed heads of a few sad deer and elk.

From our table I could see Julie and Ian in a half-moon booth across the floor. Their hands outstretched, uniting two champagne flutes together and then putting them back like a shots of Jägermeister. They were still dressed in their street clothes, so I assumed that they had found a friendly, a.k.a. easily corrupted, waitress and decided to drink well into character before hitting the slopes.

Dura looked funny in her snowboarding gear. The shop was out of her size, so she had to step it up a few. Our shitty rental pants were actually more like a one-piece overall type of deal with two elastic shoulder straps. Once we walked into the restaurant, she pulled the straps down and let the top hang, but before she did that, I had told her that she looked like Ralphie's little brother, Randy, from *A Christmas Story*. You know, in the scene where his mom bundles him up in so many layers that he can barely walk to school. She was not amused by my association.

The Little White Trip

On our last lift ride Dura and I had decided that the first thing we would order at the lodge should be two giant hot chocolates with extra marshmallows. Dura fished a couple of ice cubes from her water glass and dropped them into her boiling mug. I had been falling in the snow all day and was so cold that the scalding chocolate didn't matter. The first cup thawed me out some, and by the time the waitress returned with another, I was ready to order.

"How are the fajitas?" I asked the unsightly woman wearing a plastic tag that read, "Sandy."

She peered down at me with pupils coming in just above her brown framed glasses, and doubted, "Fajitas? Are you sure you're reading that right, honey?"

I looked again, scrolling with my middle finger along the laminated menu. I knew that I had seen them on there somewhere. I even remember thinking how out of place fajitas seemed on a menu flooded with old-fashioned BBQ dishes like biscuits and gravy, chicken-fried steak and squash, and pork ribs with corn. I found them near the bottom of the first page under skillets: *chicken or beef fajitas served with green and red peppers, onions, and sour cream.*

I pointed them out to the woman. She scribbled a few things on a notepad and turned to Dura, saying, "Okay, and for you, darling?"

Dura didn't answer. Looking at me, she said, "Oh, Matt, were you done or..."

The waitress snapped back to me with a critical stare. "You wanted the fajitas, right?" she asked, scratching her dry chin with a pencil and swaying a little.

"I don't know, maybe. I asked, *how are* the fajitas?"

Leaning over my shoulder, she gave the description a closer look, and unintentionally whispering her stale breath in my ear, read the description to herself, "*Red and green peppers, sour cream.* Yeah, sounds good. Burt, the chef, is something else. I'm sure it'll be just fine."

"It'll be fine? Well, Sandy, you've sold me. I'll take them, and you know what – I don't think I'll get a soda either. Water should do it, but thanks for asking."

She underlined my original order and turned away.

Dura laughed, and ordered. "I'll just have a number five with a Mr. Pibb."

The woman snatched up the menus and was gone.

"Wow, she sure is a pro," I said.

"Yeah, she is, and you are quite the professional asshole when you want to be."

"Whoa, whoa, I wasn't being an *asshole*. I was simply pointing out the fact that she was being an asshole, or at least bad at her job."

Dura was already over the debate. "Hey, what are you doing on the other side of the booth? Come over here with me."

Why *was* I on the other side, I wondered. Then, I remembered that I'd seen Julie and Ian as we walked into the room.

I pointed over my right shoulder, saying, "Ozzy and Sharon are right over there."

Dura's eyes followed my finger. "Ozzy and who?

The Little White Trip

There's nobody over there."

I spun around and saw that besides a small collection of bottles and glasses, the table was empty. I hated being wrong. I turned back around and pretended to have forgotten what we were talking about.

"Who are you talking about?" she asked again.

Buying myself some time, I casually knocked a fork to the ground and hunched over to pick it up. Once out of sight, I slid under the table.

Ahhh, under the table – that was a familiar place from long ago. When I was a little kid, around the holidays my parents would always pack our extended family into their brown van and terrorize some unlucky waitress in the name of Yuletide cheer. I was just a mini-Matt back then, and when I needed to go to the bathroom, instead of asking three or four people in either direction to slide out, I would just duck down and tunnel out beneath the table.

Of course, back then I was small enough, and I had long since outgrown that size, but to my eyes it was exactly as I remembered, dirty brown particle board, dried-up colorful blobs of chewing gum, and a series of dark patches where generations of hungry visitors had grabbed the table with their oily hands. And to my delight, that table lacked the popular smeared boogers left behind by little Nathan while his mom occupied herself with a hot butter rum.

Dura didn't realize where I had disappeared to until I sank my teeth into her snowboarding pants. I must have caught her skin because she threw her leg into the air, bumping my head under the solid table with a thud.

"*Ouch*, shit, Matt, what are you doing?" she yelped, snatching around under the table and seizing my shirt.

I was about to tell her that it was an accident when I heard a strange voice above the table. "Excuse me, miss. Are you okay?"

She let go of my shirt. "Oh – yes, I'm fine. I just had a muscle spasm. The slopes do it to me every time."

Turning my head, I saw a pair of black slacked legs at the end of the table.

"My name is Jerrod and I'm going to be your..." he cleared his throat, "new waiter."

"What happened to Suzy?" Dura asked.

"Suzy?"

"The lady who just took our orders."

"Oh, Sandy, yeah, she got moved to another section. Anyway, listen, your boyfriend ordered fajitas, but he didn't say whether he wanted beef or chicken. Do you know what he wanted?"

I had been poking and prodding at Dura from under the table ever since she had let go of my shirt. And she was doing a good job of keeping everything under control up there.

"Hmmm, chicken or beef, I wonder what he wanted," Dura wondered extra loud.

I think she was waiting for a signal, a tap or something like that.

She gave the choices again. "Beef?" She paused for a moment. I did nothing. "Or – chicken?"

The Little White Trip

There was an uncomfortable moment of silence exchanged above, and then I gave Dura my signal. I did so with my best rendition of a greasy, bass-filled fart. It was long enough to be exaggerated but just short enough to be believable.

"Another spasm?" the waiter inquired.

"Not quite. Better make it chicken," Dura said, throwing a kick straight out under the table and missing me by just inches.

As the waiter walked off, both of Dura's hands shot back under the table. I pulled away, sliding up onto my side of the booth. I popped my head up, but Dura's concentration was under the table, and she didn't notice. She had a real determined look on her face. Her shoulders bobbed left and right as her hands searched for me.

"Pssssst," I signaled, sitting up straight.

She paused and slowly looked up at me. Taking a deep breath, she pulled her hands out from under the table and carefully placed them to her sides.

I smiled. "Looking for something?"

"You little *shithead*, I should've just given you up," she said, trying hard to sound pissed.

"You've got to admit. That was a classic," I laughed. "There was no one else at the table – he knew it was you."

She rolled her eyes at my enjoyment.

"I think you bruised my leg," she said, leaning down close to her seat to take a look.

I felt bad. I didn't mean to get her skin.

"Yeah, it's bleeding."

I didn't know what to say.

"Sorry," I started to apologize to her empty bench. "I didn't know that I –"

My words were halted by what felt like a steel trap clamping down on my inner thigh. *I'd been had.* A brief flash of clarity was the only thing that kept me from banging her head up against the table, too.

"Sonofa-*bitch*," I cried.

The entire restaurant paused and looked over at me. She had bitten me much harder than I did her.

A pleasant giggle drifted up from under the table, and Dura followed. Squeezing onto my side of the booth, she said, "All right – now we're even."

We shared a kiss of truce, enjoyed our lunch, and debated, at no conclusion, whose leg hurt worse. I realized then that Dura was a cooler female version of me, and as strange as it may sound, I loved it.

TWENTY-ONE

After lunch, Dura and I met up with Ian and Julie at the snowboard park. Ian was attempting to showoff for Julie, but I think that his lunch of champions had gotten on top of him. Most of his tricks would come around perfectly, but his body would go totally limp when he touched down. Each attempt was the same as the last, arms flapping, body twisting, and a steady flow of cursing as he tumbled the length of the landing ramp. I thought it was safe to bet that Ian was going to be the one beat-up and staying home with Sam the next day.

We still had a couple of hours left before the slopes closed. Dura stayed at the park with Julie. Ian slithered back to the lodge, and I spent the rest of my time cruising a few of the long, scenic runs. It was a cloudy day, but we didn't get much snowfall. The less-traveled slopes were beautifully kept and immaculately fresh in some areas. Light powdered snow crept up the tall berms and bordered most of the slope's length. I carved up and down the white waves, digging trenches, and cutting paths deep in the untouched snow.

I was already in the rental shop when Julie and Dura showed up, hauling their boards, boots, and pants. After the gear was checked, the three of us waited around for Ian.

About ten minutes had passed when Julie made the suggestion to walk over to the lobby bar. "We'll probably find him there. If not, it won't be long before he shows."

She made a good point, and the smell of musky carpet and boot cleaner in the "board shack" was starting to give me a headache.

Just before we reached the lobby, a pair of black glass doors from the front entrance blew open, and a familiar boozed-up deviant came sprinting out, headed for the parking lot.

"RUUUN," Ian screamed upon seeing us. He was holding a bottle of liquor in one hand and his windbreaker in the other.

Following close on his heels, two men from the restaurant blasted out after him. One was wearing a tie, a pair of nice-ish slacks, and a collared shirt. The other appeared to be a busboy, with a stained white shirt, black apron, and a white rag clenched in his fist. I was not about to get wrapped up in whatever it was that he had gotten himself into. Besides, the manager-looking one was about level with us by the time Ian screamed. We would have been grabbed for sure. The man kind of slowed for a second looking us over. I spun around watching Ian race off into the lot of Greyhound buses, grocery-getter minivans, and raised SUVs.

Pointing into the lot, I said to the girls, "Holy shit, look at that crazy-ass kid."

They caught on quickly enough. "Yeah, it's those damn kids from the valley," Dura added.

The man lost interest in us, hurrying to join the busboy who was already in the lot.

Once inside at the bar, I wasn't exactly sure how to handle our situation. If those guys returned with Ian captive, I was sure he'd try to get us to help him. Then we'd all be in it.

I overheard the old bartender telling another man, "No, I poured him a shot. But then he couldn't come up with an ID, so I had to take it back. That's when he grabbed the bottle off the bar and ran out."

"Can I get you guys something?" the bartender asked, wearing a smile in spite of his last young customer.

"Uh, yeah, can we just get a couple – root beers for now?" I asked, in a horrible improv.

He began to fill three cups with ice, but we were gone before he came back from the soda fountain.

We found Ian back at the rental shop, out of breath and shrewdly camouflaging the hot bottle under his windbreaker.

"I already got a car service," Ian said, looking totally keyed up. "They're going to meet us out by the entrance."

"The main entrance?" I groaned. "That's like a half a mile from here."

"Well, we better get going then 'cause they said it was going to be there in ten minutes," he said, studying the hands of time.

As we walked, the daylight yawned and slipped away. Tuesday's weary sun fell dim and quiet behind Mount Agassiz. When I asked, Ian pretty much told the same story as the old bartender, except he tossed something in there about the man being racist. I couldn't help but laugh at his story. Envisioning the old bartender, I could confidently say that I didn't think he would be the flagrantly racist type, especially at work.

Our cab was waiting at the entrance when we arrived. It wasn't just any cab though; somehow, Ian had booked a huge, platinum Lincoln Town Car.

"Damn, Ian." I smirked. "Nice choice. Do we have enough money for this thing?"

Ian dug deep into his jacket pocket and produced a business card that read, "Custom Movement, *the classy cab*." "The guy at the rental shop set it up for me. He said that we could drink in the back seat."

That explained his need for the bottle. "Ian, you can drink in any cab – well, people of age can."

Ian shook his head. Doubtful, but it's true.

"Dude, you fucked up. This is going to cost us a hundred bucks."

Ian was amazed. "You can drink in any cab?"

"Why did you have to book us a fucking *Town Car*? This is crazy."

Annoyed, Ian threw the business card into the snow.

The Little White Trip

"I told you. I didn't even call for this thing. When I split from the bar, I ended up in that rental place, and the dude there handled this shit. He didn't want me on his phone."

"All right," the driver said through a sliver in his lowering window. "You guys coming or what?"

The back seat was the size of my parents' couch. Julie handed a scrap of paper up to the driver as we got in.

He studied the paper below an overhead light then twisted in his seat, asking, "What is this, some kind of prank? You guys are trying to tell me you're going to the Brinkley place right now?"

"Yeah, what's so funny about that?" Julie asked, tired from the walk.

"Who put you up to this? Was it the boys at the call station? They know I won't go anywhere near that place."

Ian had been obsessively staring out the back windshield. He stopped, whipped around in his seat and demanded, "Let's get this thing moving. Why are we still sitting here?"

Shoving his door open, the driver stepped around to the back of the car. He yanked the door on Dura's side open, saying, "All right, you guys, out of the cab. It's not even funny to joke about that place. What the hell's the matter with you kids? That bastard killed his wife, and they never –"

"Found him?" Dura said, finishing the cabby's sentence.

"So it's true?" I asked.

"Hell yeah, it's true," he said, shuffling impatiently

beside the car. "Everybody within a twenty-mile radius of that place moved out when members of the search posse started coming up missing or dead."

Mrs. Mailer had told us that the dad killed all of them, not just the wife. "So – he only killed the wife?" When stories change, they always indicate that at least one of them is a lie.

"He killed them all," he grumbled, shattering the hope for my dispelling theory. The stories aligned, or at least that part did. "The wife was the only person they found in one-piece. The rest of them, the kids, must have lasted a little longer because they were still at the cabin when the cops went in.

"He cut them up and then went crazy trying to make them disappear. He burned one. Cops found a pile of ash and teeth in the bathtub. In the kitchen, they found an arm stuffed and ground elbow-deep into the garbage disposal. The kid's pink fingernails had been peeled back with a can opener. He stayed there for weeks before anyone even knew the wife was gone."

Squatting outside our open door and seeming disgusted by his own words, the driver pulled his mind from the Brinkley cabin and went into our problem. "Now what are you guys really trying to do here? Do you need a ride or what?"

"Yes, we do," Julie said, stamping her foot on the hollow floor.

"Okay then, where are you going?" he asked in an angry calm that bordered on rage.

The Little White Trip

The dialogue was getting rotten.

"We just got picked up from the cabin this morning. The other driver didn't have a problem with it," Julie said.

The driver laughed in reply to her claim. I think he still believed that we were fucking with him.

Dura got out of the cab and tried to explain the situation. "We *are* staying at the Brinkley place. I mean we're obviously not going to anymore, but last night we did because —"

"WHAT'S YOUR POINT?" the man shouted so loudly that I winced.

Dura continued in a soft voice, "The point is this; we thought the whole thing was some kind of myth. Our friend is there and so is our car. And we really need to get back to pick them up."

"No way," he protested. "It's already dark and —"

Ian was getting so anxious that he was physically hopping in his seat. Throwing the door open on his side, he approached the man. "Listen, buddy, I'll tell you what…"

The two of them walked around the cab talking for a minute before Ian returned. The driver closed the door on Dura's side, and the car jerked forward, navigating the dark road to the Interstate.

"What did you say to him?" Dura asked.

"Well, I didn't really *say* much. I did give him a fifty dollar pre-tip for his troubles though."

The man captured his dispatch radio off the dash, calling in, "Don't ask me why, but I'm going by the

Brinkley place. If I don't confirm my drop in thirty minutes, call the cops."

The voice on the other side reluctantly agreed. Besides the purring engine, the car was silent.

Devoid of public street lamps and passing cars, Springston Road seemed beyond darkness. The car came to a halt at the opening of Brinkley Drive and began to pull a slow u-turn on the shoulder.

"Excuse me, sir, what are you doing? The cabin is still a ways down the dirt road," Julie voiced what all but one of us were thinking.

Clicking the cab light on, the man turned around in his seat, and as if he hadn't heard Julie, said, "That'll be twenty-five even."

She returned his disregard, saying, "We're not there yet. You need –"

"No, you *are* there. That was the deal I made with your buddy; he gives me an extra fifty bucks, and I take you guys to the property line – no farther."

All eyes were on Ian. "Hey, what did you want me to do? Fifty was all I had. It's better than being thrown out at the mountain."

"No way am I walking out there in the dark," Julie said, as if she had a choice.

"Well," Ian offered, "do you guys have any more cash?"

"I'm not going any closer. Not for a million bucks," the man disputed. "You guys got where you need to be. Now get out or I'm going to have to get you out." The driver was jumping out of his seat again; he was not messing around.

Ian flung his door open on the opposite side of the car, hollering, "Come on, guys, *run*."

The three of us scrambled out behind him, almost losing Dura to the man's snare-like hands.

"Hey! You kids owe me twenty-five bucks. Get back here or I'm calling the cops," he threatened, pounding the icy top of his car.

"*Fuck you*," Ian replied simply. He knew that the guy wasn't going to follow us.

Returning to his seat, the driver spun the car around. His lights beamed down the unpaved road. We dashed out of his sight, our shadowy figures bleeding black with the trees. His brights clicked on and flooded Brinkley Drive all the way down to the darkened bend. Then, returning them back to normal, the driver skidded out backward and peeled off down Springston Road.

Ian was drunk and having way too much fun. "Forget him. Fifty dollars for a twenty-five-dollar ride is more than enough."

Nobody else seemed to enjoy the situation, and when he was done congratulating himself, we were left with the cruel hum of the forest. Our four pairs of feet crunched a strange rhythm in the snow-layered ground. A full moon gave Brinkley Drive a lambent glow.

"Shhh," I called out.

The others were still.

"Did anybody else hear that?" I whispered.

Silence.

"Hear what?" Dura finally asked.

"I thought I heard another set of feet out there," I said, pointing into the trees. "It wasn't any of ours. You and Julie walked the same, and I watched Ian's, too."

"Are you sure it wasn't your feet?" Julie asked hopefully.

I started to answer but stopped, hearing the steps again. I pointed in their direction. Nobody said a word. We just stood there listening as they neared. Julie's breathing became so loud that I feared she might topple over right there in the road. It took everything I had to keep from running off into the darkness.

At that moment, just off the road, our ears where consumed by a powerful crack followed by a brittle shredding, like Velcro but amplified. Julie's scream put every muscle in my body on alert, and for no real reason, I ducked back under my jacket sleeve. Ian dropped his bottle in the snow. As Julie's breath ran short, the foreign steps raced in the opposite direction, *Clop-Clop, Clop-Clop*, galloping away and probably more shaken up than we were.

"Jesus, Matt," Ian scowled. "You put us through all that for a fucking deer."

My heart began to find its normal pace. "Deer? Shit, that was an elk or a moose. They're probably all after us because of that dead one we have over the fireplace," I joked, doing a shitty job at keeping my voice steady.

Nobody bought my casual sarcasm.

"This is crazy. We should've called Sam from the mountain. We could've picked our shit up in the morning," Julie figured, sounding as angry as she was distraught.

I could tell that if the time came, she would be the first one to crack. I admit that the whole situation was desperate, but what else could we do?

"Do you have the cabin number memorized?" I asked Julie. "Besides, we couldn't hang around the mountain. Those guys were after Ian."

Picking his bottle back up from the snow, Ian thanked me, "Thanks a lot for bringing *that* up, Matt."

"Oh yeah, now I remember. It's your fault, Ian." Julie shrieked, "Why did you have to steal that bottle when you have ten others at home?"

Cornered, Ian snapped back, "I'm the only reason we got this far, so shut up and take a drink."

He bit the cork out of his bottle and spit it into the powder ahead of us.

I reached over and tapped Ian on the shoulder.

"*What the fuck. What was that?*" Ian yelped, spinning around and raising the bottle for protection.

"Jesus, chill out. I just wanted to get a pull off that thing," I said, troubled by his reaction.

I took a couple of long gulps and handed the bottle back. I only made it a few steps down the line before I felt the drink taking lead on my vacant stomach and climbing my spine toward the control center. Ian had the right idea; my nerves instantly began to settle. The path of Brinkley

Drive curved deeper into the forest, and the moon died behind the tall trees.

"What the fuck is going on?" Julie asked whoever would listen. "Nothing makes any sense. One driver will come to the house and the other one *won't*. Wouldn't the guy from this morning have known about the cabin?"

Dura had some clue. "Well, it was daytime then. And, didn't that last driver say something about it being dark?"

Julie remembered otherwise. "No, he didn't even want to go before that. Why the fuck wouldn't this shit have been on the Internet? It obviously happened. Now that's two people who told us about it."

"Three," I said in a low voice, almost inaudible. I had to release that haunting piece of information.

"What?" Julie asked, confused. "No, that's not right. There was the Mailer couple and then –"

"No, it's three. I heard about it back at the restaurant, yesterday – at Donny's. The waiter told me."

"*What?*" they said in a shocked harmony.

"What the *fuck* are you talking about?" Julie yelled. "Matt, tell me you're kidding. Please tell me –"

"Why the fuck didn't you say anything?" Ian demanded to know.

I was ahead of the others and chose not to turn around and face them, but I knew that they were starting to crowd around me; their panicked voices were that close. Our steps had grown still, and since my confession, Dura hadn't said a thing. She must've hated me.

"We might have laughed off one person for telling us

about this shit, but if we knew that that time at the crazy house was the second warning, *we never would've come to this fucking place*," Ian screamed so loudly that I prepared myself to block a punch.

Fuck, it *was* my fault. I screwed up – badly. I didn't believe all the bullshit though. Even then, my reason still told me that we were going to be fine.

Under attack and trying to think, I said, "I didn't believe it. That's why I didn't say anything. I knew *you* would make a big fucking thing out of it. And I still don't believe it now." I wasn't entirely sure about that last part.

"Don't *believe* what?" Ian howled. "How many goddamn people have to tell you about it before you do? Would Sam's headless body do it for –"

"Ian, shut the fuck up and use your brain for a second." To my surprise, he did. "How the hell would that family have made the news for an 'arts and crafts fair' and not for their bloody murders? How does that make sense? And like Julie said, the other cab driver didn't know shit about it either. How could that be?"

Always thinking, Ian said, "This is a small town. They cover shit up – keep it quiet. Do you really think that they would want to make the national news for something like this? Fuck no. It would ruin this place."

I chose not to answer him. Julie was crying in my ear. Dura was still quiet.

My last monologue made the most sense. "Think about it, guys; small towns have all types of myths and shit. If our biggest worry is that three people out here have heard about it, then I think we're fine. Tons of people probably know about this story, in one version or another; that's how myths go.

"The first driver didn't know; the media didn't know, and our school or whoever set us up on this trip sure as *fuck* didn't know. And let's just pretend for a second that it is true, which it's not. But if it was, and this guy did kill his family here, besides being a creepy place to stay at, there's no way we'd still be in danger.

"Do you really think that this guy has been living in the snow for months watching his cabin? Fuck no – no way, he'd be long gone. Trust me; we're cool. All we need to do is grab Sam and our shit, and we're cool. We're gone." I finished, feeling a little better about our situation and about holding out the other day. Hearing the words aloud, although they were my own, convinced me that we were okay. Julie had stopped crying, and as I started down the path, I heard the others following behind.

"This is all fucked," Ian muttered, but that was the end of it.

As we tramped around the last curve, the Brinkley cabin came into view. The porch light had been left on. Julie made a break out of the darkness toward the cabin door. Dura did the same. Ian looked back at me and booked it as well. The place looked normal enough, a few lights where on upstairs but no bloody axes or shattered windows. At a glance, things seemed fine.

"Damn it the door's locked, and the car's gone," Julie cried, pulling on the copper door handle.

The Little White Trip

"Didn't you bring your key?" I asked Julie.

She looked at me as though I had just slapped her in the face.

Ian raised his bottle and, clanging it with the porch light fixture, toasted, "All right, let's hear it for Julie, today's MVP; she –"

"Shut up, *Ian*," she hissed. "You could've grabbed them from *our* nightstand, but did you?"

"Why don't you ring the bell?" I asked. "The car was in the garage when we left. Maybe he stayed home, and the car's still in there."

She rang the bell feverishly. *Ding. Ding. Ding. Ding.* I remember thinking that if he was in there, we were going to have another aggravated person on our hands. He never came out though.

"I'll go around and see if the door back there is open," I said, desperate to get away from the building drama. I could only take so much before joining in.

Sure enough, the back door was not only unlocked, but it was half open. The door screeched as I slid it the rest of the way. A very clichéd horror story detail, I thought, but I had to admit that I was pretty goddamn scared as I stepped into the dark and silent living room. There was a light on in one of the upstairs bedrooms, and I could make out the faint outline of the curved railing.

"Hello…Sam? Are you in here?"

That would be just like Sam to hide in the dark just to pop out and scare the shit out of me. That was exactly the kind of thing that he would sit around all day planning.

"Okay, Sam, I see you. The gig's up, flip on that light over there," I bluffed, and he was either holding out or really not there.

Taking a few steps around, I ended up standing at the back wall. Walking the perimeter, with a guiding palm against the wall, I found the black leather chair and then the kite string light pull. Fuck, my heart was pounding like hell, and for nothing really. I pulled the string and finally escaped the darkness and surveyed the room around me. The crew outside must have seen the light come on, and they beat the door mercilessly.

Ian and Julie were still feuding as they charged into the house. "Okay, Julie, I get it, but Sam's gone with our car, so what the fuck do you suggest?" Ian asked, lifelessly flopping over the back of the couch and resting on the cushions below.

He must have chugged a good portion of his bottle during the walk because his attitude was peculiarly detached. I never could tell with Ian; most times, he only showed what he wanted you to see.

"Shit. That's just great. Now we're *stuck* here," Julie said, looking to me for some kind of explanation. Was it my fault?

"Sam is obviously coming back; he's probably on his way now. Actually, he might even be here. Did anyone look in the garage?" I pointed my question at Julie.

"I'm not going in there by myself."

Dura started for the door, saying, "Come on, Julie, I'll go with you."

The two of them disappeared into the garage. I could hear the clanking mechanical door rolling up as I squeezed between Ian's wet shoes and the end of the couch.

"What are the chances?" Ian sighed, emptying the last amber drops of his stolen brew onto his outstretched tongue.

"I don't know. This sure the fuck isn't what I pictured our vacation to be like. I mean – if this shit happened, it would have been months ago. No way has that guy been in the forest this whole time. He'd be a Popsicle," I said, verbally lulling my uneasy stomach.

"He wouldn't have to, Matt. Nobody comes up here. You heard the cab driver; everybody in the area moved out. Who would know if he was in one of those other cabins – or even this one?"

He was right. The driver wouldn't even come near the cabin. I didn't think he could just move back in there...or that "he" even existed, but all it would take is for one of the nutty locals to try and make a myth come to life. That copycat shit happens all the time.

The door that opened from the garage swung open, and Dura appeared, out of breath and much more frantic than I'd ever seen her before. "You guys better get out here."

My brain, prompting action, prescribed a blast of adrenaline that cranked my eyes wide and lungs tight.

"Seriously, guys, I'm *not* fucking around."

TWENTY-TWO

Dura was in the kitchen, yanking cabinet doors open and tossing their contents onto the ground around her.

"What's going on," I asked. "What are you looking for?"

"We need to find a flashlight," she said, uncovering a long silver stick.

Julie shadowed Dura; she tried to help but did little more than get in the way, fretting and mumbling about what had happened outside.

"Dura – what's going on?"

She didn't answer, pushing by me and hurrying off into the garage. "Come on, they're out here," she said, stamping off through the garage and into the snow.

Ian wobbled out behind us, trailing through the white driveway.

"See that?" Julie said, pointing out a set of tire marks sunken deep into the snow.

The tracks headed down the driveway, but where the path turned, they continued straight and trailed recklessly into the open woods and darkness.

"Holy – *fuck*," Ian said, walking to the clearing of shattered landscape.

Dura walked up behind him.

Kneeling down, I studied the prints. They couldn't have been more than a couple of hours old.

"No way that's from our car," Ian said. "Maybe they're old, could be from when the cops were everywhere."

"Old?" I asked, "Why would there be tire marks in last night's snow if they were old? Look at these snapped branches and shit. This just happened."

The damage was fresh, dirt spit up from under the snow, bushes flattened, and a good-sized tree, maybe six feet tall, was snapped right above the snowline.

"What's that?" Dura noticed, shining the light on a piece of black fiberglass half buried in the snow.

I walked over and picked it up.

Julie asked what she hoped wasn't the truth, "Is that a piece of our car?"

I nodded, dropping the scrap to the ground.

"*What the fuck is going on?*" she cried.

I didn't say anything. I was still trying to figure that out for myself.

"Could Sam have gotten wasted and crashed the car? Maybe – but how would he have lost control so soon?" I wondered aloud but knew that it didn't make any sense.

Julie was losing touch, screaming and repeating herself, "*What the fuck is going on? What the —*"

I was forced to shout to be heard. "I don't know, Julie. None of us do." I felt bad about yelling, but her condition was making it impossible to think. "You and Ian go inside and call the cops. Dura and I will find Sam and the car."

"Find the car? That thing could be miles from here," Ian said in an unsteady voice. "I wouldn't go out there in the dark. I say you guys come inside with us and wait for help."

I was shocked. "What? Sam could be stuck out there, hurt, and you think we should just leave him and wait?"

He said nothing for a few seconds, but then came out with it, saying, "I don't know, man. I don't know what's going on, and I just think we'd be safer in numbers."

"Safer in numbers? Safer from what?" I asked, knowing damn well what he was talking about.

"You know — Brinkley. Sam was on his own and he got him --"

Heading him off sharply, I said, "Ian, you're fucking dreaming, man. *He* didn't get anybody, and there is no *he*. Just go inside and call the cops. We've got a car accident here."

With that said, I started off into the trees, following as much of the tracks as the raven forest would reveal. Dura ran up alongside of me and passed the flashlight over. Looking over my shoulder, I saw Ian and Julie reluctantly heading toward the cabin. I guess they would rather be two in the cabin than four in the forest.

The trees were growing dense, and I knew that the car couldn't have made it much farther.

"Shhh, listen," Dura said, clamping her hand on my shoulder. "Do you hear that?"

We stopped for a moment. I couldn't hear anything besides the hissing wind. The frozen air split and wailed, shredding endlessly through the sharp quills above.

"I don't hear it," I said, but then I almost instantly picked up on the noise that she was talking about.

The sound, disguised amongst the wind, was hard to distinguish, but it was there. It separated itself in a lower tone. I wasn't sure what its source was; it seemed distorted through the trees and the distance, but it was definitely coming from straight ahead.

Dura reached over, grabbing the flashlight, and said, "Come on, I'll show –"

Blocking her path, I said, "No. I hear it now. It's coming from up there."

I reached out to collect the light, but Dura pulled back, avoiding my hand.

"Maybe I should go first. It would be safer if I was up front," I said, continuing to hunt for the silver stick.

Dura pulled it away again and pointed the strong beam in my eyes, saying, "Safer? Safer from what, Matt? Remember, 'we've got a car accident here.'"

Swatting the light from my eyes, I admitted, "I don't know what's up, Dura, but something's fucked; that's for sure."

She lowered the light. The narrow beam reflected up from the snow and chased our blackened masks away. "Well – Matt, what the hell are we doing out here in the dark woods for, then?"

I was beginning to feel like she sounded – scared, confused, and dying for an answer. "Ahhh, FUCK," I roared into the distance. My delirious voice cracked and faltered hoarse then silent. I was letting the night get to me much too soon.

Dura stood voiceless. Her chest heaved, and her warm breath reacted pale and cloudy in the winter air. I could see that she was frightened, and her worried eyes made me wish that I hadn't snapped. I was making things worse. She gave in, handing me the light and walking ahead into the darkness, alone.

"Dura, wait," I called out, jogging up beside her. "I'm sorry."

The growling intensified as the tire tracks lengthened behind us. We had walked only a few more steps before we were right up on it. The car must have been going in reverse because from our direction, we were looking into a set of smashed headlights. Scratches and dents riddled the hood and side panels. It was obvious that the damage wasn't all from the wreck. Somebody had maliciously kicked the shit out of the new body.

The window's tint was dark, and even with the flashlight, it was hard to distinguish what was inside. The engine, stuck in some kind of high idle, rumbled an unhealthy plea. In spite of the live motor, the tires remained dead in the snow. The car's back half had basically been split in two, pinched bumper-first around a thick pine. Broken glass and scrap metal littered the snow around the damaged tree.

Entering a black glass halo, I leaned neck-deep into the almost entirely missing back window. A light popped on up front and the driver's side door cranked open.

I panicked and pulled back through the hanging glass, nearly cutting my throat in the process. My head bumped the window, raining squares of glass along my back and down my shirt. Disoriented, I fell backward into the snow. Dura was at the front of the car standing in the open doorway. Her mouth hung open, and her eyes locked steadily on the illuminated front cab. She turned to me. Her face was pale enough to match the ground with an expression twice as cold.

Rolling to my feet, I asked, "Is he in there?"

She wouldn't speak but slowly shook her head no. The door swung closed as her grip loosened. Staggering a few steps back, she hunched forward, gagging violently and coughing up a solid yellow fluid.

"What's in there?" I asked, standing between her and the mangled car. She didn't even look up at me.

As I pulled the door open, the images I was confronted with blurred into nothing. The grotesque state of the cab was enough to send my brain reeling, but one item in particular set it off. My eyes fixed on it for a second and then shutdown, refusing to compute.

I was stuck.

At first, the only thing that I could clearly register was the constant ping of the ignition bell. In a state of shock, I started to identify details from inside the car, one at a time. The front seats, dash, and windows were splattered and soaked in blood. The smell coming from inside the car was so pungent that my eyes began to water. Tears and punctures covered the driver's seat, exposing red-soaked foam from beneath the split black leather. The wipers, on full blast, screeched across the dry glass. Thick lines of blood staked their paths down the slanted windshield, clotting in pools around the dash.

Then, as though forcing myself back to it, or maybe being pulled, my eyes crept in horror to the passenger seat. I stood transfixed on an image that was hard for the reasonable mind to comprehend. Lying before me was an entire human arm. The pale limb stretched long across the bloody bucket seat, resting its dead hand half-open on the center console. The thin arm had been cut so high up that a patch of armpit hair still remained. The strands clung together, tangled in the sticky spillage. Loose tendons, slashed muscle, and bone pushed through where the filleted skin had rolled back. Blood welled in the seat, drowning most of the cold limb.

The hair and the tone and the freckles resembled those of its owner, but the fingers pointed him out more clearly. A tuft of brown hair laced the long digits, a product, no doubt, of a feeble and final last stand. The hair had probably been gripped and torn cringingly from the head of an evil mind. Besides holding the stringy brown spoils, the lifeless hand wore a bronze and silver class ring. A familiar bird and name were inscribed inside the gaudy gem border. Despite our Farrell jabs and lack of school spirit, Sam had invested in that ring. He was one of the few people I knew who had.

Fearing that I might physically collapse, I shut my eyes to the scene. But the image, persistent, was bigger than the darkness that I ran to. It followed me inside, glowing bright in my thoughts. I can still see it, and unfortunately, the only thing that would shake such a horrible image was a worse one.

Dura hacked, spitting up the last of it. With an open hand, she swabbed her glossy mouth and chin.

My stomach felt sick, threatening to spill. My head was spinning so fast that Dura's voice blurred and echoed. Her despondent sounds barely translated to earthly words. "He's gone."

TWENTY-THREE

Getting back to the cabin was like running through a dream, legs dragging behind, every sound off the path echoing like gunfire, and the weight of the world on my lungs and heart. The shock was the only thing that saved me.

Before we walked in through the garage door, I told Dura that we needed to stay calm around Ian and Julie and just wait until the cops show up before we say anything. She said nothing in response.

Inside, we were greeted with the shrill sounds of Ian and Julie consumed in yet another argument.

Ian had just come in from the deck and was trying to explain something to Julie. "They're cut, actually, more like ripped out. Shit's hanging out all over the place."

Julie was having a hard time understanding him, or maybe she just didn't want to hear what he was saying. "What do you mean *ripped*? Do you even know what you're looking for?"

The Little White Trip

The two of them noticed Dura and me standing near the kitchen.

Pulling away from their crisis, Julie asked, "What happened?"

Dura and I shared the same troubled look. We hadn't even talked to each other about what we had seen, and I, for one, wasn't sure how or even what we should tell them. I figured that they had already called the cops, and thought that maybe I should just tell them that we hadn't found anything out there. They didn't need to know; what help would that be?

Julie was out of it; I could almost see the path of her torment right through her skin. She looked as though powerful tremor was running upward through her chest, knotting in her throat for a moment before finally escaping clear and wet through her swollen blue eyes. It was as if, without a word, my expression had said it all: *Sam's dead.*

She knew the answer but insisted on asking the question all the same. "Where is he, Matt? Tell me what's out there." Shaking her head incredulously, she went on, "What did you guys find out there? Don't look at me like that Matt…this is bullshit. What happened?"

Her swinging disposition was hard to follow. Was she cracking up?

I closed my eyes, once again trying to separate myself from that night. I waited for it all to go away. The images from inside the car flashed with my thoughts. They reappeared in vivid detail, one by one, the same way I had registered them earlier. The blood, the tears, the hair, the arm, they materialized visually behind my pinched lids. Julie's panic only fueled their clarity. I had to let it all out.

I sat myself down at the kitchen table, and without looking at any of them, I began to recount bits of our find, summoning already repressed and broken recollections. "Okay...fuck, yeah, we found the car out there in the forest. It's still running and Sam's gone." I swallowed hard. "The car's fucked, wrapped around a tree, and somebody beat the living shit out of it. The seats are shredded, punctured, and covered in blood —"

I had already made up my mind that I wasn't going to mention what Brinkley had left behind, but even if I had wanted to continue, Julie had heard enough, shrieking and sobbing, "Stop, Matt, shut up! Oh, God! Oh, God! We're fucked, we're —"

"Julie. Julie." I got up and took her by the shoulders. "Julie, calm down. We don't even know what's happened yet. We just need to wait for help and —"

She shoved me away and clenched two handfuls of her hair, screaming, "We're staying in the house of an escaped murderer. Sam's missing. The car's full of blood, and you don't know what happened? I think it's pretty fucking clear." Her voice was mad, but her logic was crystal.

With the same blunt reason, I said, "All right, but there's nothing we can do now except wait for the cops and —"

"COPS? The fucking cops aren't coming here!" she

screamed, pounding both fists on my chest. "Didn't you hear what Ian said? The phone lines are cut."

"What? What the fuck do you mean the lines are *cut?*"

Okay, so we are fucked, I admitted, to myself only.

Ian, winding his arms tightly across his chest, paced around the room talking. "When we got back here and tried to call…and then there was no tone… but then outside the wires were all torn up and sliced." He continued disjointedly like that for another partial sentence or two before I stopped listening.

Praying for the obvious and forgetting what I already knew, I asked, "What about your cell phone?"

"Nope, reception's fucked out here; no signal," she countered, shaking her phone like a can of spray paint.

"You tried the other ones?"

"Yeah, Matt, I'm not as stupid as you think I am."

She continued talking about why we should have, or could have done one thing or another, but I was someplace else. My head was about to explode – car's totaled, friend's gone, no phones, the neighbors had moved out in all directions, and it had become pretty fucking clear that somebody didn't want us there. Julie was growing increasingly hysterical, and Dura was still in some kind of walking shock.

I couldn't envision what had happened while we were gone. The house looked fine, no signs of violence.

"All right, everybody get it together. We don't have many options here, and it's going to take all of us if we're gonna make it out of this cabin tonight," I plagiarized almost exactly from some shit action flick. Regardless of their origin, my words had no effect. We were apparently beyond thinking.

On the way to the hill, the cab driver had said that they were expecting a storm to blow in later, and from the looks of it through the kitchen window, things were really starting to go nuts. The wind blew swirls of white about, and a crack of lightning backlit that horrible night.

"Fuck, it's starting to go crazy out there," Ian said as he spotted what was happening through the frosty kitchen window.

Unwilling to help the others wave a blood-spattered white flag, I instigated a plan. "Ian's right; we're not going to be able to walk anywhere. The car's wrecked, and –"

Dura stepped in with her first words since back at the car. "Landlines are cut, cell phones won't work, no neighbors, and we're basically waiting to end up like Sam."

The room was quiet. Dura's eyes searched around, waiting for somebody to tell her that she was wrong. That was usually my cue, but what could I say? She was right. We really had no options.

She paced the room, and finally coming to rest at the window's edge, said, "Well…shit, Matt, I should have never let him stay home alone. I should've stayed back or made him come with –"

"Listen, Dura, it's not your fault," I started to say. "You –"

With tears in her eyes and fire in her voice, she disagreed, "No, it is my fault. He knew, Matt. He knew about us and about last night. That's why he wanted to be alone. He didn't have to say anything; I could just tell...I should've stayed."

Julie and Ian looked confused, among other things.

Shaking her head, Julie turned to me, asking, "What's going on? What are you guys talking about?"

I had been avoiding Julie's eyes since Dura's performance. Explaining my secret love life hardly seemed appropriate at the time. The expression on Julie's face was painful to look at, chin quivering, eyes swelling, and mouthing some inaudible plea. Her eyes seemed to be fixed on Dura.

As I turned toward the window, Julie whimpered, "There's a man in the –"

The kitchen window exploded into a galaxy of ice-like chips. Glass and thin strips of window framing filled the air around Dura's back and shoulders. In a cowardly instinct, I pulled back, shielding myself from the glass and the noise.

The clamorous shattering and hail brought with it a long pair of red and black flannelled arms. They erupted from the darkness, haloing Dura's slumped body in the sill. The left arm wrapped tightly around her neck. Screaming and thrashing about, she pulled forward into the kitchen light a savage-looking man. He clung heavily to her stiffened back and muscled her backward in his favor.

The freak of a man carried the strapping shoulders of an ape and a face neglected by everything but cruel time.

His oval head was patchy and matted on top. A wiry cul-de-sac of peppered brown and silver hair whipped a mist of slush and dirty storm water around with their struggle.

He leaned in close, breathing in Dura's ear. His abrasive beard scrubbed and reddened her straining neck. His eyes rolled in their darkened sockets, and his heavily bearded jowls turned up a lascivious snare-lipped grin, the kind usually reserved for the final climactic seconds of some raunchy porn. He was loving it.

Dura's wails were almost worse than the scene itself.

With desperate eyes, I searched the table for a weapon, but there was nothing. Uncertain and close to an adrenaline overdose, I lunged forward toward the window. My feet slipped on the broken glass. I fell back, smacking my head on a wooden chair. The crack of my skull against the oak echoed in my mind. An electric flash ran through my vision as I fought to pull myself upright. Julie and Ian, as if etched of marble, stood paralyzed at the other side of the room.

Effortlessly holding Dura back, the man broke into an insane bellowing laughter. His voice eclipsed Dura's and echoed against the sterile walls of the kitchen. Dura was strong, but he was stronger.

His right arm rose high above, fist clenching an enormous blade. The steel gleamed cloudy silver in my blurry eyes. In a powerful swoop, he hunched forward, burying the knife's entire length into Dura's stomach. Blood expelled from around the blade, showering the glass-covered floor and dotting my catatonic legs.

The Little White Trip

Seeing the knife and the blood, Dura seemed to give up. Her back relaxed, and her jaw fell slack. Her once kicking and flaying legs slid lifelessly through the window. But before she was gone, for a brief moment frozen in time, our eyes connected. Everything became clear in our last seconds together. I couldn't hear it, but when I saw her lips move, I knew exactly what she had said. I had memorized the movement of that word. It was my name, and she chose it to be the last thing that she would ever say. There is absolutely nothing that I could write here to explain what that felt like, and I hope to God that none of you ever find out firsthand.

TWENTY-FOUR

With my body as unsteady as my first day, I crawled forward and stood up. Mobility was back, to a degree. Sliding along the glass and blood, I pulled myself through the shattered window frame. My hands, receiving little direction from my brain, clutched the broken glass edges. I felt nothing. I tumbled through the sill, and in the distance I thought I heard Dura's cries, shallow, but I could swear that they were out there. I followed his trail of footsteps illuminated by the house lights. Then there was darkness, complete darkness. My eyes flooded with the black absence all around me.

I stopped and screamed into the frozen night. "Dura! Oh God...Dura!"

I was too late.

I raced ahead into the caliginous forest, dodging trees, stumbling over rocks, and then again, "DURA!" But she was gone.

A small break in the treetops welcomed a shaft of

moonlight. I stood in a hazy grey consumed with an emotion yet to be named, an inbred mix of the worst kind. Anger fucked depression, spawning a monster so powerful, so vile, that its first impulse was to crush the throats of its guilty creators. From deep within I could hear the evil self-abortion calling my name. It laughed, taunting me, and dangling its cold limp parents, one in each wicked fist.

I tried not to listen. My weary mind struggled to protect itself; concentrating on the fact that Dura might still be alive, that I could save her, but first, I had to find her. The wind moaned the rueful cries of truth in my ears. *She's gone; you'll never find her.* Lightning flickered low in the trees. Gasping for air, I desperately waited to hear her voice, a noise, anything I could follow. I waited in that spot in silence until my only light, my fleeting moonlit beam, dimmed shadowy then black, eclipsed and killed by a heavy winter cloud.

I broke out of the trees, heading toward the cabin. As I stepped into the lights of the back deck and yard, I saw footsteps trailing through the snow from the cabin to the forest, but they weren't the tracks that I had followed of Brinkley's. I wondered if Ian and Julie had come through there. Were they out in the trees? Did he have them, too?

"IAN…"

Nothing.

"JULIE… IAN…"

My back was to the cabin, and the sound of footsteps startled me as they broke the silence of my unanswered calls. I spun around and saw them both, Ian and Julie. They crossed the remainder of the yard between us cautiously. Julie's cheeks were glazed with tears, and her hands trembled uncontrollably. Ian had the wide-eyed look of a tweaker feeling that first big flash; I felt the same way. My heart was pounding so violently that I was afraid it might catch fire.

"What the...I mean, what the fuck is *going on?*" Ian screamed, throwing his head back to face the heavens. He was working Julie up even more, sobbing and burying her face in his windbreaker.

Ours was a hopeless scene.

"Who the fuck *was* that guy?" Ian asked a seemingly stupid question.

"What do you mean?" Julie asked, still clinging to his arm. "That's the guy they told us about. That's Brinkley."

"Bullshit – that's not the guy from the photo."

I didn't totally remember the picture, but I did remember thinking that the dad looked dopey and harmless. Then again, I had no clue how old that picture could've been.

"That was before he went crazy and killed his entire family," I said. "Who knows what happened between then and now."

"Still, the guy from the photo wasn't *that* big."

I didn't feel like arguing with Ian but did anyway. "When was that photo taken? Maybe it was a while ago. Besides, the fucking guy could've been living in the woods. He's a goddamn animal by now."

The Little White Trip

"Come on, Matt. He didn't get *taller*." Ian wouldn't give up and continued to argue with my turned back.

My eyes were again on the snow and the foreign tracks that I had noticed earlier. The sunken footpaths started from the trees and headed in toward the cabin at an angle. My brain cranked, sputtered, and then it hit me. Could it be?

Walking over to the trail, even though I knew it couldn't be true, I asked, "Did you guys come through this way?"

After contemplating the question much longer than necessary, Ian answered, "No, we came from over there." He pointed to the deck.

The prints became clear to me then, and I could see yet another set. The two other ones headed in diagonally from the trees. I followed them with my eyes toward the cabin, and about midway, the three trails became one.

"This isn't some lone madman. There's more. At least two more people here," I said.

Julie and Ian were close behind me. "What? More than one – how do you know?" Julie asked, sounding more helpless than before.

"Look at all these prints."

"How do you know he didn't just walk up to the house earlier? Maybe those were his old ones," Ian said.

"No. Look, these other two paths only go halfway before they connect with the straight one," I said, pointing up the line toward the cabin. The tracks formed what looked like the enormous lines of a peace sign. The snow was all mixed-up where the three connected.

"It looks like the two other people came out of the forest and met up with him over here." I speculated, "He probably needed them to help drag Dura away."

I figured that they understood what I was talking about. How could they not? What other explanation was there.

"Come on, guys, let's get back to the cabin and lock the doors," I said, walking to the deck.

They didn't budge. I stopped a couple of feet away and saw them, motionless, waiting near the tracks.

"*Come on.* What the hell are you guys waiting for?"

Julie looked blankly at me and then at Ian, who seemed to still be mulling my story over.

His mind was in motion, which wasn't always a good thing. "*Go inside?*" Ian doubted. "That didn't help Sam. *Lock the doors?* Dura was pulled through the goddamn window. Yeah, let's get in there and 'lock the doors.' Great fucking plan, Matt."

Throwing my hands up, I agreed, "Okay, fine, you guys stay out there in the open. Sure, why not right there, ten feet from where Dura was dragged off."

Walking alone to the deck I heard them sluggishly following behind.

Back at the cabin, Ian and I tipped the kitchen table up lengthwise to block the missing window. The table was too long to sit flat against the wall, and the cold blew in from around the table. The storm had calmed to a spell of dying wind. Although rare in the frigid skies, lightning continued to strobe dangerously low around the cabin. Dura's blood was starting to clot and dry around the edges.

"Here, Matt," Julie said, offering me a wet dishtowel.

My hands and forearms were covered in blood, mostly dried. I didn't seem to be bleeding anymore. Before wrapping my palms, I lightly rubbed them under the faucet's warm stream. They washed totally clean, no blood, no cuts, nothing.

"My hands are fine," I said, examining them more closely.

"How can that be? You went right through that broken window." Puzzled, she took one of my hands in hers. "What about all the blood?"

"I don't know. It must have been Dura's." The name triggered memories that I was already trying to forget. I refused to acknowledge what I had seen; it just couldn't be.

I felt totally helpless. I wished that we had the car, a phone, something – anything.

"We need to arm ourselves," I said, scanning the kitchen and looking over the possibilities. The need for protection was one thing that we could all agree on.

"Knives," I said, before even seeing them. "Julie, Ian, grab one of –"

My eyes saw what my brain chose to deny. The wooden block holder, that just the night before had held an assortment of blades, was completely empty.

"Where the fuck did those knives go?" I asked, as if

either of them would know.

Following my question, their eyes found the chopping block, and more importantly, the vacant knife holder.

Ian was the first to act. Turning for the silver drawers, he began yanking them open, left and right. "What the fuck? No way!"

He closed the final drawer and then slowly rolled it open, exposing the same problem. "FUCK," he screamed, slamming the drawer.

The sound of silver clanged and wood crushed as he continued to pull and slam the fancy drawer. The entire unit fell apart and ripped free of its tracks. The wooden box swung in his dying grasp. "Fucking *spoons*." He laughed – expressing anything but humor.

The object of his words spilled from the broken drawer onto the hardwood floor, glittering and chiming our dying song.

"They took the forks and knives?" I couldn't believe the reality of my own words.

We were the prize of some calculated game. The so-called madman was in fact totally prepared. He preferred his prey declawed and easy to chase. And regardless of what Ian and Julie thought, I knew that he wasn't alone. The prints wouldn't lie.

Ian kicked the worthless silver across the room. Spoons skipped and traveled across the floor between us. "Let's go upstairs. At least we'll know they can't jump in through those windows," he said, tossing the drawer and extending a hand to Julie.

I secured the doors before following them upstairs. As I reached the top of the staircase, I heard urgent voices coming from inside the master bedroom.

"Well, we gotta do something," Ian said.

"Yeah, you're right, but not that —" Julie stopped talking as I entered the room.

The two of them sat on opposite sides of the bed. Except for the blowing silk curtains, the room was totally still. The French doors which opened to the balcony were open.

"We've got to keep these doors locked," I said, closing one and then the other. I leaned back against the doors. "What were you guys talking about?"

Julie's gaze rose to mine as she informed me of Ian's horrible plan. "Ian wants to go get the car and —"

"The car's ruined. It's done."

Ian pushed up from the bed. "Why, Matt? Just because it's full of blood? Fuck that, man, this is our lives."

I could tell that he and Julie had already been arguing about it.

Julie stood up facing him. "Ian, we can't just walk off into the forest now. We'll be dead in a second. Plus, you heard Matt; the car's totaled."

"Matt — didn't you say that the car was actually running?" He didn't wait for an answer. "If the car's running, that means the engine works, so let's —"

With our noses almost touching, I said, "Ian, first of all, I saw the wreck, you didn't. The back tires are fucking sideways. He drove back first into a tree."

I was not ready to let Ian make such a stupid decision. He pushed past me. It crossed my mind to tell him about the arm, but I didn't see the point. He was going out there, and it didn't matter what I said.

"All I know is that we need to do something. I'm not all right with just standing around and waiting to be next."

He slammed the bedroom door at his back.

Julie ran to the door and pulled it open, begging, "Ian, don't go out there. Don't leave me here."

From the top of the stairs, I saw Ian already at the front door. "Don't worry, Julie. I'm not gonna leave you. I'll get the car, and I'll come back for you," he promised valiantly.

The door crashed behind him.

Julie cried out, "Ian, don't...IAN!" She must have known that once he was gone, he wasn't coming back. "Why is this happening to us? What the fuck did we do —"

I was on my first line of pacing through the room when I heard a scream outside. It sounded like Ian's voice, but muffled.

TWENTY-FIVE

I was practically in the center of the bedroom when Ian's cry stopped my pacing. In times like those it's hard to think. I know; I was there. Two quick nouns were the only things that entered my mind, *stairs or balcony*; that's it. And even with the simple true or false type of problem, I was confused. What the hell was I going to do? *God*, I wished those knives were still around. For whatever reason, I chose the stairs. I had to get out there. Then I reconsidered. I spun around toward the balcony. If I was going to be any kind of help, I needed to at least know what was going on.

I unbolted the doors and dashed out onto the long balcony. My thin rubber soles slid on the icy flagstone deck. I was going too fast. My toes slipped under the guardrail, stopping only when my shins cracked connection with the solid log post. Pain, like many of my feelings at that point, was forgotten.

Twin puffs of displaced snow, stirred by my gliding

feet, sailed from the high deck. In the motion lights they looked like two falling clouds, sparkling and glistening champagne and pearl. At first, they were the only things that I could see. No other movement was available. Leaning halfway over the pine rail, I searched the barren white yard. The falling clouds, too heavy to live, thinned and disappeared.

I called out, "Ian!"

Julie ran out beside me; she spotted him right away. "Oh my God, Matt, look," she screamed, pointing to my left.

She tagged them near the edge of the driveway. His movement had triggered a security light at the far end of the yard and brought into view a devastating scene. The beastly man was practically riding Ian. He held him down with one arm while the other was occupied by a great silver blade. Ian never had a chance; no living creature would have.

Brinkley worked his knife so savagely that I imagined Ian's spine was the only thing holding him together. He plunged the blade into his wearied body with a sexual pace, over and over and over and over; he was building toward something. God knows it had gone far beyond the killing itself.

For a second, I thought about jumping from the balcony, but ended up tearing through the bedroom and heading for the stairs instead. I bound down the set in three huge strides, covered the living room, and burst through the tall front doors.

The Little White Trip

I found myself stomping through the snow before I even knew what I was going to do. I was ninety-nine percent sure that I had no chance of saving Ian, so I guess my motive was clear. I was going to stop Brinkley with everything I had, and given my present mindset, I was willing to do whatever it took.

Racing through the shadows, I became aware that he hadn't even noticed that I was there. Rising to his feet, he passed the mighty blade through his flannel cloaked hand; the sticky steel returned chrome and clean. Nodding to himself, he carefully inserted the blade back into a belted side sheath.

Ian's head was cranked to the side, and I was spared the grim sight of how haunted his face must have frozen. Blood marred the virgin snow surrounding his curled body. My hands shivered and breathing became difficult. I prepared to meet the devil himself the only way I knew how. I said a prayer, or more of a three-word request, *God, help me.*

Running up from behind him, I bawled, "HEY!"

His head turned with the sound of my voice. My fist, clenched diamond tight, cocked back in my final stride. I felt a brittle pop above my wrist as I connected squarely with his wooly temple. The sound of my fist against his skull went straight to my stomach, and he went straight to the ground. I took a few steps back after the hit, watching his limp body fall. He met the ground with a grunt. His splayed limbs crushed a twisted silhouette in the snow.

As I realized what was happening, I became drunk

with the moment. "All right, motherfuckers, come on out," I taunted. "Come on, let's see you." Right then, the world was mine. "What are you waiting for? Come and help your friend."

I spun around, watching my back in all directions, and waited.

Heading back to the cabin, I lifted a thick piece of firewood from the top of a dense pile. I had seen enough scary movies in my day to know that you never gamble with whether or not the villain is done. I was going to do it right the first time.

Raising the heavy log high over my head, I walked out of the darkness ready to crush that bastard's head. I thought about using his knife on him, but I didn't want to get that close. If he had gotten ahold of me, that would've been it. I wasn't even near his size. I was about ten feet from him when I saw his body stir. His legs twitched, and his head tossed, burning cold in the snow.

I knew that he wouldn't be out for long.

My heart jumped, strides lengthened, and just before I reached my target, a strong hand seized my right arm from behind. The log was shaken to the ground, and my arms were yanked and pinned painfully tight behind my back. A full gut pressed high on my back: yet another huge guy. He smelled like coffee and bad hygiene. His heavy breathing, warm and fetid, stuck damp on my neck. He was that close. I didn't make a sound as I whipped and pulled, trying to free myself.

Brinkley came to and got on his feet, stumbling

around in a tight circle. He stopped, facing in my direction. He seemed confused, dizzily shaking his head and bobbing at the knees. He raised a hand, touching his tender ear and temple before realizing what was happening. Turning back to Ian's body, he effortlessly scooped it up under one arm and staggered a crooked path into the forest.

I had stopped struggling under the killer's stare. My captor had done the same. He didn't let me go or anything that helpful; actually, my momentary surrender had given him time to reset his strong grip. That was it though, just a hold.

With Brinkley's absence, the fight was back on. I threw a kick backward connecting unevenly with a sturdy leg. One of my arms was released, but at the same time, so was one of his. His free arm was quickly put back to use, wrapping thick and hairy around my neck. Another followed, locking the hold tight. I swung wildly behind my head, clenching a greasy handful of the man's hair, a wasted effort.

Pressure built dangerously behind my eyes; I closed them, so they wouldn't pop out. Blood rushed with nowhere to go. Paths pinched, head drifted, and my trembling lids opened to a white blur. I was done. My once fierce grasp released. My arms fell dead to the sides, and my body froze.

The cold and numbness of that night turned as I slipped farther into the bliss of a thermal euphoria. My body felt so much different, smaller, and everything else seemed bigger: my mom, my cereal bowl, the table. I was at my parents' house, their first place, on Kalil, and judging by the breakfast I saw spread out across the table, I would guess that I was about six years old. The refrigerator was decorated with A-plus math tests – not mine, of course – and art pieces of the public school genre – glued plastic bobble eyes, hard macaroni, and yarn.

My mom smiled at me from across the table. "Eat your orange slices, Matthew."

I did.

"Mom?" I stuffed another orange slice into my mouth. *See, Mom, I'm a good boy.*

"Yes, sweetie." *She knew I was.*

I giggled and wondered how to make my request in such a way that she couldn't say no. "Can Dura come with us to the water park?" I asked before I was even aware that Dura was at the table.

"Dura?" My mom contemplated, looking down and to my left. "Well, do you think that your parents would mind if you came along?"

I didn't even know her back then. We hadn't met until high school, but in that place, we were best friends.

"No, Mrs. Thomas, it'd be fine. They already said that I could," Dura said, revealing that we had been planning this situation for some time.

I chuckled, anxious for an okay.

Dura kicked my ankle under the table and buried her gaze back into her bowl of Cheerios, embarrassed. I

The Little White Trip

couldn't believe what I was seeing. Sitting next to me, with her proud brown ponytail arching about level with the chair's grownup backrest, was a little six-year-old version of Dura.

"Okay, honey," she said. "After you're done with your cereal, run next door to your house and make sure that it's still all right with your parents. Let them know that we're going to be gone till after dinner."

Little Dura smiled with glee and incomplete teeth. She spun around in her chair with her knees toward me, winked, and hopped down from her tall seat, skipping for the door. She pulled the heavy back door open, and the summer light poured in all around her. Her little figure paused in the doorway for second, then disappeared — actually, ran away, off to confirm the most important detail of the day.

The door never closed after she was gone, and the warm morning light flooded the kitchen like a great golden deluge. It consumed everything that ever was, hiding my mother's smile, the grade-school art, and our breakfast plates. The light sparked and flickered, yellow then blindingly white. I shut my eyes to the scene. Inside the darkness of my mind, the visions became hypnotic and psychoactive. With the melodic patterns of an aurora borealis, marbled swirls of green and silver and aquamarine consumed my thoughts, and I was back.

I awoke face-down in the snow. Julie hovered above; she thought that I was gone, too. "Matt, oh God, Matt, *please.* Don't leave me alone."

Rolling me onto my back, Julie swept my icy hair away from my eyes. Her warm hands caressed my face and reminded me that I was still alive, but why?

My eyes fluttered open, and I started to murmur, "Who were...?"

"He's gone, Matt. Ian's gone, too."

Sitting up, I saw the blood-drenched snow where Ian's body used to be. Everything started coming back to me, even breakfast with Dura.

"Who grabbed me?"

Her eyes flashed all around us.

"What do you mean? I saw you hit him and then walk off. I ran down from the balcony and found you here, and he was gone."

I felt like I was going batty. Did that really happen? I wondered.

"Didn't you see me getting choked over here?"

Looking toward the balcony, she reasoned, "No, I couldn't see this far over. I thought you were coming inside to get me."

She was right; the low overhanging roof blocked everything.

"Come on, let's go inside," she said, helping me up and sounding unreasonably collected. She was on autopilot.

Sure that I was following her, she walked off to the cabin. I hung back for a second, once again looking to the tracks for an answer. I saw the line where I had run up to the blood and then another heading to the wood pile. Confirming my recollection, there was also a set of tracks heading out from the shadows. They stopped where I was choked and trailed off again, vanishing into the darkness.

"Matt, come on."

Inside, Julie paced around the living room, talking to herself. She seemed to be losing more of her resolve with each passing second. "Okay, okay, okay, what can we do? What *have* we done, and what *can* we do?" she asked the walls, seemingly unaware of my presence.

"Did you lock the doors to the balcony?"

She was engrossed in her self-planning and didn't reply.

"Did you hear me?"

Receiving no answer, I started to feel totally alone.

I climbed upstairs and, as I had expected, the doors were fully open. As I forced the deadbolt closed, a regrettable sound filled my ears, the sharp crash of compromised glass. I darted out of the room and froze at the top of the stairs.

I couldn't see Julie anywhere.

TWENTY-SIX

She was just in the living room. "Julie!"
I tripped on a step, bouncing and sliding down the carpeted flight. Gripping the railing's end, I pull myself up from the ground. I scanned the windows to see which one could have broken, but they were all fine.

"Julie!" I called again, franticly heading into the kitchen.

I found her crouched over a pile of glass, sweeping the pieces together with her bare hands. "Julie, what happened? What are you doing?"

She looked up to me with a face that seemed to have never seen mine before.

"I need a drink. I need a drink – Ian," she said, with shivers running through her hands and voice.

"Julie, it's me. It's Matt." I could tell that she understood. "You need a drink, right now?"

I coaxed her up and hoisted her onto the countertop like a little kid. "Okay, my dear, what'll it be?" I asked, with an aching smile.

Julie's ocean eyes welled up salty and red. Her bloodshot blues looked so sad that I could hardly take it. "He's gone, Matt; they're all gone. What did we ever do to deserve this?"

I held her close. Our shaky arms clung to the last thing that we had — each other. She nuzzled deep between my neck and shoulder. Her warm tears bled through my shirt onto my skin. As I stood there between Julie's knees, with her quiet sniffles and rising pain, the weight of what had really happened took form. Like the blind depths of the ocean, that night, that pressure, was too great for a person to bear. I couldn't breathe.

Her innocent tears infected me like some inescapable virus. They traveled with my blood. Three of my friends were dead. Dura was finally mine, and I had lost her. It happened right in front of me, and I was too slow to stop it, too scared. I had wronged Sam, lied to him. That was my good-bye. The reality of all of that was bigger than anything that I had ever known. My heart hurt so bad that I thought I might die right there in Julie's arms. I began to weep and could do nothing to stop it. My sadness soon turned to anger, as it often did. Years had passed since the last time I had actually reached tears. I wouldn't allow it.

"What the *fuck*," I shook out, with hell on my breath.

I pulled away from Julie, walking toward the slanted table. The same table Ian and I had propped against the window, the same window Dura was pulled through. I was so fucking mad at myself.

"GODDAMN IT," I howled, feeling the veins bulge from my neck and snot bubble and run from my nose.

I cursed the world, spitting and throwing my limbs around. Grabbing up a chair, I lifted it over my head and smashed it onto the crooked tabletop. The legs cracked and broke loose. The thick seat held up in battle with the table, but in the end, it too came apart. I swung again and again until I was left holding only the chair's splintered backrest and a piece of the shattered seat.

Julie covered her face, and cried out, "Matt, stop it. You're scaring me."

My white-knuckled grip relaxed, and I dropped the battered pieces to the bloody wooden floor.

"*I'm* scaring you? *I* am? It's not the bearded fucking psycho who's stabbing knives into people?"

Peeping out from under her hands, she begged, "Please, Matt, you're all I've got."

Her words tranquilized me; they neutralized me and brought me back. "Fuck – I'm sorry, Julie." With pressed palms, I wiped my soggy eyes. "This is just all so fucking crazy. I don't know what to do."

I thought for a minute. Ever since we had come back to the cabin, things had been so nuts, and I hadn't had a chance to come up with any kind of plan.

"All right." I started pulling myself together. "This guy seems to know exactly what we're doing in here – when people are going outside, which door, if you're by a window – and he's not alone. He knows everything. Maybe he has cameras in here…no, where could he be watching them from? Why do they want me alive, choked, and then left alone, why?" I was reflecting aloud, and Julie was listening – I think.

She still didn't want to believe that there were others. "Are you sure there was somebody else out there?"

"Yes, I'm sure. I didn't choke myself. I saw his footprints, too."

I rested in one of the remaining chairs. I knew that somewhere, there was an out. The waiter at Donny's had laughed something about a cult, and I began to wonder what else he knew about that cabin or even about the town itself.

"One thing's for sure though; this place isn't where we should be. It's not like he can smell us," I said, coming on to something. "What if we turn off all the outside lights and make a run for the woods? We could stay quiet in the trees until morning. He would never find us."

I looked to Julie for a verdict.

"No way – he'll be waiting for us. He lives out there in the woods. Plus, if the storm comes back, we'll freeze to death."

She had a point, but I didn't want to stay in the cabin any longer. That was making it too easy. Julie slid down off the countertop and walked around the kitchen. Her wet shoes squeaked on the floor.

Emptying half a bottle of Ten High whiskey into a dirty glass, I hatched a better plan. Leaning back, with my face over my left shoulder, I smacked the empty bottle on the granite counter top. *Clink*. The stubborn glass resisted.

"Matt, what are you doing?"

I swung again, that time connecting with the solid edge. The bottle shattered, and the scent of whisky lingered in the air around me. Bits of broken glass hung from the sticky label, but the end result was perfect, a jagged glass chalice.

Disconnecting the mosaic glass flap, I explained, "This is what we'll do, then. The paved road is less than a mile from here. It's not busy, but if we get lucky, somebody will be on it. We'll sprint from the house along the path, and I'll hide this bottle in my sleeve. If he catches up with us, I'll punch this edge so far into his neck that his fucking eyes will pop out of his head."

Julie's eyes followed my barroom weapon, and as my plan darkened, she skittishly shook her head and abandoned the blood and cold in the kitchen for the warm living room.

I followed.

TWENTY-SEVEN

Crossing the long living room, with no real destination in mind, Julie listened as I further rationalized my plan. "Julie – that would work. As long as he's not right outside the door, and we get a couple seconds' head start... He won't catch us. I promise."

"I don't know, Matt. I can't think now; I just can't think anymore. There's nothing else we can do. Maybe he's done with us. I mean, he left you alone out there," she said, motioning toward the front window.

"No, he didn't. Somebody else stopped me from dropping a log on his head. They strangled me. For all we know, they thought I *was* dead."

Throwing her hands up, Julie said, "Okay, Matt. I know – I'm not making sense, but there's more of them. How many? And what if they *do* catch up with us? You're going to jab them with a *bottle*?"

A stiff chill drifted in from the kitchen and lingered eerily at my feet. The half bottle hung loosely in my right hand. I had almost forgotten about my serrated extension. Turning the broken side up, I examined the major points, six of them. The glass was thick, and even if it crumbled in action, I knew that it would do the appropriate damage. I could see it. I almost enjoyed the idea. The skin of Brinkley's face peeling back, the screech of jagged glass on bone – fuck, what a terribly wonderful thought. I was going mad.

I felt the urge to tell Julie of these things, reassure her that my bottle would do. It may not kill, but it *would* do. I knew that another gruesome thought was not what she needed, but she did need convincing. Maybe if I could find her a weapon of her own; maybe that would make her feel better. She didn't like my bottle idea, or at least she didn't take it seriously…so, what else?

I studied the room around me; the tall shag, the fluffy leather – the room was so plush and useless. My eyes climbed the main wall, consulting with the plastic gaze of a wild effigy. The old moose, once spry and bucking, was reduced to a vapid coat of dusty brown fur, ten-point antlers, and the wasted vantage point that, for the few of us left, could have supplied the answers that we so desperately needed. Those dead eyes were there in the Brinkley family portrait when the kids were happy and the couch was green.

My stare dropped to the white tiled hearth beneath the fireplace. The polished floor was speckled with the blackened embers left behind by the fire of last night. Memories of Dura hit me like those of a thirty-year widower, festering hard and permanent over time but still piercingly fresh. The look in her eyes when she knew that it was all ending; fuck, I could understand nothing more. How could I have let that happen? As I sunk deeper into those images, my depression ran so high that I wished that I could just disappear. Not disappear as in wake up or be someplace else. I wanted to vanish completely.

I shook all of that off the best I could. I needed to focus; remorse came later. I had to stay angry; I had to stay brave. Julie was depending on me. She was quiet, sitting on the second-to-last step of the tall flight. Her hunched posture fell forward, and her shaky hands massaged slow circles, moving rhythmically, against her hidden temples. Her curtaining hair, more than just pretty now, concealed her worried eyes and separated her from all but herself.

My blurred thoughts filtered, and my attention focused on several instruments of hope. Hanging on a crude metal stand next to the fireplace was a set of old-fashioned cleaning tools: a thin scoop shovel, a short bristled sweep, a pair of extended log tongs…and that's where it ended, cut short at number three. The fourth tool, a heavy steel poker, had disappeared, and I had no doubt that it was in the mysterious company of our forks, knives, and anything else that could've helped keep us safe.

The thought of our missing knives triggered something in me. I was recalling another tense situation, one from just the other night. Ian had stashed a long steak knife behind a vase at the end of the mantle. *Could it still be there?* I didn't wait to speculate; my legs went into action mid-recollection. The heavy vase wobbled as I slid it along the oak mantel and away from the wall. I could immediately see the empty space growing between my hand and the wall. There was nothing.

My brain, too busy with that simple fact, had forgotten to tell my arm to stop pushing. The vase tipped outward, dropping an elaborate blue and silver lid to the ground. I reached a lazy hand out beneath the vase, but as gravity pulled the ceramic weight past my fingers, I did little more than watch it connect with the solid hearth below.

The violent union sent shards of fractured pottery jumping at my feet. Julie's languid state exploded with the crash. Like chemical combustion, her legs popped, head whipped back, and she started a backward retreat up the stairs. She moved on her hands and heels, and her dangling hair tossed up and away from her face. Her mind was back from wherever it had run to, but the look on her face told me that she was only half aware of what was going on.

"Julie. It's okay. It's just me; I knocked the vase over."

"WHY?" she screamed, as if that mattered.

I didn't answer. Her shoulders were tense and cranked forward with each forced breath.

She rose from the steps, and crossed the length of the living room, the way that people advance on an aisle at a wake. Standing next to me, where the carpet ended and the tile began, Julie's eyes sifted through the pieces.

"What's that?" she asked, without looking up.

"What?"

I looked down, and as obvious as black smoke in a white cloud, the focus of her question appeared to me. The object out of place was thin, black, square, and upon closer inspection, I could see a tiny glass bubble at its heart. A bit of detached ceramic surrounded the glass eye and followed the shape of a half moon. Bordering the other half, where the vase had broken away from the plastic, was a patchy layer of yellowed adhesive.

At first, I felt totally indifferent toward the object pinched between my thumb and pointer finger. I didn't feel betrayed or violated, as most people do when they discover such things. As I looked into the scratched glass eye and I knew that somebody was watching me at that very second, after all that I'd been through, I just felt so very, very… And that's really the closest that I could come to describing that feeling, that deteriorated state of mind. The truth is that I still don't understand it.

Julie shuttered. "Is that what I think it is?"

"Yeah," I said as flatly as possible.

Weighing that new dagger, I thought that, given the problems we faced outside, whether or not they could see us or hear us didn't necessarily make our situation any more hopeless. But then, rewinding our night about five minutes, I remembered something very damaging. I had just recited our entire plan for everyone to hear. Seeing us leave the kitchen, they probably thought that we were on our way out right then.

"No. No, I don't think so," Julie said. "How could he...like you said, where could he watch them from?"

I remembered the statement; I wasn't thinking. "Look at this thing, Julie." I turned the ultrathin camera over in my hand. "This kind of stuff is wireless. He could probably get a feed from anywhere around here. This is all the more reason that we need to –"

What started as a faint stir in the kitchen progressed to the unmistakable sliding and collapse of the kitchen table. The window was uncovered, and the wind blew in like cold death. For a second, I believed that a gust of that size, if there was any God at all, could have possibly been the culprit. Maybe it blew over.

TWENTY-EIGHT

The noise in the kitchen got worse, and my irrational hopes were blown away as I heard the crisp sound of footsteps crunching through broken glass and heading in our direction. I didn't have to look at Julie to gauge the extent of her terror. Her first reaction was to dig her nails bitingly deep into my arm.

Run.

Going upstairs would leave us trapped or injured trying to escape. To make it to the front door we would have to pass the open connection to the kitchen, so the back door was all we had.

I dropped the camera, which Julie and I had been staring directly into, and ran full stride, almost colliding with the back wall before swerving toward the sliding glass door. Julie's claws tore from my arm as I led the way across the room. She trailed behind me, but my pace was much stronger, and I reached the door ahead of her. As she came level with the black recliner chair, I saw

Brinkley's enormous figure appearing through the archway. His head turned to the left, scanning the front door. His long arms hung a giant pair of Cro-Magnon hands just above his knees.

We had missed our chance. Using the sliding glass door was not going to be an option. We would be spotted for sure, and the whole situation would have turned into a raptorial chase. Julie would never last. I looked down at the whiskey bottle in my right hand, and passing it to my left, I used my free hand to reach out and grab Julie's wrist. I dropped behind the bulk of the leather chair and yanked her down beside me.

Brinkley stopped and leaned a huge step toward us. I reached over with my right hand and borrowed the bottle from my left. I was ready. He paused in front of the fireplace, taking in the disrupted sight at his feet. I had a clear picture of his movements through a lurid reflection in the darkened back window. Julie's eyes burned a hole in the wall beside me. Slowly, Brinkley's tall frame bent over, disappearing behind the long couch that separated us.

I didn't see him for too long and decided to risk an inch outward, exposing an eye from around a chair. Julie regained her sharp grip on my arm. I ignored it. I couldn't hear anything from his direction, and I was afraid that he might be crawling over to meet us. First, I saw the scruff of his head, followed by his arched back as he stood upright. He was holding the black contraption that we had found earlier. His shoulders jumped, and his head rolled back as he exploded into a ridiculous call of laughter. He was fucking crazy over it, gasping and continuing louder.

"Let's get the fuck out of here," Julie moaned.

I didn't respond. He was right across the room from us, and by then he was also pointed half in our direction. Our only hope was to keep still. He might not have known that we were back there, and under the guise of furniture, I'd have the opportunity to spring out from behind that chair and drive my six glass points under his grizzly chin. I would have one chance before he pulled his blade out, and then, it would be over. That was if he wasn't carrying it already.

What he did after flicking the camera to the floor was equally as insane as the bout of manic laughter that he had just recovered from. After kicking a blast of pottery and white dust across the room, he marched straight into the corner, where our wall met his. He was right ahead of us, ten feet, maybe fifteen.

As if being frisked, he raised his arms out above his head and softly placed his open hands, one on each wall. He was actually touching the same wall that the recliner faced. After forming two quick fists and easing them back to their open position, he stuffed his face as deeply into the solid corner as his strength would permit. His hairy neck strained with the effort.

He let up for a second, waiting in silence, and then his limbs were put back into strange motion. He caressed the textured wall with his heavy palms. He rolled his head back and swiveled his hips as if he was in a wild dancing trance. He took a deep gasping breath and let out the most ungodly shriek that I had ever heard. I could feel it in my teeth and in my stomach and behind my eyes. Even after he had stopped screaming, I could still hear it. As the ringing aftermath settled, he began talking. His voice started in a whisper, and his groping hands began to climb the walls again.

His neck bent backward, leaning far away from the wall. Then, throwing his shoulders forward and arms back, he smashed his face into the corner with a loud thump. He screamed with the noise. "WHY?"

His voice had such a growling, animalistic tone that it was hard to mark as human.

At first, I thought he was talking to us, but with his next outburst, I realized that he wasn't. *"Why not right now — why not inside?"*

He crashed his head against the wall again. He stepped back and shoved the wall so hard that I almost expected to see it move.

"I'm not. He's not," he growled. With no real effort, he sent his mighty right fist crushing through the wall on our side. *"He won't...I'm not gonna let him do it again. I'll pick the time."*

He was talking about me; that, I was certain of.

The thought had come over me that we may have been able to slide out of the glass door during his rant, but I was frozen, and Julie was worse. Besides that, my luck of the night was not the kind you feel comfortable betting your life on.

There was no escape.

The Little White Trip

He pulled his hand, still clenching a fist, from the shattered plaster. *"Why not in the house?"*

He stomped away from the wall toward the front door. Midway there, he stopped between the coffee table and the fireplace. He started pounding his open right hand against the side of his head, the way swimmers do to clear a liquid obstruction, but he was really beating himself. Whatever he was trying to get rid of was big.

"I'M IN CONTROL NOW," he bellowed, stomping his boot through the glass-topped coffee table.

I flinched with the shattering; I thought of Dura.

"DO YOU HEAR ME? IT'S MY TIME."

I wasn't sure then if he was talking to us or not. Those last two statements were the only ones that hadn't seemed to have been in response to some unheard voice. Julie detached her hand from my arm and had advanced to fully hugging me. Her grasp pinned my right arm, the one with the bottle, to my side. Her breathing all but deafened my left ear.

Stepping his high black boot out of the shattered coffee table, he tried harder to expel the taunting voices. He shook his head and began digging at his ear, half-pleading, *"Get out. Get out of my head. You're all out. I'll finish it my way."*

He staggered distractedly toward the center of the room, still digging at his ear. I could see then that his knife was at his hip. I had such a good view of him because, with his new positioning, the chair was no longer between us. Julie and I were right across the room from him.

Peeling Julie's fingers from my side, I shoved her away from me and against the wall. She slid behind the recliner. I did the same. Crouching as low as I possibly could, I regained my mirror vision, this time in the sliding glass door. Brinkley's small reflection was still and calm. Being between the wall and the chair, our bodies were well hidden behind the high leather backrest.

"Oh, God, please," Julie quietly begged, "Oh, God —"

I squeezed her hand, and she stopped. Seeing the same thing as I did in the reflection, she stopped everything, even breathing. He turned in our direction. I knew that things were opposite in mirrored reflections, left and right, but front and back, that was just wishful thinking.

I, like Julie, was not breathing. The choice was involuntary. Like when dropping beneath the water, even one breath could kill you. The figure in the glass grew larger as he came closer. When he was almost full-size in the reflection, hoping to God that my timing was right, I guided Julie around to the left side of the chair.

As my head lowered under the chair's arm, I saw his red and black flannel as he reached a hand to the door. I don't know how long he stood there because I refused to uncover myself and look up.

The sliding glass door never made a sound; in fact, he never opened it at all. The silence finally ended with a strident click at the opposite side of the room. It was the sound of the deadbolt being unhitched on the front door. Wishing that it was him leaving and praying that it wasn't somebody else coming in, I lifted my head in the direction of the door.

He stood in the open doorway, glaring over his shoulder into the living room. I didn't duck or try to hide. There was no need to because, once again, Julie and I were totally uncovered. He didn't seem to notice, or care if he had. He simply shook his head and grumbled something as he turned and walked outside. The door slammed behind him, and the noise shook Julie from her fetal position. She looked up to me; her eyes were cold and wet.

She didn't speak; she just stared at me as if she was contemplating whether or not I was real.

For no reason, I sat up, shook my head at Julie, and started to laugh. I laughed hardier tones than I had ever hit before – ever. "*Oh my – GOD*," I said, expressing more of a, *what the – FUCK*.

I continued to laugh, softer then, but just as ridiculously. I looked at the hole in the wall and, trying to absorb everything, just totally lost myself. A tear formed at the corner of my eye and slid down my cheek. Once the seal was broken, I really fell into it, drenching my face from both sides and laughing more and more. Julie watched apathetically. I started in with the long sighing laughs, the kind that people always end a really, really, good run with.

Our near-death encounter eventually ran dry of its manic humor, and I began to calm down and hold most of my fluids. I still can't figure out why I was crying or laughing at all; logic didn't enter into it. I swallowed hard and wiped my eyes and my face.

"What are we going to do, Matt?"

I was almost startled to hear Julie speak. I was in such a horrific place that I couldn't imagine having somebody else there with me. It was, I figure, like death or like being dealt a life sentence. In times like those, you get no partners, and even if somebody was sentenced to life by your side or lost theirs with you, would it matter? No.

The ending of life or the death of free existence allows only one through at a time. I felt that way about Julie only for a moment at the end of my delirium, but I knew, even as fucked as everything seemed, we still had a chance, and before the night was up, I was sure to have another stab at it.

"What are we gonna do, Matt? I'll listen now. Let's go Matt – *Please*. Do something."

Looking over to where the vase had fallen, I wondered how many other cameras there were. Were there microphones, too? Could they hear us? I was thinking semi-clearly again, and I wasn't sure if that mattered.

"Well," I started, "our plan is shot. If they can see us, then chances are that they can –" I paused, sizing up a new thought. I walked away from Julie.

She followed. "Matt, where are you going?"

I stopped in the corner, next to the fist hole, and waved her over. She was confused but compliant; my crazy time was over, and I think she could sense that.

The Little White Trip

She stopped before reaching me. "What are you doing?"

I took her hand, pulled her in close to me, and talking quietly toward the wall, said, "Listen, like I was saying, if they can see us, chances are they can hear us, too." She was listening, and I continued, "They probably know that we were going to cut the lights and run. And even if they can't hear us, they must have seen my bottle."

"Okay, so what do you want to do?" she whispered.

Speaking as softly as possible, I told Julie about my new plan.

We were going to forget about the lights; they would be waiting for that as a signal. The new plan would utilize both the front and the back doors. First, I was going to blast out of the front door; no doubt all of the attention would be on that move. A few seconds after I took off, Julie would escape through the back. She could cross undetected through the lining trees, and we would meet on Brinkley Drive. I would play the part of the armed diversion. I was sure of the plan, and I felt ready for whatever was going to happen next.

Right away, Julie didn't like my idea, and she voiced her reservations in a very low tone, saying, "I don't know, Matt. What if he's out back when I go – or if any of them are? If they see me…"

I knew that she was right, but I didn't say anything, thinking of our other options. My ideas were safer kept inside.

"Did he go out through the front?" Julie asked,

pointing at the double doors.

I wasn't listening, but ended up nodding the correct response by luck.

She walked away from our corner and approached the doors, warily. Her last couple of steps were quick. She reached the door and snapped the lock closed.

"So are we going to do this or what?" I asked, forgetting that I had just silently denounced the plan myself.

"I don't know, Matt, it seems –" her words died with the sight of new life.

Standing near the dusty front curtains, Julie peered through a narrow part in the cloth.

Her body stammered. Clutching the fabric, she said, "Oh my God – Matt, look outside."

I ran to her. "What? What is it?"

TWENTY-NINE

"It's a cop car, right out there in the driveway," she said, with such excitement that she actually floated for an extra second as she jumped back from the window. "They must be here because we didn't pay that cab driver," she guessed, and pulled the curtain open so I could have a look.

I didn't bother with the window. So as not to take a bullet when I ran outside, I dropped the bottle in the carpet and went straight for the door. I pulled the massive door open and exposed our newfound freedom, sanctuary. Acting solely on the thoughts of my own personal safety, I broke into an all-out sprint toward the posted squad car. Julie trailed close behind.

It was impossible to see into the cab. I rounded the grill, looking closer, but the midnight tint disguised everything. I stood at the driver's side door for a second, unsure. I knew if there were cops inside, they would've jumped out already. Considering the way I ran up on the car, they probably would've had their guns on me as well.

Leaning forward, with my nose almost to the glass, I tapped on the window. I could see the illumination of a small light burning yellow in an open compartment. From that close the light brought about the faint outline of a head and shoulders. There was definitely somebody inside.

Julie stopped just ahead of the car. She shifted the weight of her anxious mind from one foot back to the other. Her fidgety limbs were spotlit in the electric white high beams. "Matt, be *careful*."

I found the door handle and slowly pulled. "Hello, we need —"

The dome light popped on, and the first thing that became clear to me was a man pointing a gun in my face.

"FUCK." I stumbled a few steps back tossing up two meager fists. My feet caught their places, steady.

As I jerked back, the door followed, and swung fully ajar. I slowly lowered my protective fists, and through squinting eyes, I saw that it was in fact an officer sitting in the driver's seat. He maintained the same fixed position.

Inching a step closer to the car, I looked painfully at the uniformed man. His neck leaned away from me. The cop's fat head was almost cut off. His throat was bristly with stubble and sliced deeply, from ear to ear. His gullet had fallen open; cords of severed muscle and globs of orange fat glistened in the florescent overhead light. Blood dripped from the points of his stiff tan collar and trickled a stream over his gold pinned badge. His left arm held cramped and still, endlessly clutching the wooden handle of a black .357 revolver.

Like most people, I had never seen a murder victim before. Sure, I'd seen them on the cop shows. There's *some* shock in witnessing a dead hand or foot left exposed from a figure beneath a government white sheet, but even though the people on the shows are real, when you're in your house on your couch, they may as well not be.

I had seen dead bodies though, three of them. My cousin, grandpa, and uncle all passed in my younger years. I remember when I was at my grandpa's wake, I touched his skin, kind of poked at him with a finger; I was ten; I was curious. And being outside the door of that squad car, in a way, was similar to standing high on my toes at ten years old and peering at a lost member of the tree.

There was nobody crying for him or commenting on how "natural" they made him look, but to deal with such an overwhelming thing, I stepped back to a child's logic, and tried to convince myself that he wasn't dead. Maybe he was just sleeping – that's what my older sister had told me when my cousin Edward died. I wanted to believe that so badly back then. My friend would come back, and we'd build a new fort in the desert and swim at his house and shoot slingshots just as soon as he was done with his long nap. Crazy. And just as crazy and hopeful as the old days and stories, I almost fell over when my delirious brain told me that it had seen the cop's chest move. *Yes, breathe, stretch, yawn – goddamn it HELP US.* My delusions had become almost impairing. Registering a sight like that one leaves very little room in your mind for anything else.

"He's fucking dead," I said, pulling my sights away from the butchered cop. My stomach constricted, and I tried hard not to puke.

"No, no, are you sure? Matt, are you *sure* –" She stopped talking, struck silent by a great idea. "Let's take the car."

A shot of bile pushed up from my throat onto my dry tongue; I swallowed. "Yeah. But first we've –" Julie was too far ahead of me. I couldn't help her; I could barely warn her.

"Julie, look out!"

I was too late.

His eyes were about the only thing that I could make out from his shadowy figure. He bound forward into the car's lights and clung to Julie's back. As he grappled with her, my eye caught the gleam of his silver blade. Only as a form of control, he slid the steel edge under her chin.

Feeling the knife, Julie froze. "*Matt?*"

Easing the blade away from Julie's throat, he pointed the tip at me and roared, "WHY ARE YOU FILTHY KIDS IN MY HOUSE?"

Julie spun around and bit the inside of his arm. He bellowed as her jaw clenched and teeth sunk painfully deep. The blade fell from his grasp and disappeared beneath the snow.

With his free hand, he grabbed ahold of Julie's hair.

Pulling her head back to his, he snarled, "Ahhh, let go of my arm, you little bitch."

The Little White Trip

She let go and sprung forward toward me. Julie's hair was still wrapped tightly in his hand. She pulled so hard that when the golden slack was gone, she actually dragged him a few steps with her. Reeling Julie backward by her hair leash, he regained his choke hold. His eyes snapped from me over to where his knife had disappeared.

"Don't you move. I'll snap her neck," he threatened, back stepping toward the lost knife. His actions were choppy and nervous. His eyes shifted from the knife, back to me, and then through the glowing windshield at the dead cop. Following his eyes into the car, I realized his concern, the cop's black .357.

THIRTY

As I leaned, ever so slightly, nearer to the dead cop, I watched Brinkley's visual displays of panic. He could only guess whether or not I was going for the gun. With a flick of the wrist, I snapped for my savior.

I fucked up.

My knuckles cracked under the long barrel and shook the piece loose from its dead holster. I watched the heavy weapon flip, in slow-motion, barrel over handle. The gun connected with a splash, resting in a congealed pool of blood near the man's crotch. My thoughts froze and actions instinctively followed.

Capturing my mistake through the windshield, Brinkley progressed backward. Julie stomped and struggled in the other direction. I sunk below the door and collected the slippery pistol with both hands.

Raising the heavy weapon to him, I screamed, "LET HER GO, YOU PIECE OF SHIT! I'LL BLOW YOUR FUCKING HEAD OFF!"

Holding the sights fixed between his eyes, I carefully sidestepped out and around the open door. My heart was vibrating in my throat, but my hand remained surprisingly calm. He chanced another half step back, positioning himself directly above the spot where his knife had fallen.

"Let her go," I repeated calmly.

My thumb leaned forward and creaked the hammer back. *Clink*. The pistol was ready, waiting on a hair-trigger. Defeated, he unraveled his arms from Julie's neck and raised his stained red hands into the air. Julie fled to me, shaking and cowering behind my back.

"Don't you fucking move," I warned, taking a step closer.

My mind raced clear and brave. I had the power. He took a step back, and then another. Julie squirmed behind me, peeping over my shoulder.

I couldn't let him get away, not again. My finger eased back on the readied trigger. I still had *some* choice. The hammer had yet to drop. But I wasn't thinking about the gun anymore – or the man on the wrong end of it. Those lips, how she called for me, but I was too weak. If I didn't pull the trigger on him, I might as well have swallowed the barrel and taken my turn.

My decision came to life with a thunderous crash. A blast of smoke and fire consumed my sights. I wasn't completely ready for it when the gun went off. The wet steel jumped in my hands, and the booming shot echoed and throbbed in my ears. A ruby burst exploded from his chest. Besides the crumpling snow, his lax body fell silently and almost peacefully to the ground.

I killed somebody.

Julie stayed back as I crept over to his fallen body. I readied the gun. The hammer *clinked*, the cylinder spun, and a fresh chamber locked into place. My sights stayed trained on his expressionless face. Blood gurgled from the hole in his chest.

"Is he dead?" Julie asked, standing an equal distance between me and the squad car.

Honestly, I didn't know, and I sure as shit wasn't going to reach down and check his pulse. Turning my head away, over my left shoulder, I squeezed the trigger and fired another round into him. I didn't look at the damage. With a gun that big and a range that close, his face would've been nothing more than a cavernous void of bone and brain, and that was a reality better left behind me.

"Yeah, he's dead. Now let's take the car and —"

What happened next topped the night; nothing could've prepared me for it.

THIRTY-ONE

As looked back to Julie, I spotted another cop car heading up the driveway. I didn't know whether to feel relieved or horrified. I had to shoot him, didn't I? Where the fuck was that cop two minutes ago, before the gun went off? I had a dead body at my feet, a cop with his throat slit at my back, and a smoking pistol in my hand. None of that mattered though. My situation was much more complex.

A dark figure, with a woman's voice, scuttled out of the trees, saying something like, "No, uh – stay back; we're not going to need you."

Julie and I looked at each other, totally lost.

"*Who the fuck is that?*" Julie couldn't begin to answer my question, and I didn't expect her to.

I turned back to Brinkley. He was sitting up and angrily shaking his head.

He turned to me.

I raised the gun.

"All right, kid, save your time. That thing's full of blanks," he said in a New York accent.

He got to his feet, rubbing his arm where Julie had bitten him, and complained to himself, "Sonofabitch, punched in the head, bit — how the fuck am I supposed to work like this?" He turned away from me and hollered into the trees, "You people better hope I'm not deaf after all that."

Bright lights began to pop and glow high in the trees all around us. Two men hurried over to the dead cop, and when I say dead, I mean totally alive and standing outside of his car. One of the men handed him a Styrofoam cup while the other tended to his neck, removing a large portion of slashed faux fat. People were spilling out of the trees into the light from all directions. A short man wearing a ball cap, blazer, and a pair of faded blue jeans, walked into the center of things.

With the help of a megaphone, the small man started shouting to the crew in a large voice. "Okay, people, that's a wrap."

My head was spinning, sick and dizzy. I felt like I had been slipped some awful drug. I heard the voices of fact and fiction screaming from within but didn't know which to believe anymore. I started walking over to the man with the megaphone; he seemed to be the one in charge.

I put into words the only thought that my mind would produce. "What the *fuck* is this?"

Before he turned around, a couple of smiling ladies wearing headsets tried to collect Julie and me, saying, "Hi, um, can we ask you guys to wait over here for just a second? We —"

I pushed the lady's hand from my shoulder, saying, "No, you can't ask me to do a goddamn thing. What the *fuck* is going on?"

She ignored my question. From over my shoulder, she gave someone an assenting smile and then mouthed the letters O.K.

Then, looking back to me, she pointed at the short man, and said, "It's really quite amazing."

I turned to see a blonde woman towering over the little man. She was holding an oversized microphone and staring into a TV camera that was propped on the wide shoulder of a paunchy guy.

The woman began to chatter animatedly. "Hi, I'm Cindy Schwartz, and I'm here on an exclusive interview with Rex Luther. We're on the set of his newest project, which just wrapped filming a few minutes ago." She took a deep breath and continued, "Many of your peers said that you'd never pull this off, so tell us, Rex, did you ever have any doubts?" She pointed the black foam device at his ready mouth.

The man stood in quiet contemplation for a few seconds and then leisurely nodding his head, replied, "Doubt? Of course I did. Whenever someone pushes the limits and creates something brand-new, they're going to experience *some* doubt, that's what happens when people chart the unknown." He paused for a moment, waiting for her nod. He got it and went on, "You see, Cindy, other directors couldn't fathom the detail and preparation that goes into creating the world's first full-length reality movie."

Many of the people that I have told this story to ask me what I did at that point, when the "director" was answering questions and the murderer was breathing and the lights were glowing, and the answer, simply put, was nothing, or close to it. I listened. I wanted answers, and in the next five minutes the glass eye and the black foam would bring almost all of my questions to rest. Besides, I wasn't in a state of mind to really *do* anything. I wasn't angry or sad or happy. I was shocked, and shock, usually, when brought on without the elements of fear or danger, warrants no action; just shock and shock itself was enough to keep me there.

The steps that were taken to fool us were plenty, and he listed them with pride. "We had to do everything: fixing the raffle at their school, hiring dozens of actors – like the guy at a car lot where we sent the kids to pick up their SUV – the waiter at the restaurant that we arranged, the grief-stricken family where their original directions led to, and the perfect small-town murderer – just to name a few. You can't just cast, either. There's no yelling cut; we had to find the type of people who could get it right the first time and were always ready to improvise. Most of them had an earpiece to help with direction, but at times it was still a mess.

"The hardest part with a project like this were the little, unforeseeable things. And in life and in reality, everything is little and unforeseeable. Okay, example, we had a crew riddle this cabin with very high-end digital cameras in places like closets, trash cans, and crawl spaces – places that nobody would go into, or if they did, the most that we could get out of it was a quick face shot for a double angle or something. But to our surprise, and gain, early last night a cluster of those random cameras paid off and saved our asses in the process. The kids ended up finding an old box in the attic, something that should've been removed during our prep, and inside, they found a picture of Brinkley – the real Brinkley, not our murderer.

"When we rented this place for the filming, the producer liked the owner's name so much that she insisted we use it in the script. And I'll admit, *Brinkley*, it's a great name for the job. But what the hell are the chances? I mean, I've got our hired murderer that looks nothing like the guy that the kids first learned was the killer...and, well, so a stroke of genius was added. It wasn't entirely my idea, but it was great. The pop-in visitor was brilliant.

"Jim, our casting guy, got ahold of Mike Horowitz, the owner of Green Flag Talent, and we worked something out. We woke the poor guy up and had him book us an actor that same night. Somebody upstairs must have been looking out for us because Mike found us a near match to the real, much smaller and blond, Brinkley. Fucking fantastic, right? Yeah, we dragged him out of bed, but now he's a star. He was almost stabbed by one of the kids, but, fuck it, he's famous now, you know?"

She looked startled by his gratuitous use of the word *fuck* but kept to business, saying, "Yeah, I mean –"

The man wasn't actually asking her a question. He was too busy congratulating his own brilliance to care what she had to say. He went on, "We had to constantly cover our tracks around the yard, too. We had a portable snow machine specially built, so after our prep, all the tracks were buried and our secret was kept. Our tech team even rigged a lightning simulator in the trees around the house. It's rare, very rare, to see lightning in weather this cold, but every good horror movie needs it." He chuckled.

"We did our research on that school and on these kids – perfect dynamics in that crew; we couldn't have cast such a colorful bunch. They were it. Cameras followed them for weeks before graduation just to get the techniques right, and we had *hundreds* of hidden cameras, small lights, and microphones. We even special-ordered a high-end prototype tape that can be shot with very little artificial lighting and still come out crisp. I've seen it in action. It's fucking great.

"We had to capture every possible detail, even though, in the end, a lot of it will stay on the cutting room floor. We're up to our ears in location permits for quick roadside shots, private businesses, the cabins, a bowling alley, and all sorts of other spots. If they stopped there, we have to get the rights. Some will happen later. Who's going to turn us down? Everybody needs another buck, right?

The Little White Trip

"Getting the school worked out was tough to figure out, but we had a team of *don't ask* type lawyers who seemed to work miracles for us. When it came down to it, the school signed for a donated snowboarding trip and a hold-harmless film agreement as well. Companies do that kind of thing all the time at events; by participating you're giving your consent.

"We had to get people inside, like the raffle announcer and the people who made sure that he would get the gig. Money talks, and we had to pull everything together however we could. Besides that, we donated a lot of the prizes, so people at the school loved us. We had pull over there.

"This is art, and in the end, these kids are going to thank us for making them a part of it. We made history today." He tried his best to justify the gross exploitation of his project, probably expecting the inevitable next question, and then it came.

"Yeah, that's true, but you *were* filming people without pay or permission. Wasn't that an issue – legally speaking?" the woman asked, quickly returning the microphone.

Lighting the end of a cigarette and snapping his brass Zippo closed, the director shook his head, and started in, "Oh, the releases for the kids? Those were no problem. There's a scene on the way to the cabin where the girl that originally won the trip gets a call from the rental lot demanding that she either bring back the car or get the *liability* contract signed. The kids pulled off at a "friendly lot of ours," had it faxed over, signed, and there you have it, in black and white, five actors signed for scale wages. It breaks down to about two thousand apiece. Perfectly legal; check it out.

"Like I said before, normal and unsuspecting people agree to have their images used every day. Do you know that when you go to the state fair, by purchasing a ticket you're giving your consent to be photographed and filmed? It's true. What we did was merely to control the events around those people. That's what makes our deal worth the time and the millions. With the money we're going to save on royalties and wages, our profit margins are going to blow sky-high," he cackled, wheezy and dry.

Pulling the microphone back, the woman started with the next question, but the director grabbed the handle, with her hand still attached, and tugged it back, saying, "Yeah, filming the kids was easy enough. It was more the safety of the kids and the actors that we worried about. Filming and playing tricks is one thing, but if somebody really got hurt, we could lose our shirts. We took as many safety precautions as possible, but we couldn't think of everything.

"For everyone's safety, all of the house windows were replaced with sugar glass. Also, for obvious reasons, the actor that played Brinkley, Paul, was given a special rubber molded and chrome dipped blade. It looks as real as the ones the hunters use, but it's as safe as a condom."

The woman shook her head but kept up with the smiling.

The Little White Trip

He didn't notice. "You see, the blade on that thing is totally retractable. I think it works with a spring, and when you stab with it, the blade gets pushed back into the handle, and blood sprays from around the grip. I forget how they told me the sprayer works on that part – CO_2? Either way, it was *great*. Ha! We filled that thing with pig's blood to get the smell just right, a little *Carrie* inspiration.

"Speaking of knives, after an episode with our surprise visitor and the kid with the knife, we made a few changes. While the *stars* were away at the hill, we swept the house and confiscated anything that we felt could be used as a weapon, especially a deadly one. For his own protection, Paul was dressed in a thin protective vest. It's kind of like a bulletproof one but not quite as strong.

"We tried to keep his contact with the kids to a minimum, but to make it believable, he did have to be seen. There was a shot when one of the kids had been murdered and another comes outside to help. Nobody in the crew saw the boy running in the shadows of the cabin, and he got the best of old Paul for a second. We had to send one of the grips out to grab the kid in order to keep our guy's head in one piece. Paul was totally out of it when we finally got to him on his earpiece. He didn't understand us, and as far as I'm concerned, the scene had already gone south. The way he carried the dummy off didn't look very realistic either. I'm not sure how we'll cut that one.

"We also had a scene where the first girl, Dura, figured out what was going on, and she put up such a fight out back that we had to send two more guys out to help pull her away. But the worst, and this was our fault, was when Brinkley, or Paul, I mean, decided that he didn't want to let his character get spoiled by being knocked out by 'some kid.' He wanted more dignity than that. So anyway, he took it upon himself to break back into the cabin and give the world one last great performance.

"He was nuts in there, screaming to himself, punching and kicking holes in things. We just let it get too out of hand, and he wouldn't listen to any of us over his earpiece. We told him that the kid had a bottle and that the last scene wasn't set to happen in the house. He really went loony, screaming back at us. We had to finally threaten his contract to get him out of there. It was fucking brilliant film though; I'll be the first to give him that."

"Wow, sounds intense. Did everything else go as planned?" she finally asked, after mechanically nodding to the man's comments.

"I'd say so. I mean there wasn't a specific plan, more of a loose storyline. With something like this, we just had to let it happen. Yesterday, we had sent a crew into the kid's car while we *thought* they were busy in a restaurant, and things went a little haywire. You see, we had cameras planted in almost everything inside the car: seats, vents, shades, and mirrors — that thing was *custom* with those mirrors. It was like a dressing room in there.

"Now, by no fault of my own, our measurements were off, and on the ride out of town our camera angles were hurting. I had a couple of guys go in there to make the adjustments, and unexpectedly, the kids started heading out. My guys had to scramble. A door was left open, and some things inside were all out of place. I was sure we blew it. The kids noticed, but they thought the driver, Matt, had left the door open, and somebody had gone through it looking for cash. That was too close, but it's amazing how things kept working out for us.

"We had to be ready for anything. When the last kid, Ian, came running out of the house, I had a couple of our bigger guys grab him. When he saw the dummy and started catching on, he almost gave us away. We had to get him out of there quick. One of our young production guys was actually the voice we used to alert the kids inside.

"Things were always going *wrong*, if that's what you want to call it. Sometimes it would be on our end, like — okay, we had somebody at the other cabin who screwed up the name of *his own son*, idiot, but most times, it would be the live spontaneity of the kids.

"Inside the cabin, just a few minutes ago, we had a potential problem. One of the kids had improvised a weapon. He smashed a bottle and was talking about running for the road with it. Luckily, since he thought that the police were here, he came out of the cabin empty-handed. We probably would've cut the whole thing short if he hadn't. We didn't want to consider it, but I always knew that we could call in body doubles later to play the kids, for small, small bits, if we really needed to.

"But I've gotta say, I love the way it all worked out.

We couldn't have written it better. It was real. One thing that we *did* know was that the last scene was going to take place right out here in the driveway. We had the big cameras, multiple angles – the whole bit. This was going to be one of the only scenes that would be shot like a conventional movie, and it was, but it just didn't play out the way that we had planned it to go.

"The written ending was supposed to go a little differently. We wanted the whole thing to end in front of the kids in a dramatic police shoot-out, and it would involve the other car that you see down there at the entry bridge. Brinkley was going to get ahold of the gun from the cop he had killed, and eventually, he would die in the shoot-out. The kids were going to be alerted by a police loudspeaker, but we couldn't do that because we had the problem with the kid and his bottle, and then, before we knew it, the girl, Julie, had spotted the police car. So that was fucked. Also, earlier in the scene, Matt was talking about shooting the killer in the head, and when the blank was fired, the only thing that we had rigged was a chest packet. I guess we'll end up using computer generations on some of this stuff, unfortunately."

The reporter looked surprised by the depth of his answers, asking, "You're not worried about how much information you've given away here? I mean, you've described a couple of scenes as well as the ending. What's your reasoning?"

Blowing smoke in the camera's lens, the man said pompously, "You don't get it, do you, Candy?"

"Cindy."

"Whatever, honey; it's not the storyline that matters here. It's the fact that these people are *real* — that's the show. Also, along the way the viewer will see the kids start to catch on. They know something is off but never have the time to figure it out. They basically knew that the kitchen window was safety glass, and then the dad screwing up the son's name... It was all there.

"They were never supposed to think that the killer had help, but that was something that just happened. It made sense to them that way. Anyway, it only thickens the plot. Don't you see? This — thing — it's like a murder mystery, it's a horror, and the fun of it, really, is watching the characters — letting yourself become one of them.

"Fuck the clichéd plot. People will show up by the busload to see the real gut reactions these kids supply. And another thing that you may have forgotten is that before your little piece airs, I have to sign off on the interview — in its completion — and who knows; maybe I won't. Maybe I'll buy this interview from your boss someday and stick it in the DVD as a bonus feature."

The woman fired off another question but was quickly brushed off by the director. "All right there, that's enough. We have a lot of work to do here." He nodded to the camera and walked away.

She snapped back to the cameraman, talking through a smile, and said, "You heard it, folks. There's still work to be done here on the set. And we're fortunate to have gotten a glimpse at history in the making." She held her unblinking smile, just like old Mrs. A, until the camera had panned down. "*Asshole.*"

Julie's shock wasn't quite as hushed as mine. She broke into a full-fledged meltdown, right there in the snow, and they had to take her away. I didn't know what to do. I mean, really, what could anyone do in that situation? Stepping beyond the bemusement of the moment, I felt exploited and confused, but more than anything, I was happy that I could wake up from that bad dream, safe, with my friends and what was left of my nerves.

EPILOGUE

Which puts me here, about a year and a half after that crazy night in Flagstaff, Arizona. Later that night, Julie and I were taken from the cabin to a nearby rental of the production company's. Dura, Ian, and Sam ran across the opulent ballroom toward us. Their spirits matched the surroundings – bright, glittering, and filled with the excitement of newfound stardom. They knew that we were in the film. They hadn't known while it was happening, but they had since been told by the crew.

Ian, sipping complimentary champagne, threw an arm around me, saying, "Can you *believe* this shit, man? We're fucking famous."

Julie clung to his arm and didn't say much. He guided us over to a large flat-screen TV positioned between two potted palms. "Check it out. They're called the dailies or something. That's us, man." He shook his head at the image. "What the fuck man…what a trip."

The video showed a faraway angle of the five of us pulling up to the second cabin; the shots were cut roughly like a real movie. Some were from inside the car, outside coming in through the trees, and even one that cut in tight when Ian had tagged me with that snowball. My expression was true and clear.

The car was a huge camera in itself, filming both from the inside and out. They had cut together a few rudimentary scenes for the occasion. One such scene was when Dura got pulled through the window. It was shot from inside the cabin and from outside. The camera crews were basically right outside the window. It's amazing what one can hide in the veil of darkness.

Apparently, the "deceased" had been taken from the cabin to that knockoff Emmys-style party. They were told a bunch of shit, how much money they were going to get, how famous they would all be, and what a great job we had done. Sam had been told by one of the crew members that one of us had signed up to become part of the project, like we were in on it. Dura had heard the same, but I think that Sam was the one who told her. The people behind the scenes did a good job of keeping the others happy and occupied until they were done with us.

Besides the five of us, about ten or fifteen other people hung around the room, good-looking people, important-looking people. A young girl, who was supposedly apprenticing *under* the director, clung to Sam's arm and filled his head with all types of pillow talk. Speaking of Sam's arm, I found out later that he had actually given his school ring to that girl, so they could use it as a prop. He never saw it again, and it's probably stuffed in a stockroom in Hollywood, still being worn by a rubber hand.

Dura seemed apprehensive, but the ebullience of Ian and Sam was almost contagious. She told me later that, like myself, she was just relieved to know that Sam was okay, that everybody was going to be safe. It was hard to be unhappy with the change in our reality. I had seen too much though, been through too much. I was also savvy to the truth, the real truth. We were tricked. Nobody was in on it, nobody except for the people who would be cashing in on our torment.

And that was another thing; we weren't really getting paid shit either, not compared to what we had been through. No. I wasn't carted off to some party. I watched my girl die. I smelled the blood of a swine and gagged at the sight of my friend's hacked-off arm. And I shot somebody. I murdered a man. It wasn't real, but try explaining that to my crazed mind. You can call me weak, but that was too much shit for me to drown in a little champagne and sparkles.

I was so fucked up that I didn't know what to do. I started by telling Ian, Sam, and Dura everything that I knew. Their fall from fame was quick, and the bruise that it left filled them with more than just questions. Ian and Sam felt that they were owed, that we all were. They were right. Dura, as I expected her to be, was quiet. She was always one to defeat her battles on the inside. When it came to the big stuff, the real problems, she was strong.

The bubbly partygoers casually began to disappear when I started to talk. Most of them probably knew that once the truth was out, there was sure to be some drama. Ian pointed out a guy as the director. He wasn't the director that I had seen earlier, and he failed to answer any of the questions that Ian screamed at him.

"Sorry, man, I don't know anything. My agent booked me to play a director. The only thing that I was told was to stay in character." He left us alone as did Sam's groupie and the rest of them.

"So we're not getting shit?" Ian asked me.

"Nope. They'll make millions off us."

We were the only ones left in the room. Leaving people who would inevitably become furious alone in a room with so many nice things was a bad call, and it must have cost them thousands. Ian and Sam started trashing the false-party room. They kicked plants over, pitched bottles of champagne, and ripped the flat screen from the wall. I would've joined them, but it wouldn't have been enough. I chose to keep my anger.

The people behind the scenes sent an enormous guy out to calmly inform us that our ride was waiting.

Sam was crying.

Ian grabbed an unopened bottle from the bar and kicked a chair over, saying, "Fuck this place, and fuck this guy. Let's get outta here."

He walked through the rubble toward the door, but the goon stopped him, saying, "Hey, man, I'm gonna have to ask you to leave that here."

A moment went by when I thought that Ian was going to throw the bottle at the guy's face. He wanted to; I could tell.

That moment passed, and in a perfect movie line, Ian knocked back a shoulder with a raised brow to the bottle, and said, "What – this? This is just a *souvenir*."

"Give it up, buddy. The party's over," the guy said in a stiff cop-like tone. "Don't *fuck* with me, kid. I'm an off-duty officer." That explained the tone.

Ian held the foil-dressed bottle out to the man, and just before their hands met, he dropped it to the ground. The sparkling booze exploded into a carbonated shower and soaked the boot clad hooves of the angry officer. Ian reached over, took Julie's hand, and walked out through the broken green glass and wasted champagne; the rest of us covered the same path and trailed out.

We were dropped off by a driver who, much like the others, was just doing his normal everyday job. Like a guilty smile from an abusive parent, the moviemakers did us one right. They made sure that we coasted home through the pines and the hills in a black stretch limousine, a convenient end to an atrocious night. A night that we, surprisingly, ended by sleeping side by side in the back of a limo, warm with the comforts of each other and dreaming of the nights to come.

Our time on the road passed unnoticed to our resting eyes, and the morning was almost upon us as the black Lincoln snaked along the neighborhood streets and came to rest in Ian's long pebble driveway. His mom's cranberry Mercedes was pulled half into the reaching branches of a desert broom next to the front steps. She was probably just waking up from her nightly nap.

"No. Pull over there – to the guest house," Ian told an intercom that led to the driver.

"No problem."

We detoured through the side lawn to Ian's private drive. The trunk popped, and a few soft lights gradually came to life as the driver opened the side door. Julie was still asleep on Ian's shoulder.

She was awoken by a chill from the brisk desert air; it flowed in through the open door and stole our warmth. "What — where are we?" She sat up wiping her eyes.

"We're at my house, baby. Do you want to come in with me, or are you going home?"

"Of course I'll stay with you, babe."

Ian turned toward the rest of us. Dura was passed out to my left, and Sam was on my right. "You guys can come in and crash, too, if you want." His words didn't pull Dura from her dreams. Sam lethargically declined, and I just smiled. Ian ducked out through the doorway and helped Julie out behind him. The two of them walked off through the gravel to the covered entryway of his three-room abode.

My lids fluttered shut to black and then reopened with the jerk of the brakes. We were outside Dura's place. The trunk clicked, and the door was opened. The atmosphere inside the limo was dark and calm, but outside, the day was through sleeping, and the sky was glowing a dull silver and blue beyond the clouds. The birds were awake, and natural commerce had begun.

"Doora — Dura," The driver read from a piece of paper. My eyes filtered the light outside and adjusted, taking in the figures to my left and right. Sam was awake and aware but silent. Dura leaned forward, pushing away from the long seat. Her head and shoulders blocked most of the light from the open doorway, and her body was silhouetted like a long-haired apparition. The resolution of her features was hidden with the battling light and dark, but her opalescent smile was ever present.

"Miss?" the driver's voice came in from behind her. She didn't answer or move.

Considering the blood and terror and loss of that night, what had transpired between Dura and Sam and I was truthfully one of the only real things that had happened, and the weight of that thought filled my stomach and conscience. Nobody had said anything about it, or at least as far as I knew they hadn't.

Dura, probably aware that Sam and I were a mere audience, said, "Okay guys – I'll see you later."

My brain formed a perfect farewell, but my mouth produced something more like, "Yaahh."

I sat up from the bolstering cushions like an eager puppy noticing the car keys. *Take me with.* Her parents were still away in San Diego, and she wanted me along, and all I could do was watch her gather her things and walk out on me. I hadn't looked at Sam and didn't want to. We would have the rest of the drive to his house to talk about Dura if either of us wanted to. I sighed and sunk back into the leather luxuries of our final ride. The car door swung in toward us and sealed shut.

Sam's voice surprised me when I heard it. "Matt – what are you doing?"

I felt embarrassed and confused. "I don't know... Nothing."

The driver's door clamped shut, and a dim light in the

front cab went out. The engine hummed as we pulled away from the curb.

Sam pressed the intercom with his thumb. "Hold on a second. Please."

"Sure thing," granted the tired voice of our driver.

Except for the jingling of the champagne glasses at the bar and the subtle purr of the engine, the limo was quiet.

I decided to go first; anything was better than that evil anticipation. I already felt bad about how things had gone between Sam and me, but by then my senses were clear enough to feel even worse. "Look, Sam, I didn't know about –"

"Matt, dude, it's okay. Me and Dura talked about it. It's cool."

"But you told me –"

"I know what I said," he admitted, shaking his head. "I must have been high – or drunk. I was both, wasn't I?" He chuckled. "Seriously though, she's a great girl, and of course I feel that way. I'd have to be an idiot not to. But you're my best friend and so is she, and... You guys are perfect together."

"Really?"

"Yeah, really. Don't worry about me, man. Besides," he said with a laugh, "I think I might marry that girl from the film crew." He poked at the intercom button again. "Driver, pop the trunk for this prick back here. He's walking the rest of the way."

"O – kay."

The Little White Trip

Then, smiling and jabbing his bony finger into my ribs, he said, "Now get the hell outta my limo, *lover boy*."

The driver pulled the door open beside me and held it as I got out. Sam collected some pillows and sprawled out on the empty back seat.

"I'll give you guys a call later. Maybe we'll roll up to the secret spot," he said before the door closed.

As I hauled my bags across the yard to Dura's front door, I watched the ritzy Lincoln coast off to the end of the block, turn left, and vanish from sight.

After we had returned home, a couple of weeks went by before things started to feel anywhere close to normal. Julie's father didn't wait that long to start a case against the moviemakers, though. He not only went after them for the full contract wage of a big-budget star but also things like emotional distress, false advertising, all the way up to fraud and assault.

Her father just so happened to be friends with one of the top attorneys in Arizona, and he happily represented all of us as a package deal. He agreed to do the work at a discounted rate because, "This thing is going to be fucking huge – pardon my language."

After months of fighting back and forth with the film jocks and their soon-to-be-fired lawyers, they decided that too much had already been invested in the project and that its potential was too big to miss, so they settled…and did they ever. We each walked away from that deal with nine point five million dollars. Let me just say that last part again – nine point five *million* dollars. And that was after the lawyer's cut and whatever taxes or fees that they hit us with. I was never really good with complex math or the law, but my understanding is that when the movie comes out, depending on how well it does, we'll all be getting royalties as well – what a world.

Dura and our lawyer made sure that our little scamp in front of the fire wouldn't be shown, at least the second half wouldn't. I improvised when I said that the camera panned off to the flames. That's just the way they always do it in the movies.

Dura and I moved to the top of a tall green hill in Hollywood...not in the same house or anything. We're much too young for that; we do live three doors down from each other though. Our houses are modest, not much bigger than the one I grew up in, but it's always beautiful up there. At night, with the murky sky black and sleeping, the city lights come alive. Tinseltown sparkles and bustles late into the early hours. Sometimes, Dura and I sit out on my balcony and marvel at what that derelict city has done for us.

We usually spend our days – well, doing whatever we want, I guess. We've been talking about spending some time in South America soon, maybe Brazil. We're rich, young, and in love. What more could anyone ask for?

At first, my parents were uneasy with all of the legal drama. My dad never thought much of lawsuits, but he didn't seem to mind much when I finally thanked them. I did it in a card. The card read, "Dear Mom and Dad, I can't express to you how thankful I am for the life that

The Little White Trip

you provided for me. I know that you gave up a lot to raise us kids, and you did an amazing job. These days, it's rare for a kid to sit down to dinner with their parents, not to mention their original parents. I don't know exactly how to put the rest of this. I heard a saying once that went, 'If there's no God, there are still parents.' I think that says it all. You created me, you love me, you sacrificed your lives for me, both in your own way, and this is the least that I can do to pay you back."

Inside the card I left two smaller envelopes, both sealed and inscribed with a fountain pen. The names on the envelopes weren't the names that I had ever known them by. Mom and Dad, those were more job titles than names to me. My dad's envelope read Matthew and my mom's read Penelope. Beyond the forgotten names and glue, fit a light blue card. The message inside read simply, "If there was one thing that I could wish for you, it would be to find yourselves again. Be free, and live your lives as the eager twenty-year-olds who honeymooned in the islands. I love you, your son, Matt."

Now some people disagree with the way I did this next part, but I have my reasons. Folded inside my final message was a carbon-style cashier's check, one in each card. Both read their legal names and a figure of five hundred thousand dollars. I wanted to set the precedence for my mom in her new life. I wanted to let her know that even though her duties weren't payable by the U.S. economy, what she did in life dwarfed the impact of any office job. She held the highest position in my mind.

I thought about giving her the entire million. Let her feel the power from both ends for a change. But, I knew that she would've just deposited the whole amount into the family account either way; that's just the way she is.

My dad phoned his boss that day. He called the guy at his house to let him know that his son had just retired him. They begged him to stay, but he declined. I guess selling industrial carpet didn't do it for him anymore. My mom told me that he had really taken my letter to heart and had all sorts of plans cooking. Her voice was so pleasant, alive, and blissful. Can you believe that? They invested some cash in real estate and stocks, and with the money that they already had put away, life has become a breezy day for the two of them.

Doing that for my parents had always been a dream of mine. I knew that someday I was going to be rich and famous. I didn't know exactly how, but I wanted it so bad that it had to happen. Maybe not the fame part, but I knew that sooner or later I would find my niche. I would climb to the top, and everyone would be proud of me. They would say that I made it. That kind of shit was always so important to me back then. I guess I did now, you know – make it. I kind of cheated, but I'm not done yet. I have plans.

Julie and Ian followed Dura and me out here to Los Angeles. They ended up in Beverly Hills. They tried living together for a while, but it didn't last. The money, real money now, only expanded Ian's party lifestyle. He became too much for Julie to deal with, so they split up. I

The Little White Trip

went surfing with Ian a few weeks ago, and he told me that he's living on the twentieth floor of the Renaissance Hollywood Hotel. He loves it. I worry about him sometimes, but goddamn, does that kid have some fun.

After donating a nice chunk of her settlement to her favorite charity – her closet – Julie started working on opening a dainty little boutique on Melrose. Just for fun, she says. Now she "does lunch" with tons of fashion designers and industry people, which I'm sure she loves.

Sam stayed back in Arizona; he's a much bigger and younger fish out there. He's got a nice perch up on Camelback Mountain with a negative-edged pool, an indoor Jacuzzi, and his name, Canton, stamped in huge bronze letters across his electric guard gate. Dura and I went to his place a couple of weeks after he moved in. It's very modern, or that's what his snooty interior decorator told me; either way, it's nice.

He couldn't have picked a better location. His back deck and pool face to the northwest and reach daringly close to the edge of a crumbled stone cliff. There's no fence in his backyard – none needed. Unless you've got ropes and chalk and climbing shoes, you're not getting into Sam's backyard. Ahhh – the northwest, one of the only directions that you can face on that end of town and still see God's country in the nude. The houses are sparse, and the prairie dogs and jackrabbits run that end of town; it's beautiful.

The sunsets and the ancient mountain ranges don't mean anything to Sam – yet, but they will, after the glare of being rich and wanted dims a bit, he'll appreciate that stuff, too. Why start with the old, rough, and natural? Those things will always be there for him. These days Sam is better entertained with the sleek, the soft, and the hot. He picked himself up a couple of flashy cars and a few lady friends to match. He loves being rich, and having finally found something big enough to counter his bad luck, he seems to be having tons of fun. After nearly twenty years of his clumsy burdens, he needed it. I'm happy for him.

Oh my God – I almost forgot one of the best parts of all of this. Apparently, Mrs. Adams was in charge of the raffle prizes, and she failed to read the fine print on one prize in particular. To my great delight, she was fired or resigned because of it. She now works as an assistant manager at the YMCA over on 32nd Street, right next to the school. Her boss is Lenin Hayes. He's twenty-three years old and used to go to Farrell. I know Lenin; he hates Mrs. Adams and probably gave her the job just so he could terrorize her. I got a good laugh when Sam called and told me that one.

After the lawsuit, things became understandably awkward between the crew and the five of us. I have no clue what they actually caught on film besides the obvious. But, as I said in the beginning of this book, I wanted this thing to be a dedication to my group – who we were back then because God knows that it all changed that night, for the better, but still, we'll never be like that again.

Once word of our story hit the Hollywood insiders,

The Little White Trip

we were bombarded with offers from agents, managers, and future sponsors. They say that when the movie hits, we'll have more fame and endorsements than we'll know what to do with. I hear that Ian and Sam are game, but I guess for me personally, I'm just trying to enjoy being a normal guy as much as I can until that day.

Apparently, to cover our settlements, the filmmakers were forced to shop the project around to a couple of outside investors. That was a long and hard sell because the raw shots weren't available to show around or work on during the lawsuit; they were considered evidence. There was also some sort of episode with the studio. They got spooked at the sight of our lawyer's tall grey fin and shit their pants at the close to seventy-million-dollar figure that passed by his smiling rows of teeth. The director ended up finding somebody else to go with, but it took awhile.

The last thing that I heard on the actual making of the movie was that in the beginning, they were running into some trouble finding the right group of people to cut and paste the thing together. But now everything is coming along and turning out better than they could've hoped for.

I know that there are still *some* bugs in the reel because the other day Julie told me that we might have to link back up with the production crew to get some "voice stuff" taken care of. I'm not entirely sure what that means, but I think that we're supposed to repeat some of the things that we said while they were rolling. How they're going to convert those couple of days that changed our lives forever into an hour and a half presentation is way over my head. But I've gotta admit, I'm pretty anxious to see what comes of it, if anything.

So far, none of us "stars" have been told when the movie is set to hit theaters, but you can be sure that we'll all be there when it does. Oh yeah, and the question that everyone's wondering…is the book better than the movie? In this case, I don't know; I guess we'll just have to wait and see.